THE GENESIS INCIDENT

Butch Berardesco

All's Well Inc.

The Genesis Incident
Published by, **All's Well Inc.**

Copyright © 2013 by Butch Berardesco

Cover by David W Murray, Talented literary artist, former Disney Animation artist, whose screen credits include Mulan, Tarzan, Lilo & Stitch, and Brother Bear. He is also a writer for 3-2-1 Penguins, the TV series brought to you by Big Idea Productions. Murray is the author of the children's fantasy adventure novel, "Majesty the Sorcerer and the Saint, as well as numerous screenplays. He won the 2004 Golden Aurora Award for best short film. Visit his many accomplishments at dwmurraybooks.com

This book is dedicated to,

Patricia, my darling wife, my human spell check. Little did she know, that someday she would not only be my wife, my friend, my lover, but my proofreader and editor. Thank you for all your hours of labor and love, working right beside me in our office. I always knew God put us together as a team.

Table Of Contents

1

~ THE MYSTERY MISSION ~

The year is 2077 after five long years, the mystery mission is finally falling into place. All members of the team, have been selected, with each member possessing a distinct and sought-after expertise. The pilot, who will complete the crew, is in the process of being contracted.

The candidate is Axle Kade. At 5'8" and 180 lbs, he is in top physical form. His wavy brown hair has a small white patch in the front over his left eye. His brown eyes change to hazel at times, depending on the light and what color he's wearing. Today his eyes match his light brown shirt.

What this candidate doesn't know yet, is that he has already been chosen for this mission. Axle was the last choice from a list of five. The first four candidates, although more experienced, lacked some of the mandatory criteria.

It's Tuesday, and just like *every* Tuesday, Axle is at his parent's house for dinner.

"So tell me more about this potential project son," Axle's dad questioned, with a hint of doubt in his voice.

"Well, I've already told you that it's a prototype space craft, but now I think there's a mission involved," Axle replied, with a mouth full of synthetic mashed potatoes.

"A mission? You're dreaming. Test pilots almost never go on missions. In my entire career, I was only on one mission, and that was a fluke."

"Dad, please, I know the story," Axle rolled his eyes.

"Son, you're barely thirty years old, sorry to say, you just don't have enough experience for a mission," Foster said boldly, as he left the table to refill his ice tea.

"You're right! I *am* dreaming, the same dream I'm *always* dreaming; to be a part of a mission that will take mankind to other planets. I'm just like you, Dad. Your grandfather inspired you to become a pilot, and I have that same desire. *I want to go where no man has gone before!"* Axle laughed.

Axle's great-grandfather handed down a collection of rare sci-fi movies to Axle's father. They have both been watching and enjoying them for years.

Axle could hear his father clearing his throat, so he braced himself for the next barrage of questions.

"It's just that you told me about this project two weeks ago," Foster said, between gulps of his root tea, as he returned to the dining room table. "Do you know what type of craft it is yet? Have you found out anything about the client? Have you learned anything more over the past two weeks?"

"Why do I feel like I'm being cross-examined? Can't you just be happy for me? I already explained it's a prototype. I haven't seen it yet. And, I told you who the client is."

"I did some checking, Axle. None of my contacts ever heard of the TMA. I am just trying to understand why this so-called Time Management Agency, would need a spacecraft!"

"You did some checking? Dad, they are a top-secret agency, and I can't tell anyone, *anything*! This could jeopardize my being selected. For the past two weeks, I have signed every non-disclosure document known to man I even got to write on real paper. The background check has been so thorough I think my security clearance has now risen to just under secret agent!"

"Calm down, son. You know my contacts are very discreet, and I wouldn't do anything to compromise your chances of getting the job. I'm on your side, but I wanted to know more than you were telling me."

"Dad, I'll tell you everything that's happened so far, if you promise to stop checking up on me."

"I'll try," Foster nodded with a slight smile.

"Okay, I've had every possible test; from hand-to-eye

coordination, physical stamina, and speed of my reflexes measured to the thousandth of a second. The reason I think it's a mission is the extensive psychological testing they put me through. I'm thinking; if the project is just to get the bugs out of the craft, why give me a psych test at all? I'm excited. I want this job. I need this job. I'm almost broke. I don't even have enough money to pay for all the new flight certifications coming up," Axle said, all in one breath.

His father paused, and felt a split second of envy as he realized that this may *actually* be a mission. His mind was flooded with the facts. Axle is young; the older a person gets the more cautious they become. He is willing to take a chance. Axle is single, no special person in his life. He lives alone. Minimal repercussions if something goes wrong. This could very well be a dangerous mission.

Foster is now faced with the possibility of losing his son. He felt his chest tighten, but knew that any negative response now, would classify him a paranoid father. Nothing he could say would change Axle's mind, anyway.

"I love you and I worry about you, son. Just be careful and remember..."

"I know!" Axle interrupted with a laugh. "Keep my finger on the eject button. Anyway, I'd better take off now. I have another interview tomorrow at 1 PM. I have to travel into downtown LA, and that always takes longer than planned. I have to find the Nico Mas building."

"That should be easy. It's a newly renovated, 40 story building. It has that new state-of-the-art rainbow-tint glass that changes color as the sun moves. I saw a special on it. It also has the new style transport tubes. You won't have any trouble finding it. Now, go say goodnight to your mom before you leave. She's waiting anxiously in the den downstairs. She knew I wanted to talk to you alone," Foster said while hugging his son.

"Dad, you won't tell mom anything, will you?"

His father's expression reassured him that this was *their* secret.

~ ~ ~

Getting into the city was as grueling as Axle expected. He made his way downtown and found the Nico Mas building. It was not as easy as his father made it sound. As he entered through the automatic doors, he saw a small crowd impatiently waiting for the transport tube.

"What's going on?" Axle asked to no one in particular.

A young man spoke up, "We've been waiting more than ten minutes. They must be having air pressure problems again. If I wasn't going to the 32nd floor, I would have already taken the stairs," he laughed.

"Where are the stairs? I'm going to the third floor, and I only have three minutes!" Not waiting for an answer, Axle searched the map posted between the transport tube doors. He made a mad dash. "Oh great, I wanted to arrive calm and collected, instead of sweating and gasping," he said aloud as he took the stairs two at a time. Catching his breath, at exactly one o'clock, he opened the door to suite 306.

The waiting room was as narrow as the hallway. On each side of the door were four metal, government-issued, dark green cushioned chairs-eight in total. The beige walls were bare. The lack of reading material was obvious-not even a brochure, or a table to put anything on. *Either they just moved in, or they're not staying long,* Axle thought.

He approached the receptionist seated behind the glass partition directly in front of him. She was a heavy, middle-aged woman, with fiery red hair. Her mouth turned downward, giving her a natural frown. Her blouse was so loud, you could almost hear it. Around her thick neck was a thin strand of pink pearls, that nearly disappeared in the folds of her loose skin.

Axle's eyes darted past her and scanned the hall directly behind. He counted six doors; none bearing a name or marking of any kind.

The receptionist glanced at him and pointed to a

screen on her desk with his picture on it.

"Sit," was all she said as she motioned him to an empty chair along the sterile-looking wall.

There were two other men waiting. They watched him as he turned from the desk and sat down. They nodded but did not exchange names or pleasantries. Then they returned their gaze straight ahead. He wondered if they were being considered for the same position and were meeting with Mr. Martin.

Up until this point, Axle hasn't spoken to anyone from the TMA. His hope is that this will be a face-to-face interview, and not an appointment with another doctor or lawyer.

Less than a minute later the receptionist tapped her earpiece and said, "Yes sir."

The three men in the waiting area looked up. She made eye contact with Axle and gestured him over, still not using his name. She slid a badge under the glass and buzzed him in. As soon as the door closed behind him, she whispered, "Third door on the left."

As he approached the door, it opened. A male voice said, "Right on time, Mr. Kade. Please come in."

Axle was surprised to see just who it was. He recognized him from the media. *Franklin St. Marten,* not Mr. Martin. He won the Nobel Peace Prize five years ago for his work with the environment. He seemed a bit heavier. His hair was showing some gray, but he appeared to be quite fit for a man in his late forties.

He shook Axle's hand. Axle was utterly speechless! He motioned Axle to sit in the empty chair. He then positioned himself on the corner of his light brown, marble desk, one leg dangling.

Axle tried to steady himself and not show his nervousness. He stumbled a bit and almost missed the chair. *If St. Marten is involved, this is a major project!* He thought.

"Mr. Kade, I am Franklin St. Marten."

"Yes, I know, sir," Axle replied, his voice cracking

ever so slightly.

"Let me get right to the point; you have been chosen to be part of a team. After reviewing a multitude of profiles, I have come to believe that you are the man for this project. This mission is extremely discreet and has the potential to be highly dangerous. Because the ramifications of this project are so significant, *if successful*, you will be very well compensated."

St. Marten stood and walked over to his window, facing the street below. His light tan suit had a slight sheen, which enhanced his ebony skin tone. He spoke with a slight Caribbean accent. He continued to enjoy the view, as if seeing it for the first time. He was allowing Axle to absorb some of what he just said. Without turning, he asked, "Do you have any questions?"

Axle's gaze was fixed on *him* the entire time. He broke the silence with, "Sir, did you say *if* the mission is successful? Where am I going?"

"I'm not at liberty to reveal that at this time. But, you have been chosen to be part of the first team we're sending. I *can* tell you this; if the project meets our expectations," he continued with a smile, "and we calculate a 90% chance that it will, let's just say, your compensation could easily reach into the millions."

Long silence.

"How *long* is this mission?" Axle asked hesitantly, thinking, *I'll probably return an old man!*

"About a month, maybe less," St. Marten answered.

It was all Axle could do to maintain his composure. He wanted to scream, *when do I leave?* But not wanting to appear too anxious, he paused and held back his reply. He was expecting St. Marten to ask him to *think about it for a few days, then make a decision.*

Instead, St. Marten said "I'm sure you have already reached a decision. Are you in?"

He was right. Axle had already given this plenty of thought. Millions for a months work? What kind of mission could pay that much?

"This sounds like a once in a lifetime offer, and *if* it doesn't involve nuclear waste, I'm in. When and where do I report, sir?"

St. Marten chuckled at the nuclear waste comment, tapped his earpiece and said, "Affirmative." Then he turned to Axle and said, "Now! There will be a hover shuttle on the roof in five minutes."

"Five minutes? I don't have anything with me," Axle stammered.

"Everything you need has already been prepared for you. I'll see you when you get back. Good luck, Axle." St. Marten smiled, shook his hand firmly, and put his arm around his shoulder as he quickly ushered him to a private transport tube that took him directly to the roof.

Axle stepped out onto a shuttle pad. The view of the city was spectacular. He could see the building he was standing on, in the mirror tint of the surrounding buildings, reflecting a multitude of brilliant colors.

I can't believe all the preliminaries I endured that led to a five-minute interview! I said yes without knowing anything about the project. Except for the part about being set for life. Now, I'm on top of this Nico Mas building, waiting for a shuttle to take me to-who knows where? Axle's thoughts were suddenly interrupted by the sound of the hover shuttle.

2

~Hangar 14~

The landing wasn't smooth at all. The shuttle hit right rear corner first coming down with a crunch. The rear entry ramp slid out. It was a typical twelve passenger shuttle, except more streamlined than Axle was use to flying. It had twelve bottom thrusters instead of ten and the two rear thrusters were now replaced with four. But, it was essentially the same shuttle.

The rear door slid open. Axle hustled up the short ramp, bypassed the empty passenger seats and stepped right into the cockpit, taking the co-pilots seat.

The pilot appeared to be about 22 years old. He was thin, good looking, with jet black hair and not a hint of facial hair. His name tag read Justin Sonmire.

He looked over at Axle, stunned that he was in the cockpit beside him. He opened his mouth to speak as Axle blurted out, "I use to fly one of these." Then without taking another breath he asked, "So, where are we going? And, is anyone else joining us?"

"Hangar 14, sir. My only scheduled pick up was Mr. Kade, 1:15 PM, Nico Mas building," the young pilot answered as they took off.

Well that clears everything up, Axle thought.

"And, just where would Hangar 14 be, Justin?" he pressed.

"It's approximately 45 minutes northeast, sir."

"Where are you coming from?"

"Hangar 14, sir." He was a little nervous.

Axle turned his head, looked out the window at the beautiful, peaceful surroundings. A wave of concern came over him as he thought, *Mr. Kade, 1:15 scheduled pick up!*

This was already in the works, even before my 1 PM meeting. That's why the offer was so high; they wanted to ensure I would say yes. What kind of mission is this?

Axle glanced at the pilot and decided to put his own mind at rest for the next 40 minutes.

"So, how long have you been flying, Justin?"

"As you can tell from my landing, probably not as long as you, sir," Justin laughed.

"Would you like a few pointers?"

Justin nodded and smiled.

Axle began teaching him several maneuvers using the controls simultaneously.

"And this one could save your life, if you ever stall and go into a free-fall. Keep all the thrusters pointed straight down; they will cool off quickly that way. Don't panic. When the temperature is green, do a cold start. Even close to the ground, the initial thrust, will act like a cushion. Go ahead, try it," Axle coached him.

"Are you sure this will work? It seems risky."

"Trust me, go ahead. Stall. That's it," he assured him.

"The ground is getting close really fast sir," the pilot's voice trembling ever so slightly.

"Not yet, not yet," Axle said slowly, as he watched the pilot's eyes widening. "Okay, now! Cold start!" he shouted.

The blast from the thrusters brought the shuttle to a smooth, but rapid halt, as if diving off a cliff into a pool of water. Smooth!

"That was amazing! Thank you, sir," Justin said with a shaky voice.

"The more you practice, the easier it will be to remain calm. So tell me, what's at Hangar 14?" Axle pressed again for information about the mission.

"I heard it was a ship, sir. Not even the guards have seen it. The security clearance is extremely high."

"Is it a military operation?" he questioned, hoping Justin would open up.

"I'm not sure, sir, but there are more civilians than military personnel. I don't know much more."

Axle sensed the uneasiness of his young pilot. He decided not to press for answers.

"How often do you get to make the LA trip?" Axle asked, wanting to put Justin at ease.

"At least once a week, sir. I love flying over Apple Valley. However, I still can't figure out how it got *that* name."

"Well, many years ago, long before I was born, this whole valley was filled with orchards. There were thousands of apple trees as far as the eye could see."

"What happened?"

"California's increasing water demand has always exceeded its resources. Farm supply companies introduced Genetically Modified Organisms; which altered the DNA of the seeds themselves; making the crops more resistant to pesticides. It seemed to be a brilliant idea at the time. As it turned out, the GMO seeds had a shelf life and they ended up contaminating all the seeds, giving *all* the crops a shelf life. The health department became concerned over a sharp rise in obesity, diabetes and other diseases. The GMO seeds were placed under scrutiny. All the crops in the entire country and most of the world had expired. The soil became contaminated. A few organic farms and some green houses survived. But, their food supply wasn't enough to prevent the world-wide famine," Axle stated.

"How do you know so much about it? It's recorded that no one knows why the crops failed," Justin inquired.

"I know because my great-grandfather was on a team that traveled to the most remote parts of the earth, searching for uncontaminated seed. I read his journals. He documented about the large numbers of fish and animals becoming extinct. He described how people were eating anything they could find. The cattle went first, naturally. Next to go were the domestic animals. Before it was over, people were eating rodents. That's when companies developed the refining process of turning bugs into the food that we eat today. I'm glad the crops are starting to come back, and that only natural pesticides are legal. Many of the preservatives are outlawed. Foods are much healthier now," Axle replied.

"Obesity certainly is no longer a problem," Justin remarked. "Real food might be healthier, but who can afford it? I heard no one would eat bugs before the famine, and now insects are considered a food group," he laughed. "By the way, wait until you eat the food at Hangar 14."

"Is it disgusting military food?" Axle smirked.

"You'll see," Justin said with a smile. "Here we are now, sir. Hangar 14. There it is, down on the right."

It appeared to be a totally abandoned air base.

Axle's first thought was *if this is all they could afford, how are they going to pay millions?*

The buildings were dilapidated. The runway was overgrown; it looked as if it hadn't been used in 25 years. They hovered over a road that ran alongside one of the hangars.

"Sonmire, Shuttle 02 returning."

"Affirmative, Shuttle 02, you're clear to land."

Axle glanced up at the control tower. He saw shattered windows on the degrading structure that had been reduced to a giant bird house. He observed a few large nests on top of the wall that still held pieces of the decaying roof.

The hover shuttle landed on the road, right next to a set of double doors, located at the middle of the Hangar.

They exited the rear of the shuttle. The pilot walked swiftly in front of Axle to open one of the double doors, allowing Axle to enter first. Inside, about four feet ahead, were another set of doors. Axle reached for the handle, but the pilot blocked his arm and said, "Just a minute, sir. Those will not open until the door behind us closes."

When the doors behind them were completely sealed, and it was totally dark inside, the handles on the second set of doors suddenly illuminated.

A woman's voice said, "Welcome, Gentlemen."

There was a soft click, and the pilot opened one of the

doors.

It was brightly lit inside. In an instant, Axle knew there was no expense spared.

"Incredible!" Axle exclaimed, grinning from ear to ear. Doubts about getting paid quickly vanished. His eyes were darting in every direction, not knowing where to look first.

"I love watching the reactions of newcomers seeing Hangar 14 for the first time. Follow me, sir," Justin said.

Axle hesitated, letting his eyes soak in the elaborate interior. The Hangar was divided in half by the long hallway they were standing in. The wall to their immediate left crossed the entire width of the Hangar and reached the high ceiling. It was constructed from 4 x 8 foot, highly-polished, stainless panels. Diamond shaped brass hardware connected the panels at the corners.

The intricate recessed lighting in the ceiling was projecting a white silhouette of the American Bald Eagle. It covered the entire wall. Laying on top was a smaller silhouette, a little darker, leaving the outer six inches exposed. At least thirty layers of silhouettes continued getting smaller and darker. It not only had a three-dimensional appearance, but as the light shifted ever so slightly, it gave the impression of the Eagle soaring through the air.

"Impressive!" Axle exclaimed, catching the attention of two armed guards, who were positioned on either side of the doors, two thirds of the way down the hall.

Partenza Hall was written above the entryway. The guards quickly looked their way. Justin nodded to them. They returned their gaze to straight ahead.

"That must be where they keep the ship," Axle declared. "Partenza Hall!"

Justin smiled. "Yes, sir, and on this side are your living quarters, an office complex, the mess hall and just about everything else."

On the right side of the hallway, the walls were ten foot high and made from tinted glass. Four corridors branched off the main hallway, about forty feet apart. The glass took on a shimmery tint as they walked by. As long as they were moving, it gave the illusion of water falling.

"Follow me, sir." Pointing toward the wall, he added, "That's one-way glass and anyone in there can see out."

Justin guided Axle to the reception area on the right. It was a ten foot alcove, recessed between the second and third hallway.

"Hi Ivanna, this is Mr. Axle Kade," Justin said with a broad smile on his face, never taking his eyes off her.

She was young, probably only twenty years old. Her light brown hair had blue streaks that matched her nail polish. She was well dressed in a stylish pink suit. She suppressed a smile and said, "Hi, Justin," trying not to look at his childish grin.

Axle showed his identification. She tapped her screen and his picture appeared. She broadened her smile, "Good afternoon, Mr. Kade, this badge will allow you access into your living quarters, mess hall and Room 47. Have it on you at all times, security can be fierce."

"Thank you, Ivanna. May I ask what's in Room 47?"

"You may ask, but I have no idea," she chuckled.

Justin Sonmire escorted Axle down the hall directing him to his living quarters. They shook hands.

"Goodbye, Mr. Kade, good luck," Sonmire turned and quickly headed back toward Ivanna.

There's no leaving now, Axle thought. As he approached his door, a red light scanned his badge. When the light turned green, the door unlocked. He stepped inside and surveyed his surroundings. His room was comfortably furnished.

It was stocked with military issued socks, underwear, and toiletries. Everything was in green tubes, with generic lettering stating its contents and a reorder number. The clothes were much nicer than what he owned. There were several pairs of black slacks, numerous collared pullovers in a variety of colors and all in *his* size. They knew!

He quickly showered. The entire time his mind kept racing, trying to imagine what was in Room 47. He left his quarters and traveled swiftly down the hall. As soon as he approached Room 47, his badge automatically activated the door lock. He entered.

Directly in front of him was the next generation flight simulator. It was glossy white and had a spherical shape about eight feet in diameter. A series of circular bands, approximately ten inches wide wrapped the sphere completely, allowing it to move in all directions. It was perched on a three foot square pedestal and was already in motion.

Axle approached and tried to peek through the small window on the top part of the door, as it went by, straining to see who was inside.

Suddenly, he heard a voice to his left. A man peered out from behind a three sided control booth and said, "Just making a few last minute adjustments."

He was an Asian man, in a Lieutenant's uniform. He was well built, with thick, black, short hair. He put his hat under his arm and extended his hand. "Mr. Kade, I heard you arrived. I'm Lieutenant JoeCat, from Honolulu. I have been sent here on a special assignment to train you. I will be your instructor." He shook Axle's hand and then motioned him to enter the flight simulator. He immediately began to brief Axle on its capabilities.

"You will be working with eight propulsion motors that swivel in all directions, independently or grouped together. The controls are called rockers."

There were two pads about eighteen inches apart with the imprint of a hand, approximately one half inch deep in each pad. The imprint of the thumbs, were about two and one half inches wide, with a sensor imbedded in each one.

"Place your hands, palms down, on the controls. Pressing down with the heel of your hand will bring the nose of the simulator up. Pressing down with your fingertips will bring the nose down; pressing with the side of your hand will turn the ship. Anyway you rock it; the ship will take that direction. The speed is controlled by sliding your thumbs. You have the ability to configure the controls any way you like, within the parameters of their functions. The left and right rocket thrusters are located top center. Do you have any questions?" JoeCat grinned.

"Several," Axle said, looking through the program menu. "The foremost being; just *where* am I going? The simulator has thrusters, yet I don't see any programs with outer space scenarios."

"I do not have that information. I just design the flight simulators," JoeCat replied, still smiling.

Axle suspected that he probably did know, but may not be able to say. Either way, he's still in the dark.

"The controls will take some getting use to, but the design is brilliant," Axle stated.

They spent several hours going over every touch sensor on Axle's control panel. And just about every piece of equipment that would be within Axle's realm.

"We have a very rapid training regiment planned, so you will need to stay focused on this, and nothing else," JoeCat said emphatically.

"How rapid is that?"

"You must complete your training before all the mission details are ironed out. Just follow my instructions exactly, and you will succeed. I think we should end for today, Mr. Kade. Meet me here tomorrow a few minutes before 0700. Our morning meal time is from 0700 to 0800 hours."

"You can call me Axle, sir. I look forward to working with you."

Axle quickly returned to his quarters and collapsed on his bed. He could sense his mind beginning to race. His thoughts turned to the magnitude of a project that demands so much secrecy.

He wished he could speak to his father.

He closed his eyes and began to drift off.

~ ~ ~

Axle awoke early and hungry. He missed lunch and dinner the previous day. He showered, dressed and left quickly to meet JoeCat, in Room 47.

"Right on time, Mr. Kade, you look well rested. Let's go." They made their way down a network of corridors. "The mess hall is just ahead on the right. Wait until you taste the food!"

"I guess it's not typical military food," Axle grinned, remembering a similar remark from the pilot.

"You'll see," JoeCat smiled.

They entered through the open doors of the military mess hall. There was a long serving line to the left, and to the right, there was an abundance of rectangular tables, each seating eight.

They proceeded to the food line. JoeCat grabbed two trays and handed one to Axle. The smell of bacon and eggs grew stronger as the line moved forward.

"Wow! That smells like the real thing," Axle exclaimed.

"It *is* the real thing. Well, almost. The eggs are a 60/40 synthetic mix, very close to the real thing. The bacon is close to being pork. Meat is still a little hard to come by," JoeCat laughed.

At the first station, a server placed a scoop of fluffy, yellow scrambled eggs, accompanied by a decent portion of hash browns, on Axle's plate. Axle hesitated not moving his tray, as a large variety of vegetables just ahead, caught his attention.

The server added another scoop of eggs and potatoes, thinking he wanted more. Axle moved his tray ahead to the next server, who quickly dropped three strips of bacon on his eggs. He motioned Axle to choose what vegetables he wanted.

Axle waved his hand indicating he wanted a scoop of everything. As the server was loading his plate, he asked JoeCat, "Are the hash browns made from real potatoes? And, what are the vegetables made from?"

"All the vegetables and fruit are real," JoeCat laughed.

"Fruit, where?"

JoeCat pointed to a kiosk in the middle of the room. It was piled high with a variety of fruit!

Axle's face lit up like a child at Christmas!

"Haven't eaten any fruit lately?" JoeCat remarked, grinning.

"I can only afford to look at fruit; and to see it fresh is a bit overwhelming. Pears, grapes, bananas, even apples. How did they get so large?"

"We have a Botany Lab on premises, where it's grown for experiments. We get fruit several times a week. Don't worry, they are completely safe, and they taste great," JoeCat said, while popping a small piece of bread into his mouth.

By the time Axle made it to the end of the line, there wasn't any room left on the plate or tray.

"Axle, you know you can go back for seconds if you are that hungry. Pace yourself, " JoeCat smiled, broadly.

"I wish I had more room on my tray," he laughed.

"There are seats at the end of that table in the corner," JoeCat, motioned to his right.

Axle spotted Justin with a small group of men, seated at the next table. The wings on their lapels indicated they were all pilots. He nodded. Justin glanced up and waved back. Axle sat down and could see Justin out of the corner of his eye talking to his friends and glancing over at Axle. No doubt telling them about yesterday's maneuvers.

"Axle, I have a progress meeting at 0800 hours. It will give me a chance to find out how the other departments are progressing. I need to get an idea of how much time we have left," JoeCat said.

"I haven't even been here one full day. How much progress could I have *made*?"

"You will do fine. I just need to know if we will be working ten-hour days or twelve."

"Twelve?" Axle's voice cracked a little.

"Just enjoy your meal. I will meet you back at Room 47 after the meeting." JoeCat finished eating and excused himself.

Axle finished what was on his tray. He exited the mess hall and went straight to the simulator room. Not knowing how much time he had, he wanted to make every minute count.

Coming up with the best motor configuration wasn't going to be easy. Working with eight motors, the combinations were endless. From here on, it would be trial and error.

JoeCat's face suddenly appeared on the monitor inside the flight simulator. "Good news all around. I have plenty of time to get you ready, and we will work twelve hour days." JoeCat smiled, obviously enjoying his profession.

Axle kept a record of each motor combination. He pushed himself relentlessly to develop the perfect configuration that would allow him to navigate through every disaster scenario. Some configurations worked well for certain situations but not for all.

He continued going back and forth. During the first three days, he constantly encountered crash after crash. On the eleventh hour of the third day, he finally found the configuration that worked for 90% of the scenarios. He knew the other 10%, would probably never happen. But he had an alternate configuration ready, just in case.

"I found the best system, I'll use the two front motors for pinpoint steering with my right hand. The remaining six motors, I locked together, so they would move as one, for speed and general direction with my left hand. Rocket thrusters would also be controlled with my left hand."

"Yes, that will work nicely," JoeCat said in total agreement. He was obviously proud of his student, as well as his own teaching abilities.

3

~ THE SHIP ~

On the fourth day, Axle breezed through every possible disaster the flight simulator could inflict upon him. He worked steadily without incident. After he had aced his final test, he exhaled a sigh of relief.

"Great job, Axle," JoeCat said encouragingly. "You look as if you need a break. Let's get lunch."

They entered the mess hall, grabbed their trays and went down the serving line.

On their way to their usual table, someone motioned to JoeCat from across the room. JoeCat quickly set his tray down. "The Commander wants to see me. I will be right back."

The Commander was about 5'8, white hair, olive skin, muscular build. He had a broad smile on his face as he spoke with JoeCat. They both seemed excited.

JoeCat nodded and walked quickly back to Axle. He placed both palms on the table, leaned forward and said in a low tone, "I have news."

With that, he sat down, placed the napkin on his lap and began to eat.

Axle remained motionless. His gaze fixed on JoeCat.

Finally, JoeCat looked up at Axle with his usual smile. "At 1400 hours, we will be attending the official unveiling of the ship. You will be briefed on the mission, and meet the rest of your team. I am excited for you, Axle. I have trained many pilots, and you are more than ready. You will do very well, I'm sure. After lunch, go shower and change. I will meet you at 13:45 in the simulator room."

"I know that I have been trained by the best. I just wish I had *one more* practice- session."

"Axle, it's just the unveiling. You're not taking off," he said, trying to suppress a laugh.

Axle quickly ate and returned to his quarters to shower, shave and dress. He took a few moments to get his excitement under control. The anticipation of seeing the ship, meeting his team, was a bit overwhelming. Up to this point, no one has spoken a word about the crew or the assignment. He ran his fingers through his hair one last time and headed out the door.

JoeCat was waiting in front of Room 47 as Axle approached. "Are you ready?"

"Oh, yeah!"Axle grinned.

They proceeded down the corridor and joined a small group waiting in front of Partenza Hall. They nodded, no one spoke a word. The doors opened slowly. They were greeted by an attractive woman, who appeared to be in her mid twenties, with shoulder-length black hair. She had a blend of Asian and American features. On several occasions, Axle noticed her passing through the double doors of Partenza Hall. He attempted to greet her each time, but she always avoided eye contact.

"Welcome to Partenza Hall, right this way," she said.

Directly behind her was a partition that obstructed the view of anyone passing by when the doors were ajar.

They followed her into a state of the art workshop and technological laboratory. Partenza Hall was immense.

Axle gasped and turned to JoeCat, "Now, *this* is impressive!"

To the left, was a transparent, freestanding conference room, twenty-by-twenty foot square. The long table and matching chairs inside that room were also made from the same transparent material.

On the outside, of the conference room wall was a shelf, two inches thick and eighteen inches wide; it ran the entire length of the wall. The shelf was desk height and angled down slightly. A row of eight chairs on rollers, were neatly tucked under the shelf, creating a long corporate work station for the engineers.

The walls on the right side of Partenza Hall, were lined with metal shelving, filled with a medley of parts and spare pieces. The shelving stretched from the floor to the ceiling and rotated, allowing any particular shelf to be brought within reach. Metal work tables were placed opposite the matching shelves.

In the center of this large room, directly in front of the Hangar doors and fully concealing the ship; was a three-dimensional hologram. It was twenty feet wide by eighty feet long. It took on the appearance of swirling smoke or fog, mixed with sweeping colors of blue, purple and yellow. Occasionally, you could see a partial silhouette of the ship through the hologram. The assembled group was staring at the rear of the ship.

To the right of the hologram, facing the side of the ship, were four rows of chairs. A few select guests were already seated. There were several men and woman in lab coats, a small group in business attire, along with two men in military uniforms. Chatting amongst themselves were four men in ground crew uniforms.

With the sound of three soft chimes, they all took their seats. Their attention was now directed toward the ship. The lights dimmed.

A man stepped forward and stood directly in front of the hologram and introduced himself. "Good afternoon, my name is Jack Brock. I am the Mission Director."

He spoke in quite a serious tone, without the slightest hint of a smile. He was dark-skinned, handsome, well built, approximately 5'9", and appeared to be in his late forties. His closely-shaved face could not hide the shadow of his thick beard trying to emerge. He sported a military haircut that suited his nondescript attire; black pants, white shirt, black tie.

He nodded to one of the four ground crew members, standing off to his left, whose name tag read 'Piper'. He was holding a remote control, almost entirely concealed by his large left hand. With one short tap, the hologram slowly disappeared, from the top down.

Axle couldn't believe what he was seeing.

The ship was magnificent!

"XODIS" was written on the side of the craft.

The ship was sitting on an old-fashioned, modified flatbed, railroad car, with steps surrounding it. The steel wheels were sitting on tracks that disappeared under the closed Hangar door. The ship did not look aeronautical in design.

The first thirty feet of the nose of the ship were transparent; top, sides and bottom. A clear band three feet wide wrapped horizontally around the entire ship. It sat on four round telescoping pads, so it could be leveled on rough terrain. The command stations were clearly visible in the nose portion. The rear portion; top and sides, above the clear band, contained what appeared to be the next generation solar cell.

There is no way this could be powered by electric motors, Axle thought. *It would never lift this ship off the ground. How is this ship going to maneuver? Its shape isn't streamlined enough. The nose is only slightly rounded. What if we run into a meteor shower? Is that glass?*

He had a million questions but remained silent.

Brock stepped up on the platform, stood alongside the ship and waited patiently for the initial commotion to quiet down.

"The oxygen level in the earth's atmosphere has been slowly declining through the ages. It is now down to 15%. If the oxygen level continues to drop, biological life on earth could become a thing of the past."

Brock continued, in a monotone voice, for what seemed like an eternity, with a lot of technical speculation of why this is happening.

Axle wanted to scream, *tell us about the mission*! His mind drifted to an old sci-fi comedy. The plot was to steal the oxygen from another planet. Their ship transformed itself into a giant vacuum cleaner and was sucking up all their oxygen. He had to keep himself from laughing out loud as he thought, *where do we go to get oxygen, and how much can we possibly fit in that ship?*

"The mission," Brock stated, "is to go back in time and find high-oxygen-yielding plants that have become extinct."

"Go where?" Axle blurted out. He looked around and realized he was the only one surprised. His eyes began to search for hidden cameras, thinking, *this must be a joke or another test. This guy Brock can't be serious. This can't be a time-travel ship! How did we get time-travel technology?*

Jack Brock interrupted Axle's thoughts.

"Please, hold your questions till the end, Mr. Kade. At the present time, massive green houses are being constructed in strategic regions throughout the earth. They will house the plants that are collected. We will recreate the condition of the earth in the greenhouses, at the time the plants were flourishing. Hopefully, they will adapt to grow in present-day conditions. We want the oxygen level to stabilize and begin to elevate." He paused and looked intently at the guests. "This ship is capable of going back *millions* of years. We have determined 20,000 years should be enough to find the plants we are seeking."

Axle scanned the room again, trying to read the others expressions. Their looks of concern added to his apprehension.

"This ship is powered by electric motors to prevent a traceable exhaust signature." Brock continued. "They are powered by the latest solar cell technology. The ship can operate in total darkness for more than a week without recharging. It is also equipped with booster rockets, should it be necessary to leave the earth's atmosphere. The ship's sensors are a technological marvel. They can measure all atmospheric conditions; oxygen, nitrogen, carbon dioxide, and temperatures from 300 degrees below zero, to 4000 degrees. They can even test soil and water conditions *out of phase*."

Axle knew exactly what *out of phase* meant! After all, he's a sci-fi buff.

Jack Brock continued to explain in full detail. "Time-travel is a two-step process. The first step is to *break phase. Phase* is a term used in time manipulation. *Out of phase* is when the time inside the ship is different from the time outside the ship. When the ship is *out of phase*, technically, it is not actually there yet. So when the ship is *out of phase,* the autopilot has time to react to conditions outside the ship. A few seconds are all that's needed to keep from landing inside a live volcano, avoiding a meteor storm, or anything that may damage the ship and prevent its safe return. $1/10^{th}$ of a second *out of phase* is enough to render the ship invisible. However, at $1/10^{th}$ *phase* you will be able to enter and leave the ship. It will leave an impression in the ground. Objects can run into it. It will be vulnerable. It can be destroyed. The ship must be *out of phase,* before the actual time-travel sequence will operate. The pilot will have a remote control that can move the ship in a limited capacity, from the outside, while the ship is in $1/10^{th}$ *phase*."

"How do I see it, to operate it?" Axle uttered, loudly.

Ignoring Axle's outburst, Brock went on to say, "Each member of the team will be wearing a contact lens tuned to the energy signature of the ship. They will be able to see the ships outline, even in total darkness. Now, to ensure the pilot does not lose the remote, it is small enough to be surgically implanted in his left forearm."

"Whaaat?" Axle, impulsively spoke out again.

Brock continued, now staring directly at Axle, "The Captain and the navigator will also have remote control implants, should we *lose* the pilot."

Everyone glanced in Axle's direction, smiling.

"The ship was not designed for easy maneuverability *in phase,"* Brock went on. "However, in an emergency for a short distance, it can. *In phase,* the ship weighs several tons.

Out of phase, it's weight is no longer a factor. The windows are truly a work of art." He picked up the control to demonstrate. "They have been developed specifically for this project. They are constructed from a combination of glass, plastic, and liquid crystal. It's called Y3-Glass. It is stronger than steel. The windows appear to be one piece; however, they are three foot panels. Each panel is a four-pane system. The two interior panes have tint sensors that add shade, varying from very dark to crystal clear."

Brock tapped the control illustrating the capabilities of the window tints. "A variety of colors can be added for light spectrum experiments and enhanced night vision. We have incorporated a new laser technology into the night vision that creates enough ambient light for limitless sight. The panels can be controlled individually or simultaneously," he stated. "The dark tint can be set to trigger automatically, to protect against an unexpected blinding light. The double outer pane systems are equipped with a replaceable clear coating on the outside of the outer pane. The coating can be repelled from the pane with an electrical charge; along with any dirt and debris that may have collected. A new coating will be sprayed on automatically."

Brock stopped to sip water, allowing them a little time to assimilate all the information.

Axle wondered if his colleagues are as anxious as he is to operate the controls.

"Once the conditions are determined to be safe, the ship can land in $1/10^{th}$ *phase*. After landing, the atmosphere will be checked for air quality, toxins, viruses and other factors too numerous to mention," Brock stated. "The ships sensor capabilities are at 100% when it's in $1/10$ *phase*. Anything we can touch with a sensor beam will be analyzed instantly. It can detect life signs. It can also determine not just plant or animal life, but the species of both. The ships sensors can reach around the planet and into space. A hand held model has been developed with a functional range of ninety feet."

Unbelievable! He just described a tricorder from an old sci-fi movie, Axle thought.

Brock resumed, "It has a flexible telescoping mechanical arm that can reach sixty feet in all directions."

Piper demonstrated the mechanical arm's capabilities with another remote.

"It has sealed interior and exterior doors to create an air lock. The air lock procedure is as follows; the interior door remains sealed while the exterior door is open. The mechanical arm collects and deposits the item, then the exterior door is sealed. Decontamination then takes place. When the green light flashes, it is safe to open the interior door." Brock paused, then spoke in a slow, deliberate tone, "Before opening the main door *no* detail can be overlooked. If anything were to happen to you and the ship were to be found, history could be changed, altering the future. We may not exist in *that* altered future."

This is sounding riskier than Axle had first thought.

"As a precaution, the ship is equipped with a self-destruct mechanism. The Captain and the navigator will have the codes. The ships computer is programmed to bring you through the Coalter D Security laser grid, upon your return," he added.

Brock studied their faces, then went on to say, "The ship has a small galley and is stocked with six weeks of food. That should be more than enough. Make sure on your return that you arrive at least five minutes after your departure time. Any sooner might create the problem of two objects occupying the same space. Although, this ship has had limited testing, it will travel back through time. However, it does not travel *forward* through time."

"Why not?" a male voice off to the right spoke up.

"I'm sorry, sir. You have me at a disadvantage," Brock stated. "Please tell me what exactly is your function here?"

"I am Oden Zadok," he stated, as he rose to his feet. "I represent the North American Union. I am handling the financing between our joint Governments."

"I have been looking forward to meeting you, sir. Your reputation precedes you," Brock replied.

Oden Zadok now seated, was an impeccably dressed man in his late fifties. His hair white and thinning, his face evenly tanned, with a broad confident smile.

"The answer to your question is simple," Brock continued. "The future hasn't happened yet, so there is nowhere to go. Time-travel has been a quest for many years and I would like to introduce the brilliant scientist whose life-long dream is about to become a reality. Less than five years ago, he cracked the time dimension. He also convinced someone in our government, whom we just had the pleasure of meeting, to give him the grant to build this magnificent ship. Mr. Dom Brothers, please stand," Brock said, as he began clapping.

A gentleman in a lab coat, with the next generation zeo-pad in hand, rose from his seat. He appeared to be in his late forties, just a hint of gray in his light brown hair. Like the others, he was in top physical form. He had a decidedly unassuming appearance. It was evident that he was not comfortable with receiving compliments.

He smiled slightly and said, "None of this would be a reality without my personal assistant and computer scientist, Miss Rebecca Weege."

A lovely, dark haired woman, with large black eyes and flawless complexion, rose to her feet. She was in her early forty's and possessed a warmth that radiated throughout the room. Her gaze added a hint of mystery that invoked curiosity. She smiled, nodded and took her seat quickly. She was seated between Oden Zadok and Dom Brothers.

Jack now directed his comments to the ship's crew. "This is the first operational time travel ship. Six of you have been chosen to operate it. When I call your name, please come forward. Captain Hunter," Jack Brock announced, proudly.

A man from the back of the room walked slowly

forward. His stride was long and deliberate. He was as least 6'6, with dark blonde wavy hair. His features were chiseled, with deep set blue eyes. His shoulders were extremely broad, and his biceps protruded out from under his short sleeved shirt. He appeared to be in his late thirties.

He was intimidating! One look at him and you knew *who* was in command.

"He will be giving the orders; the rest of you will be following, without question.

The ship's Science Officer is Miss Qui," Brock continued.

The pretty Asian woman who greeted the group in the hallway walked forward. She looked around the room and nodded to everyone, finally making eye contact, even with Axle.

"She will control time manipulation, as well as internal and external sensor readings. She will keep the Captain informed of potential hazards."

Axle liked the Miss part.

"The Navigator is Mr. Grant. He will merge space-travel with time-travel. He can operate internal and external sensors. He is also able to function as pilot and time manipulator in a limited capacity. He can bring the ship back in an emergency."

Mr. Grant stepped forward grinning. He appeared to be in his early thirties and approximately 5'9. His unkempt hair, with mixed shades of blonde and brown, was in need of being cut. A deep scar on his neck, poking out from under his collar, was a bit distracting. His clothes were mismatched, as if he were heading to the beach to surf. He had no sense of style. Judging from his dishevelled appearance, he's probably single. He seems to be a bit out of place for this mission. He's obviously an interesting character.

"Dr. Lucas, will attend to your medical needs."

Surprisingly, another woman came forward. She was well-dressed. Her clothes looked expensive, probably tailored. Her hazel eyes were enhanced by her teal blue suit.

She wore a single tear drop diamond pendant, and small matching earrings. She had beautiful, long blond hair that swayed as she walked. She was fit, trim and very well proportioned. She stood almost 5'6 and possibly about thirty-three years old. She had an air of extreme confidence. Very classy!

"She is an expert in viruses and every biological life form known to man. We are fortunate to have her join us. Next, is Dr. Doe, the Mission Botanist. She is the foremost expert in carbon dioxide-to-oxygen."

A lovely young lady, about 5' 2, stood to her feet and went forward. She had medium length, wavy brown hair. She didn't appear to have much make-up on, just a little lipstick. Her large, dark eyes somehow 'sparkled'. She seemed to be the youngest of the crew, mid to late twenties. She has an attractive, wholesome look. Her clothes were a bit plain, but *she* wasn't. There was something else about her, she was intriguing.

Axle recognized her as the cute girl behind the glass in the Botany Lab. While exploring the Hangar one day, he noticed her busy at work surrounded by plants. He was just about to tap on the window, when security caught up with him and escorted him out of that area. He had no idea that she was a crew member.

"Finally, we have Mr. Kade, your pilot. He has endured extensive training and has demonstrated superior skills. He proved his willingness to join us with only five minutes notice; thus the government issued clothing."

They all laughed as Axle stepped forward, and everyone was put at ease. It broke the ice.

"Be assured," Jack Brock stated, "you have all been selected because you are the foremost experts in your field." His attention now turned to his distinguished guests. "Ladies and Gentlemen, that concludes our formal presentation. Thank you for your participation. Please enjoy the rest of your time here. I would now like to meet with the crew in the conference room."

Those that were seated, stood and erupted into applause, as the crew was ushered behind the glass walls.

Once inside, they formally introduced themselves to each other; shaking hands, smiling and making small talk. Jack Brock was the last to enter the room, by now everyone was seated.

He remained standing as he addressed them. "You will now have the next two days off. Avoid contact with the media. If you violate your non-disclosure agreement, legal action could be taken. We will be forced to discredit you, using any means necessary. Of course, you understand our position. By now you can appreciate what is at stake here. I will answer mission-related questions upon your return. At that time, you may also ask questions of each other. I look forward to meeting with you in two days. Thank you."

Jack Brock's tone and body language let them know the meeting was over. No questions were to be taken.

"I wonder why we're getting two days off?" Axle asked no one in particular.

Mr. Grant, walking alongside him answered, "To see your family and get your affairs in order."

Axle stopped. Grant kept walking.

"Get my affairs in order?" Axle exclaimed.

4

~ NEXT OF KIN ~

"**D**ad, I have great news. I've been selected to fly the prototype."

"That's wonderful, Axle. I'm proud of you, son. We were hoping that's why we hadn't heard from you. What's the project and when does it start?"

"It starts in two days. I've been training all week. But I can't talk now. I need to see you and grandpa, and maybe get a loan to cover my bills until I get paid."

"I'll meet you at your grandfathers. He's having a little get-together tonight with his retired buddies. Can you get there early? I want every last detail."

"I can leave now."

"Me too," Foster said excitedly.

Axle boarded a hover shuttle from Hangar 14 and gave the pilot the address. However, this time instead of taking his more familiar seat in the cockpit, he found himself in the regular passenger compartment, lost in his own thoughts. He realized, that in many ways, the old time sci-fi movies laid the foundation for this project and others like it. So now, there is a time-travel ship with underwater and outer space capabilities.

His father is going to have a million questions. Being retired has never stopped Foster from keeping up with the latest technology. Especially, being a sci-fi buff. He loves to discuss how technology has increased throughout the years. Axle can't wait to tell them about the ship. He arrived before the other guests and joined the two men waiting in the den. They were gripped with anticipation.

"Start with the ship, son," Foster demanded.

"The ship is unbelievable. It's eighty feet long, sixteen feet wide and sixteen feet high. The entire nose section is clear. You can see right through the floor. The windows can change colors and repel dirt. The solar cell technology is next generation." Axle spoke rapidly with excitement.

"Are you just going to test run it, or is there a mission?" Foster asked.

"It's a mission. That's all I can say."

"Don't leave us hanging, where are you going?" Grandpa Vinny questioned.

"It's a secret mission. I can't tell anyone. I can be sued for violating the non-disclosure agreement."

"And just how much would they get if they sued you?" Vinny laughed.

"I'm *not anyone!* I'm your Father!" Foster interrupted the playful banter. "I know how to keep quiet. Where are you going?"

"You guys are not going to believe it," Axle laughed.

"Come on, where?" they both shouted.

"Back in time, to get some plants that will add oxygen to the atmosphere."

Stunned silence, then laughter.

"How far back are you going?" his grandfather asked.

"Did you just ask him how far back? You really believe that nonsense?" Foster questioned.

Vinny, arms folded across his chest, looked intently at his grandson and asked, "Axle, are you telling the truth?"

Axle nodded.

Vinny looked directly at Foster and said, "Yes, *I* believe that!"

"So, let me get this straight; you say you are being sent back in time, and you didn't want to tell us, because we *might* tell someone? Who would *I* tell? Who would believe *that*? Except for your grandfather, of course. Is that what you're saying?"

"Your right, Dad, I'm still not sure *I* believe it."

"Plus, if something were to happen to you, we aren't bound by *any* non-disclosure. We need to know what you're involved in," Foster said, sternly.

Grandpa Vinny cut in, "Well, how far back?"

"They said 20,000 years should be enough."

"Come on, Axle, you are not going back 20,000 years," grandpa bellowed. "I've been telling you all your life that the Earth is less than 10,000 years old. And, there is plenty of proof that supports my position."

"Grandpa, I know about your position, but *everyone* has a theory that can be backed."

"I need more details, son. Explain this mission fully to us," Foster interrupted.

Axle took the next forty-five minutes describing in detail, the events that led up to his visiting with them today. He began with the meeting in the Nico Mas Building and the hover shuttle whisking him off to Hangar 14. He told them about Room 47 and his instructor, JoeCat. He described meeting Jack Brock and the crew.

The men listened in silence, absorbing every word. Axle was sure they had questions, but they refrained.

Suddenly, his grandmother yelled from the kitchen, "They're here. Axle, honey, get the door, please."

Grandpa Vinny immediately removed a chain, having a gold rectangular charm with a leaf design, from around his neck, and placed it around Axle's. "I want you to promise that you will wear this for good luck." He hugged his grandson and said, "Be careful."

Axle assured them both that he would be back in a few weeks.

As his father was hugging him, grandpa said softly, "I know you will."

After Axle left the room, Foster said to Vinny, "When he told me about the project, I knew it was going to be extremely dangerous. But going back in time? This gives a whole new definition to the words, ext*remely dangerous!* How can we get him to change his mind?"

"We can't. He won't," Vinny stated, emphatically. "I remember a time early in *your* career, when you were testing the..... "

"Stop right there," Foster interrupted his father. "You always bring up the surveillance glider incident. Who could have known the ejection seat would malfunction? Look at the bright side; safety precautions were heightened and there hasn't been a mishap since."

"So when did you downgrade it to an *incident*?" Vinny balked. "Listen, son, it was a very serious crash. The doctors are still trying to figure out how you survived. I tried everything to get you to change your career after that. Nothing I said or did had any effect on your decision. And *you* turned out very well."

"That was different," Foster stated.

"Why, because it was you? I have a very good feeling everything is going to work out just fine. Have a little faith in your son's ability. He might just surprise you. Now, let's go join our guests," Vinny said with a reassuming tone.

5

~ TWO FACES ~

Rebecca Weege spotted Dom Brothers in the mess-hall, enjoying his morning meal.

She quickly took a tray and hustled through the line, selecting one slice of toast, several grapes, three chunks of pineapple and a large coffee.

Dom was seated with three lab techs discussing how well yesterday's presentation went.

"And I thought Brock was only direct and to the point in a one-on-one scenario. It was surprising to see him that way with an entire room of people," Powell Tomlin laughed.

Powell is an R and D technician in his late forties with salt and pepper, wavy hair. He spoke with a hint of an Irish accent and had an infectious laugh. He was always a few minutes early, and willing to work late.

"Yes, but you must admit, he pulled it off flawlessly," Dom nodded. "It was motivating to see him in action, not the slightest bit intimidated. A strength I wish I had."

Dom glanced up just as Rebecca was approaching his table. "Good morning, Rebecca. Did you eat too much yesterday?" he said with eyebrows raised, looking at her sparse tray. "We were just discussing Brock's presentation. What's your take?"

She slipped into the empty chair next to Dom, removed the plate from her tray, and neatly arranged the silverware. She sipped her coffee, knowing full well that Dom's eyes were on her, and he would patiently wait for her answer. "I think it went so well, that future funding for any project, will never be a problem for you," she winked.

"Well, speaking of projects; it would be beneficial if we were able to communicate with the ship. If that's at all possible," Dom stated.

"Is there time to do that before the launch?" Nadia Reed questioned.

Nadia is the Thermal Physics Engineer. She is in her late fifties with straight shoulder-length, silver hair. She is stunning for her age. She was recruited, due to her outstanding achievement in Thermionic Space Applications. She speaks seven languages fluently, including Gala Mas. She is proving to be quite an asset to this team. Rumor has it, Ms. Reed never married. She wears a pin on her lapel that was a gift from her first love, some thirty-odd years ago. Apparently, he died before the wedding. Her grief propelled her into long-term education, thus her distinguished career.

"No. The launch happens in a few days, no matter what. I meant for the next endeavor," Dom said quickly.

"Talk about job security," Rebecca laughed. "That could take another five years, if it's even possible at all."

"I'd like you to begin thinking about it. I only want to start compiling some ideas, that's all," Dom explained.

Rebecca wanted to talk to Dom alone and needed to separate him from the others. She had a little coffee left in her cup, and as everyone stood, she intentionally spilled the coffee on him.

"I am so sorry, Dom. You probably need to get a clean shirt, I'll walk with you," Rebecca apologized. Then looking at the techs said, "We'll catch up with you in Partenza Hall."

The three techs took the corridor to the Hangar, while Rebecca and Dom headed for his quarters.

"Sorry about the coffee, but I had to get you alone," she said, apologizing again.

"You did that on purpose?" he asked, puzzled.

"I had no choice."

"This better be good. What's up?"

"Over the last 5 years you have probably figured out that I have the special gift to know when people aren't being completely honest. The main reason I joined with you in this project is, it is very refreshing to find someone that is easy to read, trusting and has nothing to hide."

"I haven't mentioned it, but of course I know about your gift. I also know you have used it to save me from some potentially embarrassing situations on more than one occasion."

"Dom, you have no idea. The occasions are way too numerous to mention. Promise me you won't get upset? It's about Oden Zadok, he had an ulterior motive when he asked the question about going forward in time."

Dom stopped in his tracks and turned to Rebecca.

"What was Oden's motive?"

Not good! On his way out he made a call, the line was unsecured so I recorded it. Listen!"

"Maiyorka? Oden. I'm at the Bella project. Tell them negative to traveling forward in time," click.

"You're just experiencing a touch of paranoia "He's my friend! We've been working together for five years now, and he's the only one that would even take a look at my project. Not to mention, he got an agreement for government funding in just two days. Rebecca please. Why would Oden do anything to harm the project?

"I knew you would say that. You always think so highly of everybody. However, I was able to track down this Maiyorka."

"You did what?" Dom exploded.

"Just look," Rebecca turned her zeo–pad around to show Dom the images and intel she collected to support her suspicions. "It turns out, that she is part of an elite group of venture capitalists. They operate world–wide. It appears that Oden Zadok could be part of it."

"And that's another thing," she persisted, "how could anyone get two hundred billion dollars in government funding, in just two days? Something is not right with this guy, and we are running out of time. The ship is ready to take off. It could happen as early as tomorrow."

Dom, trying to absorb what he just heard, replied, "Just what are you suggesting we do?"

"It will take a little time, but I could come up with his

passwords and hack his files."

"Again, he's my friend! Do you really think we need to go that far, Rebecca?" he questioned her once more.

Dom, trying to absorb what he just heard, replied, "Just what are you suggesting we do?"

"It will take a little time, but I could come up with his passwords and hack his files."

"Again, he's my friend! Do you really think we need to go that far, Rebecca?" he questioned her once more.

"Dom, if he is your friend, then why does he have his own code name for your Project? He called it the 'Bella Project'! He has two faces."

He groaned, then took a moment to ponder the next course of action. He stepped closer to Rebecca, placed his arm around her shoulder and whispered, "Can you breach his files without him knowing it?"

"Probably, but I'll check him out first, okay?"

"Alright," Dom replied. "Be discrete. If you're right, he will already have someone on the inside. We could be under surveillance right here."

"Look who's being paranoid, now? Not a chance. That's why I approached you in the hallway. Hangar security sweeps out here regularly. It's Partenza Hall, I'm worried about."

They walked in silence. Dom's head was down.

6

~ ARE WE THERE YET ~

Shortly after Axles' arrival back at Hangar 14, Justin approached saying, "I took LT. Cat back to Honolulu yesterday, he wished you good luck."

"You mean JoeCat?" Axle questioned.

"He never told me his first name sir."

".Because I'm a civilian, he used his first and last name. So this whole time I;m calling him JoeCat and he never correct me." Axle shook his head and Justin laughed as they made their way to Ivanna's station. Axle upgrade his badge and went into Partenza Hall leaving Justin gazing at Ivanna.

Captain Hunter, Dr. Qui, and Mr. Grant were visible in the nose section, busily working. The Captain was standing in front of his station, consulting the zeo-pad in his left hand as he calibrated the controls in the arms of his chair, with his right. Mr. Grant, was laying on his back under one of the stations. Miss. Qui, seated at a station flashing images on the nose of the ship.

No one noticed Axle approaching until he waved. Marcella glanced and ignored him like a distraction. With that Mr. Grant picks up his head and waves with a tool in his hand. The Captain motions Axle aboard. Axle climbed the flip-out stairs looks left down a narrow hallway toward the back of the ship. Three doors on the left a labeled bathroom, shower, bathroom. An opening at the end of the hall with no door labeled Galley, it stretched the entire width of the ship. Coming off the galley, on the right two doors marked 'crew Quarters'. A large room, stretched from those cabins to the rear of the cockpit, marked 'Botany Lab and Plant Storage'. It had sliding, stack-able doors.

Across from the Lab and to the right of the stairs, was large compartment labeled mechanical arm and equipment room.

It was the ship's brain.

Axle moved turned toward the nose section in awe smiling, as he stood behind the captain's chair. The other 5 stations were typical with minor differences.

"This is a lot different from the flight simulator. I can't believe what I'm seeing," he exclaimed, smiling.

"I have never seen anything this technologically advanced, and I'm the first one to fly all the latest crafts. This could easily be mistaken for an alien space craft."

Everyone smiled and chuckled.

Captain Hunter remarked, "I said the same thing. Your station is forward center."

Axle's station was impressive! He was front and center, with an unobstructed view. His control panel was similar to the other four stations. The exception being; his steering rockers and thumb speed controls were mounted to the sides of the control panel. Just like the simulator.

Two feet behind him, to his left and right, were two more stations. The Captain's chair was positioned in the center of the craft two steps higher than the other station; allowing him to oversee the mission. Two feet behind the Captain's chair, to the left and to the right, were two more stations.

The 5 stations were transparent and constructed from Y3-Glass. All the stations were mounted to five inch diameter columns.

Coming from the equipment room, was a large color-coded, fiber-optic wiring harness that ran under the floor and narrowed, as it's cables branched off to feed each station.

The console design was a semi-circle. The three forward consoles had a strip of clear material eight inches high by eighteen inches long, that were attached to the straight edge of the console.

"Why do these three stations have an extra piece?"

Axle inquired.

Mr. Grant walked over to Axle's station and touched his console; it lit up. Each icon was labeled and color-coded. By touching RV, the component became a view-screen.

"That's a rear view. We can see behind us," Axle stated excitedly.

"You can also focus in on just the Captain or anywhere you like by sliding your finger on the top edge." Grant demonstrated.

"Impressive!"

"You haven't seen anything yet," he quipped.

At this point, everyone but Miss Qui, was intently watching their interaction. Axle realized the others had been in the dark, as well.

"All the stations are interchangeable. I can move my console to this station. I can even run my screen along side this screen. Hopefully that won't become necessary." Mr. Grant continued.

Axle Laughed. Max looked puzzled.

"If anything happens to the pilot it's a safe bet it will happen to all of us.

Captain Hunter smiled and laughed. "Well said."

Max smiled and proceeded with the tour. "The base of the column is stationary, but the console can turn 360 degrees, and adjust up or down. The chair can move with the console, or it can be turned around and used as a padded leaning post. Also, the pad can drop down and become a stool, or it can swing out of the way. But, you have to be seated to be strapped in." Grant demonstrated as he spoke.

Can a chair have any more functions? Axle thought.

"What Mr. Brock did not show you, is that all the Y3-Glass panels on the inside, convert into a view-screen that can zoom in on what's taking place outside." Grant touched the console, and they had a panoramic, magnified view of the inside of Partenza Hall. "It can use all the panels or just one. Zoom-in, zoom-out, any questions?"

"Yes, what's the reason for all the fiber-optics? Why

isn't everything wireless?" Axle asked.

"Everything is wireless. But, because there are so many unknowns, we hard-wired all the systems in case something jams the signals. That was a good question. When in doubt, ask. Our lives depend on combined knowledge," he replied.

"I agree," Captain stated.

As they returned to their stations, Mr. Grant asked Axle, "What motor configurations will you be locking in?"

"The two front motors for steering; operated with the right rocker pad. The six rear motors for speed and general direction; with the left. Sliding my thumbs inward accelerates on both," Axle stated confidently.

"Good! A wise choice."

"Would you like me to demonstrate?" Axle asked.

"That won't be necessary. I designed the rockers and the motors. But, by you choosing the 2 - 6 combination, gives me confidence that you know what you're doing," he smiled.

"Wow, that was awkward!" Axle grinned, a bit humbled. "But, thank you. I appreciate that."

After just two days of training, Axle knew everything there was to know about the console and certainly had no doubt in his own ability.

On the third morning, as the crew was finishing breakfast, they were interrupted by Jack Brock's voice. They looked to see his unsmiling face on the mess hall monitor announcing, "Its time! I didn't tell you yesterday, because no one would have slept last night. In 15 minutes, at 0900 hours, you will board the ship and go through the pre-launch checklist."

"Does he ever smile?" Axle remarked, to no one in particular.

"If I found you the least bit amusing, I would smile."

The monitor abruptly went blank.

Everyone in the mess hall laughed!

"We go back a long way," Captain Hunter broke in. "I thought I saw him smile once, but he was just fighting something stuck in his teeth."

Still laughing, they rose from the table and quickly headed toward Partenza Hall.

Suddenly, Axle was flooded with fear, excitement and apprehension. His heart was racing. He even felt a little light headed. *"Control yourself,"* he uttered under his breath. He attempted a smile as to appear calm. He looked around, hoping no one could tell what he was going through. All his colleagues had the same nervous expression. Relief! He was not alone.

They approached the stairs of the ship in silence. No one made the first move to board. The possibility that they may never return was apparent.

Axle now realized why Franklin St. Marten was not able to reveal that the mission involved time-travel. As a test pilot, he is fully aware of all the possible degrees of danger with *any* prototype. But with *time-travel*, the unknowns are endless. No wonder it will pay so much. There is a good chance they won't have to pay at all.

After an awkward moment, the Captain pushed his way through saying, "What's the holdup?" Appropriately, he climbed the stairs first and then turned to extend his hand.

Miss Doe took it quickly and then climbed on board. Axle, giving in to a wave of exhilaration, filed in right behind her. Mr. Grant followed. The Captain helped Dr. Lucas and Miss Qui aboard. They seated themselves quickly and strapped in.

Brock's face suddenly appeared, covering six panels, six feet high and nine feet wide. His forced smile was artificial, as if it was painted on. It made them roar with laughter. It calmed them.

"There, I'm smiling! The plan is to break phase, roll the platform out of Partenza Hall on the tracks. Once the ship is clear, you will have a mild lift off. Our research scientists assured me that there has not been a significant terrain alteration in the last 20,000 years. A few thousand feet would be enough altitude."

"If it's all the same to you, I would like to go up at least three miles, to stay above the Rocky's."

"You're the Captain," Brock responded.

"Miss Qui, break phase now!" Captain Hunter just gave his first command. After a short pause, "There's the signal!"

Brock, holding his thumbs up, alerted them that they were *out of phase.*

"We can see them so clearly. It's hard to believe that they're unable to see us at all," Mr. Grant exclaimed.

"I'm sure Brock is wearing one of those special contact lenses, so he *is* seeing us," Miss Doe chimed in.

They watched as the ground crew opened the Hangar door and slowly rolled the platform out with the invisible ship on it. Axle laid his hands lightly on the rockers, but had to add downward pressure to keep them from visibly shaking.

"Mr. Kade, take us up three miles. Begin ascending, now!" Captain commanded.

"Yes, sir."

It felt like they were floating. There was virtually no noise. The electric motors lifted the ship effortlessly.

"Miss Qui, what is the fastest we can travel back through time?"

"We should be able to reach 1,000 years per second, sir," she replied.

"Good! Dr. Lucas, what side effects, if any, can we expect?"

"We have no way of knowing, sir. I'll be documenting the side effects, assuming, we survive," she replied smiling.

"Okay, that's reassuring," Captain Hunter said, with a touch of sarcasm in his voice. "Everyone, brace yourselves for the next 30 seconds."

"Mr. Grant, set the controls for minus 20,000 years and begin jump now!"

"Yes, sir."

The G-Force worked in reverse. They should have turned their seats around. If it weren't for the harnesses, they would have been sucked forward and stuck to the nose of the ship, in a big pile.

The women screamed, the men groaned as the belts pressed unbearably tight against their chests.

Mr. Grant yelled, "Just a few more seconds."

Their bodies abruptly settled back into their seats.

"Is everyone, alright?" Captain Hunter asked.

"You mean, other than our stomachs being left behind?" Axle joked.

He ignored the comment and asked, "When does the visual come back on?"

Outside, the ship was pitch-black. Not a hint of light.

"The visual should still be on. There must be a malfunction. I'm working on it." Miss Qui replied.

"Are we inside a mountain? Three miles high should have been enough clearance," Captain Hunter questioned.

"Whatever we're in, it's jamming our instruments. They aren't functioning at all outside the ship," Qui stated.

"Mr. Grant, go to night vision," Captain commanded.

"Yes, sir."

They gasped!

"Where on earth are we?" Captain questioned.

They were completely surrounded by chunks of chopped, oily, green gelatin.

"The green is coming from the night vision," Mr. Grant answered.

"I'm not 100% sure," Miss Qui interjected, "but I don't think this is earth."

"Mr. Kade, move the ship out of here," Captain Hunter commanded.

"Sir, the motors are running, but we're not moving. I'll try a short blast with the rocket thrusters. Nothing! How is that possible? We are dead in the water."

Miss Qui chimed in with panic in her voice, "I detect no water, no air, no dirt, no space, or anything else. We are in some kind of a void that our sensors can't measure."

Captain Hunter yelled back, "You're the Science

Officer, figure out what happened."

"I'm working on it, but I believe we somehow jumped dimensions. That's what's causing our instruments not to function outside the ship," she said, sounding more alarmed.

"Jumped dimensions?" he shouted in disbelief. "Get us out of here! This place is eerie! And did I hear you say there's no space? How could there be no space? What am I looking at?"

"If there was space, I would be reading space," Miss Qui shot back. "That's why I think we jumped dimensions. In this dimension, there is nothing! Not even space."

"Explain that!"

"Captain, it's like trying to grab a handful of helium, it's not possible. Nothing in our dimension is able to touch anything in *this* dimension."

"I'm still not getting it!" he shot back.

Trying to remain calm, she said, "It's like jumping into a swimming pool with a thin air space around you that keeps you from getting wet. You don't sink to the bottom, because there is no gravity."

Captain stared at her blankly.

"Or, we see the reflection of an object in a mirror, but when we try to touch the object, we find in *our* dimension, it is just a reflection. But, in its *own* dimension, it's an object. The truth is, there is no way to describe it. We are the first to ever see another dimension."

"How do you know the objects *are* out there?" he questioned.

"Because, that is what we are seeing through the night vision. Objects from this dimension are taking up all the space. They just don't have any weight that we can measure, so they're not considered matter. They're not three-dimensional. This ship is the only three-dimensional object in this place. And my guess is, the only reason we are still alive, is because we are *out of phase*," she replied, apprehensively.

"Miss Qui, can we still move through time?"

"Captain, we are not caught in a period of time, which

we can control," she stated firmly. "We are caught in a dimension where time does not exist, and never will! We can't travel through something that doesn't exist!"

"I'm open to suggestions. Does anyone have a suggestion?" Captain Hunter asked, looking around. "Miss Doe, you've been pretty quiet, do you have anything?"

"Me? I do plants, why would I have anything? This certainly doesn't fit in my line of work."

"Mine either," Dr. Lucas said sharply. "Call me if you start to get sick."

Axle interjected, "I don't know *much* about the science or time part. . .

Miss Qui, rudely cut him off. "Much? You don't know *anything*, except up, down, and around!"

It appears Miss Qui panics easily and has a bit of a temper.

"Hey, I'm stuck here too," Axle said. "You may be a brilliant Science Officer, but even in my limited intellect, I can see you're lacking in common sense."

The others nodded in agreement.

"I just wanted to suggest that we ease it forward, about a thousand years a minute and see what happens," he advised. "After all, we found a way in, so common sense would suggest there *is* a way out."

"You don't get it!" Miss Qui snapped at him. "Nothing is going to change the fact, that we are stuck in another dimension. And nothing from our dimension is going to work *here!*"

"Just give it ten to fifteen minutes," Axle pleaded.

"I say we try it, till someone else has a better idea," Dr. Lucas added.

"I like it. Make it happen. Can you set an automatic stop if the outside sensors come back on line?" Captain asked.

"Of course, I can." She tapped her monitor. "There, it's done. But we are still going nowhere!"

"Brace yourselves," Captain yelled.

"That won't be necessary," Miss Qui stated. "We'll be traveling sixty times slower, and I am able to adjust the interior conditions to compensate for the pressure."

"Why didn't you do that before, when we were being sucked forward?" Captain Hunter asked.

"Because I needed to analyze a test run."

They stared at her in shock!

"Start to move us forward," Captain commanded.

"I already did. We're just *not* going anywhere."

"Oh, it's going to be a long fifteen minutes," Dr. Lucas sighed, folding her arms.

Fear was setting in. The silence was thick.

We could all die here, and I don't even know their first names, Axle thought. He could see Miss Qui was visibly shaken. *Maybe if I get her to talk, she'll calm down,* he reasoned.

"So, Miss Qui, tell us a little bit about yourself?"

Mr. Grant nodded his approval.

"What do you want to know?" she said suspiciously.

"Anything you want to tell us."

"There's nothing to tell."

"Oh, come on. I'm stuck here with all of you, in an alternate dimension, for what might turn out be a very long time, and I don't even know your first names or anything about you," Axle remarked.

She rolled her eyes and huffed in annoyance. "Okay, my name is Marcella. I was born in Hawaii, and I graduated college at twelve."

"That's remarkable!" Dr. Lucas exclaimed, clapping.

They all joined in. Marcella Qui actually smiled.

She graduated college at twelve? She probably didn't have much of a childhood. Now, that would explain her lack of social skills, Axle thought.

"I had a lot to do with the creation of this ship. I'm 27 and single," she added, less defensively.

"Do you have a boyfriend?" Dr. Doe asked.

"No, I've never had the time."

That's sad to hear. She's so beautiful, Axle thought.

"Captain, we're still nowhere!" she announced.

"When I want a progress report, I'll ask," Captain snapped back, frustrated.

"What about you, Dr. Lucas?" Mr. Grant asked.

"My name is Patricia, but my friends call me Doc. My mother died at an early age from a disease so rare, almost no one ever heard of it. I was inspired to go into medicine and find cures for rare diseases. I excelled and here I am."

She, too, probably didn't have much of a childhood.

"I've spent most of my career in the lab or around the sick. So, this was a welcomed change. I'm 33, also single. I've had a few boyfriends, but not right now," she added.

She is very attractive, very personable, why isn't she married or engaged? Axle thought.

"Hey! Wait a minute," Axle broke in, "is *anyone* here married?"

They all shook their heads!

"That's why they picked me! Being single must have been a pre-requisite. I must be the best *single* pilot they could find," he laughed, and they joined in. "My name is Axle, and I'm 30. My father was a test pilot, and I was born to fly."

Mr. Grant jumped in. "My name is Maxwell, call me Max. I excelled in electronics-to-mechanical application. I helped develop a lot of the systems on this ship; without even knowing it was capable of time-travel. I'm 31, and being single is probably why they picked me, as well. They were afraid we'd tell our spouses about the mission."

"That's not why!" Marcella said sarcastically. "They think we may not make it back, and it looks like they're right!"

"Marcella, that's enough," Captain reprimanded.

"What about you, Captain?" Axle asked.

"Not much to tell," he replied. "My name is Eli. I'm 38. I was married at an early age; never had any children. I gave up my wife to chase my career, or so *she* said. She's remarried and has the family she always wanted. I have the career I always wanted, and we are living happily ever after. Just not together."

The mood just lifted a bit, as they all laughed.

"Miss Doe, your turn," Axle said.

"Don't laugh. My name is Jane. And, yes, I have a brother named John."

They roared!

"That's okay," she said. "I'm used to that."

"Please, continue," Max said a little curious.

"Well, I have always been intrigued by the intricate design of things that grow. I am 29, a single mom, with a 7-year-old daughter, who is dying from a rare disease. Doc has been looking for a cure through medicine, and I have been searching for a *natural* remedy through plants."

Doc interjected, "We have a few theories that look promising."

"This is the chance of a lifetime for me," Jane added.

"What's your daughter's name?" Axle asked.

"Tori," she said proudly. "She's a delight."

Doc added, "She is! Tori just lights up the room when you're around her. Even though she is in so much pain, her smile never dims. She is the epitome of inspiration for me. I promised Jane, that I am committing everything I can to developing a cure for Tori. I share the same level of determination as Jane."

Plain Jane Doe? There doesn't seem to be anything plain about her. Quite the opposite, there's something extraordinary about her. I would never have taken her for 29, Axle thought.

"Did you just say *intricate design*?" Marcella questioned.

"Yes, I said design," Jane replied.

"There's no proof that things were *designed,*" she snapped. "Scientific theories say, *everything just happened!*"

"Marcella, creation makes sense! The 'everything-just-happened-theory', makes *non-sense!*" Jane laughed a bit.

"From a medical perspective, Marcella," Doc jumped

in, "there's a better chance of a fully functional android robot happening by accident than a single strand of DNA developing on its own. We *know* it's a design. Each cell carries the blueprints of your entire body in a six foot strand of DNA. Can you imagine *accidentally* cramming thirty miles of wire inside a cherry pit? We just don't know who, how, where, when, or why. The *alien* DNA theory seems plausible to some, but then we have the problem of where that DNA came from.

Marcella remained silent.

"I like Axle's theory," Jane said.

"What theory?" they asked in unison, including Axle.

7

~ THE GENESIS CHIP ~

"**W**ell, Axle, do you want to tell them your theory?" Jane asked.

"I don't have a theory," he stammered.

"You have the Book of Controversy with you."

"No I don't."

"Well, what's this?" She pointed to the pendant around Axle's neck.

"It's from my grandfather. He gave it to me for luck."

Jane laughed.

Axle pulled it from his shirt to take a closer look. He tugged the bottom of the ornament; it separated, revealing a computer chip.

Grandpa! he thought.

"My dad gave me one a long time ago," Jane said. "They took it when I tried to bring it on board. They said no personal computer chips."

"My aunt put one in my bag," Doc added. "They confiscated it, as well. She called it the Genesis Chip. She claims *time* was created, just like everything else. And we might finally find out the truth on this mission."

"You told your aunt?" Captain Eli questioned. "That sounds like you violated your non-disclosure agreement!"

"I'm not concerned. Who would believe her anyway?"

"I felt the same way, so I told my family too," Jane admitted.

"Same here," Axle added.

"Ditto," Max chimed in.

Even Marcella admitted telling her family.

Captain Hunter just smiled, shaking his head. "Well, it looks like we might have plenty of time to check out *everybody's* theory. Marcella, do you have anything yet?"

"If that's a joke, I don't get it, sir," she quipped.

"How long have we been here?"

"Just over twelve minutes, sir. It may as well be twelve years," she replied, her words trailing off.

"Give Axle's suggestion another five minutes. Then we'll try another solution. In the meantime, I expect you to stop being so negative and start trusting your colleagues," Captain warned.

"I'll try, sir," she said with a smirk.

"Captain, everything we have done has been recorded. If we retrace our steps exactly, we might just get back," Max suggested.

"Keep recording. We are not ready to go yet. We haven't accomplished our mission. That *is* why we came."

"Yes, sir, I meant only as a last resort..." Max stopped mid sentence as a vibration overtook the ship. It began to rotate.

"I feel motion, we're moving," the Captain shouted.

"We're rotating slowly, sir." Axle added.

"Marcella, give me a time check."

"13 minutes, 17 seconds, Captain."

"Well? What's happening?" he asked loudly.

"I don't know, sir," Marcella said.

The autopilot put them at minus 24 seconds, *out of phase*. The outside changed. The green gelatin took on a different form. It was frightening. A strange substance began bleeding through the cracks and compressing it. It resembled the inside of a beehive.

"Marcella, are the sensors picking up any of this?" Captain Eli yelled.

"No!"

"Care to speculate?" he shot back.

"Not yet, sir, but it seems to have stopped."

Finally, the ship halted its movement, and everything became acutely still. No one could speculate what would happen next.

There was silent anticipation.

Outside the ship, something was surging through the beehive, almost like bubbles bursting and splattering everything; leaving what looked like a residue everywhere.

"Well, anyone?" Captain Eli shouted.

"Oh no, brace yourselves!" Marcella yelled. "I'm picking up traces of energy, and I think I know what's happening. Everyone fasten your seat belts."

"Do it!" Captain Eli, shouted, turning to Marcella, "What's happening?"

"We are witnessing different dimensions coming together, and a transformation is taking place," she said with fear in her voice.

"So what's with the, '*brace yourselves, fasten the seat belts*'?" Max questioned, frantically.

As soon as he got the words out of his mouth, black lightning bolts, pushed through every hole. Instantly, the ship was tossed like it was shot out of a cannon.

Marcella shouted, "The sensors are online!"

"Captain, I have propulsion, should I try to slow the ship down?" Axle asked.

Before Captain Eli could answer him, Max and Marcella both shouted at the same time,"*No! Don't touch anything!*"

Axle jerked his hands from the controls.

"Sir, we have expanding space and rapidly moving matter," Marcella replied excitedly. "If we were *in phase,* we would have already been crushed to dust."

"Axle, if we slow down, everything moving behind us will overtake us, and we will be destroyed. Or, if we alter our course the slightest bit, we could miss our dimension," Max said. "But why can't I get a reading on our speed?"

"Because our speed is too fast to measure," Marcella answered.

"Can you estimate?" Captain Eli questioned. "The ship isn't designed for light speed."

"I don't know how it's happening," Marcella said, "but judging from the point of origin of the explosion, we're traveling at many times the speed of light."

"We must be moving with the expanding space, because if we were going *through* space, the ship would have already come apart. The space must be expanding like a wave, and we're caught in it," Max exclaimed.

"The matter seems to be traveling with us and at the same rate of speed. That's probably why we're still alive. All the matter I am able to scan so far has a spherical shape of every size, which could explain a lot," Marcella said.

"Meteors and asteroids are not round!" Jane yelled.

"It seems everything started out round, but things collide. The explosions at the point of origin are continuous," Max interjected. "We must have caught the first wave. We've almost come to a complete halt. How could we have stopped that quickly?"

"I was hoping *this* was our dimension," Marcella said.

"We have matter and expanding space; why *couldn't* this be our dimension?" Captain Eli questioned.

"If it is, we are in serious trouble," she answered.

"Why?" he asked anxiously, frustration mounting.

"We have no way of knowing where we are. We could be anywhere! We were just shot halfway across this dark galaxy. I'm reading all the elements of our dimension, but there's no Earth, moon, planets, or sun, not even light! All the matter is molten and should at least be glowing. We should be seeing this without night vision. I'm reading hot stars everywhere but without light."

"Could that have been the Big Bang? It's accepted that the Big Bang is the explosion that created the universe, right?" Captain Eli asked.

"That could not have been the Big Bang," Marcella answered.

"Why not?" Doc asked.

"Because, the Big Bang happened 40 billion years ago, for one. And it didn't create the universe," Marcella responded, clearly agitated.

"Then what did the Big Bang do?" Axle inquired.

"The Big Bang Theory summarizes that either a giant piece of matter, or all the matter in the universe, was compressed into one very heavy dot," Marcella answered emphatically. "Then it exploded, and the universe was formed."

"However, a few problems have always been attached to that theory. Matter can't be created or destroyed, for one," Max added.

"So, where did the giant piece of matter or the very heavy dot come from?" Jane asked.

"Well, that is one of the mysteries that we hope to solve, along with all the heavenly bodies not spinning in the same direction," Marcella answered.

"Some other puzzling questions are," Max chimed in, "why is everything a spherical shape? Why aren't all the blue stars burnt out, since they burn too hot to last billions of years? Also, an explosion doesn't explain where all the elements came from."

"I can't believe what I'm hearing," Axle exclaimed.

"Which part?" Marcella asked.

"*That's it? That's* the scientific Big Bang Theory?" he responded sarcastically. "A giant rock? Or better yet, a little dot that contained all the matter in the universe? No one knows where it came from? But it was eternal, because it was always there? That's the most ridiculous thing I've ever heard!"

"Axle, take it easy." Captain commanded.

"I'm sorry, sir, but I've had many heated arguments with my grandfather defending this so-called Big Bang Theory. It was presented as an explosion that started everything. I never heard about the little dot or giant rock; that must have been in the fine print. And, if there *was* a giant rock or a little dot, then it wasn't the beginning, was it? The scientist that came up with *that one* crossed the line from science, to philosophy, to science fiction; because he certainly did not have any facts. I can't believe I got sucked into that nonsense. I feel duped!"

"It's considered a viable theory," Marcella added.

"Then, Marcella," Captain Eli interrupted, "what was it that just exploded? After all, we didn't see a giant rock or anything else. We were in the green gelatin, it started changing, and now we're here; in what seems like our own dimension. And if we didn't have sensors or enhanced night vision, we wouldn't be seeing any of this."

"Max, you *did* record everything, didn't you?" asked Marcella.

"Yes, I did," Max assured her. "I'll put it up on sixteen panels, so we can get a better perspective. There."

The screen was massive at four panels across and four panels high. It took the entire width and height of the front of the ship.

"That's the dimension we were in first, then as each dimension is introduced, a transformation takes place," Max explained.

"I count at least five different dimensions, plus whatever it took to create the energy," Marcella said.

"See, at this point we didn't have matter, space or sensor readings," Max added. "Now, I'm moving forward. Watch closely, any second now. Right there. The explosion! And immediately, we are in *this* dimension." He stopped the recording.

"Why didn't we hear the explosion?" Captain asked.

"It's not that kind of explosion," Max answered.

"I didn't think there was more than one kind," Jane remarked.

"Well, it's like mixing two chemicals in the lab; it produces an endless amount of foam," Max said.

Everyone looked at Max, puzzled.

"What?" Doc said.

"I'll take it from here, Max," Marcella chimed in. "It would seem that five or more dimensions were mixed together. Matter is not what's exploding. The explosions, for lack of a better term, are literally creating the matter. It is also creating the expanding space, time and everything else in this universe. It's like properly mixing oxygen and hydrogen and getting water."

"Now *that* makes sense," Axle broke in.

"It only makes sense because you saw it happen," Max added. "But it still doesn't explain how we got mega millions of light years from the point of origin, in just a few minutes."

"Max, move the recording forward, slowly. Max, I said slowly," Marcella pleaded.

"Marcella, that's frame by frame."

"What? How is that happening?

Their distance kept doubling from the point of origin. As if they were jumping through space.

"Look closer," Max said. "Each frame shows twice the distance from the point of origin."

They weren't jumping; space was literally unfolding, like a bed sheet. Each time it unfolded; it doubled in size. It appeared as if they were dropped around the eleventh fold.

"Uh-oh!"

"Why the uh-oh, Max?" Captain asked quickly.

"The explosions at the point of origin haven't stopped. Here comes another wave unfolding. There must have been collisions. I'm reading asteroids and meteors now. *Brace yourselves!*" he shouted.

Instantly, the autopilot threw the ship into erratic movements. Without any warning, it sporadically changed speed and direction. The body harnesses were cutting into their flesh, again!

Axle felt like he was being worked over by a karate expert. He can't imagine the women taking much more of this pounding. It was like trying to dodge shrapnel from an exploding hand grenade.

The *out of phase* time delay made it appear as if they were being hit continually. No one had any idea the ship could maneuver in such a way. The wave finally started to subside and the ship began moving normally.

"My body can't take it, and my mind can't look at it

anymore," Jane winced.

"I cannot do that again. I kept covering my face expecting to be pulverized any second! We are caught right in the middle. Can't we move to a safer place?" Doc pleaded.

"This *is* as safe as it gets," Marcella answered. "It's happening all over, as far out as our sensors are able to scan."

"Captain, we can't last another wave, we've already burned 63% of the rocket fuel. When we run out of fuel, time delay or not, that's it," Axle stated.

"Axle, south-southwest, full speed," Captain ordered. "Something huge is being dropped at 1 o'clock."

With his right hand, Axle mashed down hard on the rocket thruster control and held it. The outside of his left hand was pushing down holding the south-southwest heading.

The women were gasping.

The sphere grew bigger and drew closer toward them.

Axle held the thruster down. "I'm at full speed."

The sphere immediately stopped growing and began to shrink. Axle backed off to conserve fuel, as he braced for another wave coming. He was able to put the sphere between them and the incoming debris.

"Don't get too close, it's pretty hot," Eli ordered.

"Yes, sir."

He backed off and got under the sphere, adjusting the distance to burn the minimum amount of fuel.

"Captain, the fuel is down to 16%. But, even if the tanks were full, there's no place to go."

"We will have a place to go, Axle, when my Science Officer figures out where we are."

Marcella cut in, "We can't land. Everything is molten. Again, we should be seeing this without night vision."

The atmosphere was eerily dark.

"Captain, I am 99% sure this one is going to be Earth in a few million years, after it cools. It has the same mass and diameter. Wait, I'm registering a drop in temperature."

"We should be safe here for the time being, Captain.

I'm holding at the edge of the gravitational pull, and I'm able to drift without using the rocket thrusters."

"Good work, Axle! Max, how long before the solar cells are drained?"

"About three to five days; if we conserve everything, except climate control and life support."

"Captain," Marcella shouted, "the temperature has dropped rapidly."

She began to read spacial distortions totally covering the planet. The entire surface became liquified.

"It's water!" Marcella exclaimed. How is that even possible? Water only exists between 32 and 212 degrees."

"Captain, judging from the other spheres that are being dropped," Max jumped in, "this solar system is taking form right before our eyes."

"Can this be Earth?" Marcella said shocked.

There was no sun, no moon. Not even land. Just water!

"We have light!" Doc shouted excitedly. "Everything is pure white. I have *never* seen anything like this! There is *no* color. It's so bright and yet, it doesn't hurt my eyes. Where is it coming from?"

"Max, tint the windows."

"This is as dark as they get, sir. I had them set for automatic. This light isn't even registering on my sensors."

"Where is the light coming from?" Captain Eli asked.

"I can't explain it. The light seems to be coming from everywhere, except there are *no* shadows. Look under your feet!" Marcella remarked.

"How could there be no shadows? A minute ago we couldn't see anything because it was so dark, and now we can't see anything because this white-light is so bright."

"It's so beautiful," Jane said smiling. "Just relax and enjoy it!"

"I'm feeling an exaggerated sense of well being. No stress at all," Axle interjected calmly.

They all agreed. Even Marcella!

8

~THE FIRST DAY~

"Captain, the light is becoming directional; we're getting shadows," Marcella said calmly.

"*And there was light!* **The First Day!**" Jane announced, stunned.

"What do you mean the first day?" Max questioned.

"Of course, that must be it. **The First Day!** Axle, give me the Genesis Chip!" Doc said excitedly.

He pulled the chip from its holder, dangling around his neck, and handed it to her; his hands shaking.

"Axle, I owe you an apology, I underestimated you. I was rude."

"That's okay, Marcella. Tensions were high."

Marcella apologizing? She's not the type. It must have something to do with the light.

"Why were you so sure we would return to our dimension, Axle?" she asked.

"We know time is a dimension, and I was just hoping we would run into it. And when you said the only reason we were still alive was because we were *out of phase*, I realized that the *phase* control was functioning in that dimension."

"That was a well thought out deduction," she smiled.

"Didn't you say matter couldn't be created or destroyed, Marcella?" Captain Eli asked.

"It can't, sir. I have no logical explanation for what happened."

"I do," Jane broke in. "Matter cannot be created or destroyed; *by us!*"

"Here, put the chip in, maybe we'll find something we can use," Doc said handing it to Max.

"Okay, I'll put it overhead on two panels."

"Read it," Captain Eli commanded.

"I will," Jane volunteered. **"In the beginning God created the heavens and the earth. The earth was formless and empty; darkness was over the surface of the deep, and the Spirit of God was hovering over the waters. And God said,** *"Let there be light",* **and there was light. God saw that the light was good"**

"Good?" Axle blurted out. "That's an understatement. The light is great!"

Jane continued, **"And He separated the light from the darkness. God called the light "Day", and he called the darkness "Night". So evening and the morning were the first day."**

"Isn't that pretty much what just happened?" Doc interrupted.

"No, that's *exactly* what just happened," Marcella interjected. "What's next, Jane?"

"Then God said, *"Let there be an expanse in the midst of the waters, and let it divide the waters from the waters."* **And God made the expanse, and divided the waters, which were under the expanse from the waters, which were above the expanse: and it was so. And God called the expanse "sky". And the evening and the morning were the second day."**

"If something like that happens tomorrow, we'll know for sure the chip can be trusted," Captain said.

"I've always had a problem understanding just what that means," Doc stated.

"If the Genesis Chip is correct, then the clouds and the atmosphere happen tomorrow," Max added.

"That's not the way I'm reading it. Aren't the clouds *in* the expanse? It said divide the waters below the expanse from the waters above the expanse. It's very confusing," Doc reiterated.

"I don't care what kind of atmosphere it's talking about, as long as we can stop using the rocket thrusters. Marcella, inch us forward four hours a minute. Axle, take us to two thousand feet above the water."

"Yes, sir," they said simultaneously.

It was suddenly pitch-black. They were peering into a totally dark universe. The only light came from within the ship.

"This is so hard to comprehend," Marcella said. "I'm glad this will only last a few minutes."

Suddenly, there was pure white-light!

"Look? The water is being drawn up right past us. Where is it going? That's too high for clouds!" Max exclaimed.

"Max, display it on the ceiling panels, magnify and add contrast, so we can see." Captain Eli ordered.

"I don't see any clouds," Jane said.

A canopy of water formed above them and an ocean below them; and they were *right* in the middle.

"Now that matches what we just read. But how is the water staying up?" Doc questioned.

"I'm not sure yet, it could be some kind of surface tension. Max and I are working on it," Marcella answered.

"If it *is* surface tension, it could be very fragile. Axle get closer, but avoid puncturing it," Captain Eli said.

"Captain," Marcella interrupted, "it's not fragile. It appears there are at least three forces present. Gravity is holding the canopy from drifting off into space."

"The Earth has no tilt and is spinning at 1200+ mph," Max jumped in, "creating enough centrifugal force to hold the canopy up."

Marcella interrupted, "And there's *just enough* ice, so the magnetic polls of the Earth are repelling it, keeping it stationary."

"There could be more forces at work here. Forces we don't even know about yet. It would take a lifetime to study this," Max added.

"This is incredible! As a scientist, everything I have learned is through trial and error. There is no experimentation here!" Marcella exclaimed in awe.

"There's no way of comprehending how the water is

suspended," Max added.

"There's no scientific explanation for it," Marcella went on. "It's too complicated for our minds to comprehend; and to be done *without* technology is out of the question. This is *no longer* science. This is a different realm. What we just witnessed is an act of *absolute perfection.*" She paused. "I am undone!" She began to weep.

"Marcella, pull yourself together. We need you," Captain Eli said sternly.

"What would be the purpose of a canopy of water around the earth?" Axle asked.

"I don't know yet, but I'm working on it," Max answered. "Everything looks normal. Wait, the atmospheric pressure is too high. It's over 21 lbs per square inch. It should read 14.7 lbs. Marcella, double check."

She remained motionless.

"Marcella, please snap out of it."

"I'm trying, Max," she said sniffling. "I have 21.4 lbs per square inch, and stabilizing. But what difference could that make?"

Doc interjected, "Viruses cannot live under that much pressure, it's a germ-free environment."

"The water stopped rising, and it's getting dark," Jane added.

"Jane, continue reading," Captain Eli requested.

"The third day!" She began reading. **"And God said, *"Let the waters under the sky be gathered together into one place, and let the dry land appear"*, and it was so. And God called the dry land *"Earth"*, and the gathering together of the waters he called *"Seas"*. And God saw that it was good. Then God said, *"Let the earth bring forth grass, the herb that yields seed, and the fruit tree that yields fruit according to it's kind, whose seed is in itself, on the earth"*, and it was so. And there was evening and there was morning- the third day."**

"It looks like tomorrow is *my day,*" Jane added excitedly.

"I want to see how dry land could just appear. Where does the water go?" Max asked.

They watched in awe as the white-light ushered in the morning and seismic activity followed immediately. A series of underwater earthquakes, each one triggering the next, created circular waves moving outward from a central point. The waves grew and picked up speed.

"Is this going to be a tsunami?" Axle asked Max.

"There's no land to slow these waves down. Their growth is going to be limitless. This is going to make a tsunami look like a ripple in a pond."

The waves encircled the entire planet. The seismic activity increased, and the waves became immense! The water gathered in one place.

"Axle, take us down for a closer look," Captain Eli ordered.

"Look at this! Once the circular waves get past the center of the planet, the circle gets smaller. The waves are growing even higher," Max said excitedly. "And the speed is increasing tremendously!"

"Axle, don't be over the waves when the circle closes. There is no way of knowing how high the water will shoot up when the waves crash in on themselves," Marcella warned.

"*Here it goes*!" Max shouted.

The waves reached four miles in height and shot up another mile and a half. The weight was enough to knock the earth on its axis!

"It's crashing down!" Max shouted. "The tremendous weight and downward pressure is forcing water to go about fifteen miles below the Earth's surface."

The water pressure literally lifted up a layer of earth. The Earth itself swallowed up the water, as if simple hydraulics made the land appear. A layer of water formed approximately ten miles under the ocean and encircled the entire planet! The crust of the Earth took shape right before their eyes.

"That layer of water was not there when we left

home," Marcella said astonished.

"What do you mean?" Axle questioned her. "We have underground water, underground water tables. We even have underground springs."

"Yes," Max said, "but nothing of this magnitude."

What they were witnessing was the equivalent to an underground ocean. The hydraulic pressure pushed up a vast amount of dry land. The Earth was now almost 70% land, instead of 70% water. They all stared in amazement!

"You could literally walk anywhere on Earth, and I'm already registering vegetation," Jane said. "How could it be growing so quickly? I've got fully grown fruit trees. We're still only traveling at four hours per minute, aren't we, Marcella?"

"Yes."

Plant life grew underwater, as well. Everything was still pure white to the naked eye. They could barely distinguish grass from trees, or water from the land.

"If we didn't add contrast with the panels, we would be missing most of this," Captain remarked.

"That's it," Jane exclaimed. "Photosynthesis! Plants turn sunlight into food. This light is the ultimate banquet for the plants. Marcella said the light wasn't registering, it's because it's off the charts."

"Off the charts!" Captain Eli yelled. "Max, check the solar cells."

Max ran back and checked the temperature, and quickly closed the solar panel covers.

"They're real hot, but not fried yet!" Max shouted. "That was close. But instead of a weeks worth of power, we probably have more like a year."

"Max, didn't you have a scar on your neck?" Jane asked.

"Since I was a kid, why?"

"Well, it's gone now," she remarked.

"What?" Max felt his neck. "It's gone! That was not a little surface scar, I almost cut my jugular! I got my belt caught on a strand of barbed wire climbing a fence, when it popped loose, it cut my neck. I almost died!"

Doc started scanning the crew. The look of shock on her face was making them nervous.

"Tell us, please," Marcella begged. "What's going on?"

"We're all in perfect health!" Doc said amazed.

"We were in perfect health when we left. Our medical exams were extensive," Axle joked.

"No, we were in *acceptable* health. No one is this healthy!" Doc chuckled.

"Axle, are you looking down your pants?" Captain Eli asked, laughing.

"The mark from my appendectomy is gone."

Doc scanned Axle again and said, "Well, that's because your appendix is back!"

Marcella whispered in Doc's ear. She scanned her abdomen and said, "Everything is normal."

Marcella's eyes welled with tears.

"What's going on?" Jane asked.

"I had some female problems," Marcella replied.

The men stared blankly at her.

"Now, I'll be able to have a family when the time comes," she responded through her tears.

Doc embraced her. They all smiled, except for Jane.

"I wish there was a way to go back and pick up my daughter," she said, not expecting an answer, tears streaming down her face.

Captain Eli smiled and tried to comfort her, "Maybe next time, Jane."

They spent a few minutes looking for old scars. Even their complexions were clearer.

"Did anyone have cosmetic surgery?" Doc asked.

"We're not going to see anybody's old nose grow back, or anything like that, are we?" Axle joked.

"Or worse yet, implants lying on the floor?" Max added.

They were laughing together.

Axle is beginning to see his colleagues as friends. He wondered if the "light" is having other effects on them, as well.

Captain Eli gave them several more minutes to enjoy themselves, before interrupting. "What comes next, Jane?"

She read: "**And God said, *"Let there be lights in the expanse of the sky to divide the day from night; and let them serve as signs to mark seasons and days and years, And let them be lights in the expanse of the sky to give light on the earth"*, and it was so. Then God made two great lights: the greater light to rule the day, and the lesser light to rule the night. He made the stars also. God set them in the expanse of the heavens to give light to the earth, and to rule over the day and over the night, and to separate light from darkness. And God saw that it was good. And there was evening, and there was morning - the fourth day**.

Jane sounded tired.

Captain Eli glanced at her and then his crew. "You all look a little weary. It's been a long day. Let's stop and get some rest. Marcella, keep us *out of phase* and put us on real time. You all performed well beyond my expectations. Congratulations," he said, proudly.

"Where do you want me to land, sir?" Axle asked.

Jane interjected quickly, "I wouldn't land yet. We could wake up tomorrow beneath ten feet of vegetation, as fast as things are growing."

"We have enough power to hover on autopilot for weeks," Max suggested.

"Axle, do it. Now, what is there to eat? I'm starved," the Captain said with a sigh.

"I have a surprise! I brought the ingredients to make a special eggplant dish for our first meal together, assuming we lived!" Doc laughed. "It will only take about thirty minutes. If you're too hungry, you can have dehydrated food and bags of liquid protein. Does anyone mind waiting?"

"Absolutely not!" Captain replied, quickly.

"That sounds delicious. I never learned to cook. I'd like to help," Marcella said.

"I cook a little, if there's room for me," Max added.

"Sounds great, I need you both," Doc replied.

"Okay, let's take our turn showering, while we're waiting," Captain Eli said to the rest of the crew.

The galley was tight, but nicely done and very well thought out. It crossed the entire rear of the ship. It was sixteen feet long and seven feet wide.

As you entered through the hallway, the right half of the galley was the dining area, with a booth totally constructed of Y3-Glass. Thick red cushions were attached to the bench seats and backs for comfort.

The left half of the galley was the food preparation area, in the shape of a 'U'. There were counters on all three walls. The overhead cabinets were stocked with dehydrated foods and bags of juice. A custom refrigerator, freezer and other state of the art appliances, were built in under the counter of the rear wall. The cabinets under the adjacent counter contained the necessary cooking and eating utensils.

The double sink, connecting the two counters, had a bio-degradable neutralizer. The three-foot space between the counters allowed easy access to anyone in the galley.

"Where do we start?" Marcella asked as she opened the cabinets and stared blankly at the cookware.

It was obvious that Doc knew her way around any kitchen. She was in full command and began immediately putting Max and Marcella to work.

~ ~ ~

Axle was the last to shower. He was anxious to use the sanitation station that he saw on the first day of training. It was a glass cubicle inside the shower cabin. With a wave of your hand, a door opened, allowing you to hang your used towels and days clothes. Then with another wave, the clothes and towels were sealed, and the decontamination process began. Taking all but 30 seconds, the glass door opened, and your articles were cleaned and ready to wear.

Axle was now showered and dressed. He was immediately enticed by the aromas drifting from the galley.

"Something smells incredibly good back there. Is it ready?" His appetite now awakened.

"Almost. Max, remove it from the oven. Marcella, spread the grated cheese and put it in for one minute. Everyone, come and sit down," Doc called out.

Captain Eli and Jane were already seated across from each other, when Axle arrived. He slid in next to Jane. Doc and Marcella were carrying the food to the table while Max was bringing their drinks in thermo-bags.

When everyone was seated and ready to dig in, Jane said, "Is it alright if I say a blessing?"

"What for?" Marcella asked.

"Because of that statement Doc made. She said *'assuming we lived'*. Well, we survived, I don't know how, but we did! This being our first meal together, I feel it's appropriate!"

They immediately bowed their heads.

"Thank you God for this food and bless the hands that prepared it. Amen."

"Wow, *my* hands helped prepare it," Marcella said, pleased with herself.

All six took their first taste of *'Eggplant Ala Doc'*, nearly simultaneously.

Axle chewed especially slow, enjoying the flavors of a home-cooked meal that seemed to be intensified by their near *Lost in Space* predicament.

"Delicious! This tastes even better than it smells. Where did you learn to cook like that?" Captain Eli asked.

"My grandmother was Italian. She taught me if you cook because you want to, you cook with love."

"How many more meals like this did you smuggle aboard?" Captain inquired.

"Sorry, but this is all that I could carry on. If you promise to get us home, I'll do this again."

He smiled and winked saying, "I promise."

They savored every mouthful and enjoyed each others company. Their friendship was growing.

After dinner, while the other three were showering and getting ready for bed, Jane and Axle cleaned up. They didn't say much, but he genuinely enjoyed working along side her.

~ ~ ~

The men's cabin was plain, tight, yet comfortable. There were three bunks that flipped down from the wall. Captain Eli was lying on the bottom bunk. He barely fit. Before Max left for the bathroom, he claimed the center bunk by placing his zeo-pad on it. Axle would have chosen the top bunk anyway.

After the men had settled in, Captain Eli asked, "Everyone alright?"

"I'm okay, just hope the worst is behind us," Axle answered.

"This was *some* day," Max chimed in.

"I know it was harrowing for awhile. Traveling faster than the speed of light, dodging the meteors and asteroids," Captain said laughing.

"Yeah, and not knowing if we were even in the right universe. Man, that better *have* been the worst of it," Max said laughing, as well.

"I knew it was going to be harder than, *'grab the plants and be back before lunch';* the way Jack Brock made it sound," Captain said laughing a little harder.

"But other dimensions? I wasn't prepared for *that*," Axle joked.

"How could anyone be prepared for *that* kind of unknown? So far, this journey has raised the bar on *that* word. I thought unknown meant unfamiliar but possible, or at least within specific parameters of a speculative idea. Except *this* time," Captain Eli remarked.

"I am so amazed the *white-light* restored us all to perfect health, and the scar on my neck is gone. I wanted to have it removed so many times, the cost was just way more than I could afford. I feel empowered! " Max laughed. "Maybe now, I'll have the confidence to ask Marcella out. I wanted to, ever since I first met her."

"Just go for it, Max," Axle advised.

"Good advice from someone still single!

"Good point, Max. You're a lot smarter than you look," Axle joked.

Eli laughed loudly.

~ ~ ~

The girls were pleasantly surprised to see their cabin. The walls were mirrored. Their bunks were cushioned with colorful, plush linens. They had a closet with shelves. A woman must have designed this!

"What an awesome day it's been. My whole life will change, now that I'm able to have children. I avoided potential opportunities for a serious relationship, because it was always in the back of my mind," Marcella said.

"Marcella, I am so happy for you. You have so much to offer. You're so right; your healing is life changing. And, now that you feel whole, another opportunity for a great relationship will appear," Jane said reassuringly.

Doc was nodding in agreement, smiling.

"I thought I would have all those bruises from the safety harness for weeks," Jane added. "They're completely gone. I thought it was over; dodging *all* that debris! Even though, Jack Brock explained the autopilot using time delay, the pounding looked so real."

"I was nodding the whole time Brock was talking, but I didn't quite get it," Doc admitted.

"Me neither! But we sure do now," Jane laughed.

"It would have been helpful if the chairs were made to hold your head still. I thought my neck was going to snap," Doc went on. "It's a miracle! I am grateful we're still alive. I had my eyes closed most of the time, trying to come to terms with the fact, that I was going to die. I felt a glimmer of hope when the Earth was shielding us; until the '*low on fuel, no place to land'* report came."

The girls were giggling now.

"I really admire the way you were able to stand your ground. You kept analyzing and reporting as if nothing was going on around you. You figured out this was Earth! Marcella, you were amazing," Jane said.

"I just know how the time delay works. But how were *you two* able to keep your cool, when we were in that first dimension? We could have dematerialized and been killed instantly. We could have been stuck there for eternity. We could have aged to dust in minutes. We could have run out of power and froze or starved to death in the dark. The possibilities were endless," Marcella poured out.

"What? I didn't know the possibilities were endless. Did you, Jane?" Doc asked.

"No, I thought we would live or die, not be *tortured*."

"Marcella, your knowing all those possible outcomes, must have been terrifying. Thank you for not sharing them with us. It was hard enough trying to trust God and my colleagues, without *that* knowledge," Doc added.

"Your welcome," Marcella chuckled. "I'm really looking forward to tomorrow. The water canopy is really mind boggling; it's too much to comprehend. How could science be that far off?"

"Be careful, you'll get Jane going," Doc laughed.

"Well, she asked," Jane jumped in smiling. "Marcella, there are two kinds of science. One is Operational, which allows us to discover medicines, and build a ship like this. The other is Historical Science, which is *pure* speculation and takes a huge leap of faith. The Big Bang Theory has been your starting point, but no one ever witnessed it."

"So, what's *your* starting point?" Marcella questioned.

"Genesis," Jane responded softly.

"And that's *not a huge leap of faith*?"

"Not when seen as a history book. Operational Science confirms the history written in Genesis. If it didn't, I would have to find a new starting point. My duty, as a botanist, is to find out how to use that information in my experiments. Genesis, as a history book, has never been wrong," Jane stated.

"I would love to get into this, but I'm exhausted. Let's save this for another day, okay?"

"Agreed," Jane smiled.

"Thank God!" Doc chimed in.

"Wow, you're right! Thank God!" Jane added.

~ ~ ~

Axle awoke the next morning to the brilliant white-light. He appeared to be well-rested as he easily hopped down from his bunk. Before sauntering into the bathroom, he greeted the others with, "Does anyone else feel supercharged?"

Max yelled from the galley, "Yeah, I feel like my brain has been scrubbed clean."

"Exactly," Doc chime in. "As if my mind and body have been totally revitalized."

Max and Doc were already seated at the table enjoying a cup of coffee, as Axle entered the galley ready for the day. He was pouring himself a cup of coffee, as Jane approached. He handed *her* the cup and quickly poured another. She sat. Axle slipped in next to her. Marcella was serving herself and Captain Eli, who had been waiting patiently at the doorway for his crew to gather.

"Why are you smiling, Jane?" Axle asked.

"I had a great dream last night. My daughter was running, skipping and playing with other children."

"What a sweet dream."

"It was, until it changed and I saw a shield wrap tightly around the ship and fingers without a hand, reset the phase control to....."

"To minus 24?" Axle interrupted.

"Exactly! Minus 24, how did you know?" Jane said astonished.

"I had the same dream," Doc said amazed. "Any less than minus 24..."

"And we would have been vaporized," Max interrupted. "That was my dream, too."

Captain Eli said slowly, while sipping his hot coffee, "I had that same dream."

Marcella chimed in, "Me too. No wonder the phase jumped to minus 24 seconds. I set it to minus 5 seconds, when the autopilot triggered."

"Why didn't you know to set it for minus 24 seconds, Marcella?" Captain Eli expressed his concern.

"Because, minus 5 seconds is more than enough to protect us from any predictable event," she answered, smiling.

"So," Captain said slowly, "I've never heard of six people having the same dream."

"Well, in the Book of Controversy, God used dreams a lot," Jane said. "He would give the same dream to multiple people for several reasons; to either predict what was about to happen, so they could prepare, or to confuse apposing armies so they could be conquered."

"Let's hope this dream was meant to *prepare* us for things to come," Captain Eli remarked.

"Do you think *He's* trying to tell us something?" Max questioned.

"If *He is, I'm listening!*" Doc quipped.

"You know, my dream ended with a list of self improvements that I could make. I better note them, while they're still fresh in my mind," Axle stated, while reaching for his zeo-pad.

"My dream ended with the assurance that if I overcome some trust issues, we will *not* perish." Marcella paused, and then added "But, what's with the term '*perish*'? I know fruit perishes. It sounds unsettling; being used in conjunction with human beings. Why would my dream even have the word '*perish'* in it? I mean..." she babbled on.

No one paid any attention to Marcella; they were all busy making entries into their own personal zeo's.

After a few minutes, Axle leaned over to Jane and

whispered, "You seem to have all the answers. I don't remember much of what I learned in Sunday school, would you mind if I asked you a few questions?"

"All the answers?" Jane laughed. "How sweet. I've never been accused of *that* before. I wish I had all the answers. But, you can ask me anything, Axle. I'll do my best," she smiled.

9

~ THE NURSERY ~

"Marcella, set manipulation to one hour per minute and engage."

"One hour per minute engaged, sir!"

After a few minutes, the white-light began to fade. All the stars in the heavens were brilliantly lit; as if they suddenly ignited, casting a light of their own.

"Max, are you getting all this?" Captain asked.

"Oh, yes I am."

"Marcella, now that the stars are lit, can you establish a time line?"

"I can get within a few hundred years, things are still falling into place, sir. I'm getting roughly 4200 BC. That's not possible!" she said, shocked.

"Look at the moon? No craters. Not a mark on it. Pristine," Max said astonished.

"No dust, either," Marcella added.

"Well, I guess that solves the lunar dust mystery," Max said smugly.

"Are you kidding me? There's a mystery about the dust on the moon?" Captain Eli joked.

"Yes, it's been a very real mystery. We know that dust settles on the universe one half inch every thousand years," Max answered.

"So, what's the mystery?" Axle chimed in.

"The first lunar landing was prepared for thirty five feet of dust, in line with the old Earth theory," Max replied. "What they found was only three to five inches of dust; meaning, the moon is six to ten thousand years old."

The light from the sun suddenly began to overpower the brilliant light of the stars.

Captain Eli shouted urgently, "Marcella, real time!"

"Oh my," Jane remarked with tears running down her cheeks, "the first sunrise."

As the sunlight forced its way through the canopy, a whole spectrum of muted colors appeared. Within seconds, they became vibrant. The shadows began to slowly dissipate.

The sky was a deep, clear blue, without clouds or distortions of any kind. The shadows withdrawing from the vegetation left a multitude of bright greens of every possible shade.

The crystal clear oceans revealed a host of plant life. The colors varied and were darkened as they peered through from the deeper parts of the water. Patches of white sand in an array of shapes and sizes marked the foundation of the ocean.

"According to the position in the solar system, this is Earth. The land is completely covered with vegetation," Max announced.

"I'm not reading any biological life, yet. That's why everything seems motionless," Doc added. "The silence and stillness is eerie."

"All human life is missing," Axle said.

"*Everything* is missing," Marcella remarked with a little wonder in her voice. "There's nothing but plants, there's nothing that has a voice. There are no structures of any kind. No mountains. Not even the hint of a desert. There is nothing but treetops covering the entire planet."

"When do the mountains form?"

"Captain, I don't know any more than you about upcoming events. I have been wrong about every Historical Science issue so far. I can only speculate on cause and effect issues. And, I see no cause that will have a mountain effect. It's very frustrating for me to be in the dark," Marcella answered.

"I'm comparing the size of the sun, in both time periods. I calculate a shrinkage of 0.16 - to 0.20 second's of arc per century," Max stated.

"Which is consistent with Gilliland and Stephenson's

theory. And now their calculations have just been confirmed," Marcella declared.

"Is that a lot?" Axle asked.

"Yes, it's a lot! Many scientists posted claims that the G and S findings, were based on faulty speculation."

"Oh, this is not going to sit well with the scientific community," Max quipped.

"It would seem that 'Old Earth Theories' have just ended," Marcella pronounced, emphatically.

"I don't get it. How does it put an end to *that* theory?"

"None of us get it, Axle," Captain Eli stepped in.

"Because, it proves the sun is shrinking at a specific amount," Max answered. "Millions of years would have put the earth inside the sun!" He glanced over at the Captain, just in time to see him shaking his head in disbelief.

"The sun is immense; it takes up the whole sky. How could it have shrunk *that* much in just a few thousand years? And, why am I able to look directly at it?" Axle questioned.

"Now, that's a question I *can* answer," Marcella jumped in, happily. "The water canopy is acting like a giant magnifying lens. The canopy must also be filtering out some of the sun's harmful rays. That's why you can look directly at it."

"Max, can you find out which harmful rays are being filtered out?" Doc asked.

"Okay, let's have a look. That's strange. It seems all the UVC, UVB and even the UVA rays, are filtered out. We are just getting light," he answered.

"Max, what about heat? Where is that coming from?" Doc asked.

"It seems the sun is heating the canopy. The canopy can't overheat because it rotates with the earth. The canopy keeps the inner-atmosphere between 73-80 degrees. Everywhere! What a system! Simple, yet perfect."

"Marcella, what is the oxygen level?" Doc asked.

"Almost 34% and rising. Oh my, that's more than double!" she said shocked.

"It's called oxygen saturation!" Doc said stunned. "No harmful rays from the sun are entering the atmosphere. Plus, over 20 lbs per square inch of air pressure kills any viruses. There's also a lack of temperature variation. The water canopy is creating all these conditions."

"It's set up like a terrarium. It's the perfect environment for plants," Jane said, excitedly.

"And humans, too," Doc added. "According to my calculations, our life expectancy just jumped from 75 to about a thousand years. With the oxygen at saturation level, you could run a 100 mile marathon and not get winded."

"As scientists, we have all the data from recorded history at our command. With a lifetime of study, we never could have imagined this perfect beginning. All the books written and lectures given, are now just futile speculation," Marcella expressed in total disbelief.

"We thought we were experts. We were just fools!" Max said, astonished.

"I'm here, and I can't begin to understand the purpose of it all," she added.

"Marcella," Jane encouraged, "when you're a parent, you'll understand."

"Are you saying that by birthing a child, I would better understand what I am seeing? Why would having a child help me to understand?" she shot back, annoyed.

"You would understand the care that parents put into a nursery. The preparation they go through before bringing home the newborn, especially the first-born. We are looking at a nursery with the perfect environment. The child was originally created to live forever. Even after studying the Book of Controversy, I would never have speculated anything like this," Jane said in awe.

"I've been looking at science with a limited perspective," Marcella added sadly. "I feel like I missed it. My life-long beliefs have just been dispelled. I don't know if I can handle that reality."

"Marcella," Captain Eli interrupted, "get a grip and

keep analyzing what is going on around us. It's not about you, right now. It's bigger than all of us."

"I'm beginning to realize that, sir. I had a college roommate that believed God created everything in six days. I told her, I couldn't believe that without seeing it. And now I'm seeing it," she paused and then added, "and I'm still having a hard time believing it."

"I have *always* believed the book of Genesis, but witnessing it, *is* unimaginable. You are not alone!" Jane said, laughing while shedding tears.

"Everyone, analyze yourselves later," Captain Eli snapped. "I need to know what is going on *outside* the ship. Don't fall apart on me now. And, Jane, start looking for the plants we came for."

"I will, Captain," she said drying her eyes. She cleared her throat, and then began to give orders. "Marcella, I need to be at 1/10th phase, real time. Axle, would you take us down a little lower? Good! From this altitude, I can accurately scan a 200 mile radius. I need you to sweep back and forth, as if you were mowing a lawn. Most of the vegetation we are seeing is now extinct. It all has a much higher reading, but I was hoping for better. Axle, bring us to the right and then back a little."

"You mean starboard and aft?" Captain corrected her.

"If you mean to the right and then back a little? Then yes!" she said with a smile.

"Don't worry, I have been adequately schooled in both terminologies," Axle joked.

They laughed, including Captain Eli.

"Down, right over there," Jane pointed, now quite excited. "The oxygen readings are off the charts. I need to take samples, right now!"

"The jungle is too thick for me to land there, Jane," Axle replied.

"Get as close as you can, we'll go on foot," she said with determination.

"Okay. This clearing is as close as I can get, because

of the dense trees," he stated, as he landed the ship.

"Max, do you want the honor of opening the door?" Jane asked.

"Not so fast," Captain Eli broke in. "I want everything double-checked. Max, Marcella, make sure there is nothing unusual out there."

"Captain, *everything* is unusual out there," Max said. "But we're reading only plant life. No toxins of any kind. It's a perfect environment. What could happen?"

"It's unbelievable that we would be the first human beings to set foot on planet earth. Max, if all systems are go, open the door," Captain commanded.

Max pressed the door release button, but the door remained in place.

"Max, go ahead, open the door!"

"I just did, Captain, nothing happened."

"Use the manual control."

"Okay, sir," Max said grunting as he tried to open the door. "I can't move it."

"Let me in there. I'm 6'6" and I haven't found a door yet, that I can't open," Captain Eli said, pushing Max out of the way. He took a deep breath, gripped his fingers tightly on the wheel and tried to turn it, grunting loudly. "This is a first for me, I can't move it either. Marcella, do something! We didn't come all this way, for the door to malfunction!" He tried the door again. "Max, don't tell me to be patient. I'm the Captain; I don't have to be patient!"

"I didn't say it, sir. It must have been someone else, because I heard it too," Max responded.

"Who said it?

No one answered.

"Who heard it?" Captain Eli demanded.

"I did." They all said in unison, now glancing at each other.

"Oh, we better be careful. This could be one of those trust issues that keeps us from perishing," Marcella interjected.

"Max, forget the door. Try the mechanical arm. See if that will open. Don't force it," Captain Eli said, hesitantly.

"It opened, sir, and the arm is operational."

"Jane, you'll have to do the best you can with the mechanical arm. Use the air lock procedure to bring anything on board." After a pause, he continued, "I wonder what we are being protected from. 'Be patient' infers that, at some point, we will be able to open the door," Captain Eli thought out loud. "Max, read what happens next."

"I'm busy helping Jane with the mechanical arm, sir."

"Axle, you read it then," Captain Eli commanded.

Axle displayed the words on the panel directly in front of him and began reading; **"And God said, "Let the waters teem with living creatures, and let the birds fly above the earth across the expanse of the sky." So God created the great creatures of the sea and every living and moving thing with which the water teems, according to their kinds, and every winged bird according to its kind. And God saw that it was good. God blessed them, saying, "Be fruitful and multiply, and fill the waters in the seas, and let the birds increase on the earth." And there was evening, and morning- the fifth day."** He clicked it off the panel.

"Jane, take your time, but let me know as soon as you are finished. I want a panoramic view of this," Captain said.

"Sir, the mechanical arm doesn't reach the plants we need," Jane replied. "We'll have to come back when we can get the door to open. For now, we have a few specimens the arm could reach. I'll make some comparisons."

"Sounds good, Axle take us up 2000 feet. Marcella, set time manipulation at four hours per minute."

"Captain, I could use some help back here handling these plants," Jane said.

"Axle, you go. Max can move us if necessary."

"Okay, Captain," He replied cheerfully, wanting a chance to talk with her alone. Axle quickly made his way back and began lifting the plants off the floor, as she placed them on the shelves in the storage room.

"Jane, do you know why the door didn't open?"

She didn't answer.

"You do know, don't you? Come on, tell me. What are we being protected from?"

"I just have a theory, that's all. But if I tell you, you *cannot* tell the others. They'll just think it's crazy."

"You can trust me."

"Okay, this is what I think; we're not being protected from what's out there," she whispered. "What's out there, is being protected from contamination by us."

"What do you mean by that?"

"Like I said, it's just my theory. We'll see how it plays out. So, Axle, what's the first thing you're going to do when you get back?" she said, trying to change the subject.

"How does "Second Day, White-Light Excursions" sound? I can only imagine how much money someone would pay for perfect health!"

Jane laughed!

"What's so funny?"

"Captain, Marcella and Doc were talking about the same thing. And I'm sure Max is thinking about it, as well."

"How about you? Are you thinking about it?"

"No. I'm just grateful to be here. But, I'd like to send my daughter on your first excursion."

"Only if you come with her," he said with a wink.

Marcella interrupted the moment with "It's almost morning, Captain."

"Good, slow us down to one hour per minute. Axle, if you're finished, get up here and be ready to move."

"My sensors are picking up biological movement, sir," Doc exclaimed.

"Marcella, slow to real time. Axle, take us in closer."

"I see it," Doc said. "It looks like the sand of the entire ocean floor is coming to life. My sensors are reading all the sea life as fully-grown."

"Max, put it on 16 panels," Captain ordered. "I want

to see the actual process. Zoom in. I can't make out a thing. The sand is churned up."

"I think I see a few flashes of white-light," Doc said. "But, I can't be sure. Look at how the sea life is feasting on that vegetation? Captain, I'm reading birds to the north east."

"Axle, go!" he commanded. "Max, clear the four lower panels, so I can see."

"There they are, sir, port side. They're coming from that clearing by the edge of the water," Axle pointed out.

"Get closer, Axle. Marcella, come *out of phase*. I don't want the birds to hit us. Max, 16 panels zoom in and record. I want to see this in slow motion. It's happening way too fast," Captain ordered.

Birds of every kind seemed to be flying up, out of the ground, in a blur. Max replayed the sequence of events.

"Back it up, play it slower," Captain Eli ordered. "Freeze it right there. Now go forward, frame by frame. It looks like an outline of a bird appearing in the dirt."

"Sir, sensors show it to be more like a 3-D sculpture," Marcella interrupted.

"There's the light," Captain Eli continued. "Magnify it, Max. The light is hitting the dirt and somehow a fully-grown bird flies out. Save the pictures, nobody is going to believe this! And, how does it already know how to fly?"

"I've recorded everything outside the ship from the time we left, Captain," Max assured him.

"I'm reading a large variety of birds; one male and one female of each kind. But, only one pair from each species," Doc commented.

"What does that mean?" Captain inquired.

"There are hundreds of variations of finches," Doc answered. "But here, there's just one kind."

"We never came *out of phase*. They're flying around us. How do they know we're here?" Marcella questioned.

"What goes on tomorrow? That's the last day, right?" Captain Eli inquired, excitedly.

"Yes, sir. Would you like me to read it?" Jane asked.

"Absolutely!"

She pulled it up on her station monitor.

"And God said "Let the earth produce living creatures after their kind, cattle, and creeping things, the beast of the earth after their kind", and it was so. And God saw it was good. Then God said, "Let us make man in our image, in our likeness, and let him have dominion over the fish of the sea, and the birds of the air, and over the cattle, and over all the earth, and over every creeping thing that crawls upon the earth." So God created man in his own image, in the image of God created him; male and female he created them. And God blessed them, and said to them, "Be fruitful, and multiply, and fill the earth, and subdue it and have dominion over."

"There's a term you don't hear any more," Doc cut in. "Be fruitful and multiply. Not with the problem of over population that we have."

"Over population isn't a problem, Doc," Marcella remarked.

"Don't you keep up with world events?" Doc quizzed.

"Of course I do. The truth is; less than 3% of the land in the US is populated. The entire *world's* population could fit in the state of Texas."

"In highrises, right?" Doc quipped.

"No! In their own homes, with a yard and front lawn!"

Doc just stared at her in amazement. "Marcella, if it was coming from anyone but you, *I* wouldn't believe it!"

That put a smile on Marcella's pretty face.

"Jane," Captain interrupted, "it didn't say the woman was made from the man's rib."

"Chapter one is an overview, but chapter two goes into more detail."

"Then just give me the highlights of chapter two."

Jane skimmed, "Okay, **seventh day God rests; blessed it; no body to work the ground; no rain, the mist**

comes out of the ground; Lord God forms man from the ground; breathed in his nostrils the breath of life; living soul; God plants a garden in Eden."

"The Garden! That's where we'll find the plants we came for!" Captain Eli exclaimed.

Jane continued, **"Tree of Life; Tree of Knowledge of good and evil; four rivers; God puts man in the garden; warns him not to eat from the evil tree; on that day you will surely die."**

"What does that mean?" Captain Eli interrupted again. "How long does he live?"

"Let's see," Jane scrolled ahead, "960 years."

"That doesn't make sense," Max chimed in. "How could you die on that day and live to be 960 years old?"

"No one knows. At least, not yet," Jane answered.

"There were *two* trees? I heard of the Tree of the Knowledge of Good and Evil, but I never heard of the Tree of Life," Captain Eli said. "If we could get a cutting from *that* tree, it would probably solve more than just Earth's oxygen problem. Marcella, let's go. Set the time for ten hours per minute, hold for three minutes."

Jane began to skim again, **"Not good to be alone; Adam names every living creature; a suitable helper; deep sleep; takes a rib; creates a woman from it; brings her to Adam. He says what we say at weddings; 'bone of my bone, flesh of my flesh'; he calls her woman; leave your parents and become one flesh."**

They traveled thirty hours in just three minutes.

"Okay team, what's happening? Doc, any signs of human life?" Captain asked.

"Not yet. But, I am reading lots of species of animals to the east, 260 kilometers."

"Axle, take us there. Get closer. Max, sixteen panels and zoom in right there. It appears to be the same process. The light hits the dirt, a second later an animal runs out, like he just climbed out of a hole," Captain Eli said astonished.

"Are you reading dinosaurs yet, Doc?" Axle asked.

"No, but, I am reading an abundance of pretty big lizards that are now extinct. They have many of the same characteristics of dinosaurs except size; they are much, much smaller. Given the atmospheric conditions, especially the oxygen content, the biggest dinosaur *only* had nostrils the same size of a horse's. How they breathed, was always very puzzling, until now. I am working on a theory about that."

"What's the theory, Doc?"

"Axle, reptiles are different; they grow from the minute they are *born* until the minute they *die*. So under these atmospheric conditions, with a 1,000 year life span, there is no limit to how big each generation could get. We're probably looking at the very first dinosaurs."

"Doc, are there any human readings yet?"

"I'm no longer reading animation, sir. Let me broaden the scan a little. I'm getting something now," she said excitedly, "3 kilometers north."

An air of mystery and excitement swept over them. The level of anticipation was growing rapidly; all sensing what they were about to witness.

"Axle, take us there. Marcella, slow the time, 10 to 1. I *must* see this! It's clearly a sand sculpture of a man lying down. Now that pure-white light is above him. It's as if he's being scanned. The light is starting at the feet and moving upward. Doc, do I see the feet completely formed on one side of the light, while there's just dirt on the other side?" Captain Eli asked incredulously.

"Yes, Captain, not just feet, but every bone, muscle, blood vessel, and drop of blood, right down to the hair on his toes. Now the legs are being formed! The blood is vibrating; there's nowhere for it to flow. Look at that! The bottom of the kidneys and digestive system are now complete and yet the top half is still dirt. How could this be happening? It's all the same dirt, yet different body parts are being formed!" Doc exclaimed with skepticism in her voice."

"Doc, the light seems to be passing through the dirt at varying speeds and intensity," Marcella broke in. "Each bone, organ and even skin and hair, has its own wavelength, which manipulates the dirt differently."

"Of course, every body part is like a separate life form," Doc interjected, "that works interdependently in unison with the others, creating systems within systems, then being brought together to create one human being! There's the heart off to one side, protected by the ribs. Everything is alive and just waiting to start functioning. The brain center is being completed now. There's a pure *white mist* forming over Adam. The man's lungs are filling. His blood is flowing."

"This must be it! *The Breath of Life!*" Jane wept openly.

The crew all quickly looked over at Jane, and then back at Adam, trying to comprehend the realization of what was taking place.

"He's living," Doc said crying.

The moment was intense!

"I am overcome! Dirt became man! Man invents. God *creates*!" Max said, his voice trembling.

"It's almost frightening," Marcella whispered.

"I read that we are fearfully and wonderfully made," Jane added, amazed.

"That describes it exactly," Max answered.

They were all weeping.

No one uttered a word.

The silence was deafening.

After what seemed like an eternity, Captain Eli broke the silence. "He's standing! He's walking! How is that possible? And look, he's smiling."

"The perfect physical specimen," Jane said.

"I'm mesmerized!" Marcella added.

"I'm in awe!" Doc chimed in.

"I know, ladies, but stay focused," Captain Eli broke in. "I wasn't expecting him to have dark skin."

"It makes sense! As the people migrated to colder climates, their pigment faded," Doc said.

"The mist is covering him again, and the man is being

lifted off the ground. He's gone! He just disappeared! Max, track him quickly. He's going to the garden!"

"Already en route, sir," Axle reported. "There he is. Wasn't he just naked? Where did he get clothes? They cover his neck down to his knees and half his arms. When his arms are at his side, his whole arm is covered."

"His clothes are continually changing color, like moving liquid," Jane added, astonished.

"Sensors *aren't* showing any clothes," Marcella said.

"I noticed the color was darker on his torso; so I tried a light spectrum," Max interjected, "and sure enough, it's light! I traced the source thinking it was a reflection, but get this; the source of the light is somehow coming from *inside* the center of his chest. His clothes are coming from *inside out*!"

"What? I can't even comprehend how something like that could be possible," Marcella said, staring at the screen. "Why are his clothes changing color?"

"Emotions! The colors must be changing with Adam's emotions," Doc broke in. "He is wearing his emotions on the outside."

"What if everyone's feelings could be seen? Wouldn't that be great? Everyone would have to be open and honest," Jane remarked, innocently.

They all stared at Jane, then looked at each other and laughed loudly.

"Our culture wouldn't last five minutes if something like that were to be dropped on them," Captain Eli quipped.

"Our emotions need to be locked up tightly inside, where they belong," Max chuckled.

Everyone roared.

"Here comes the white-light," Axle said, breaking the moment. "Oh, yeah."

"Look? The garden!" Jane suddenly broke in. "It's growing quickly all around us. I can't wait to see it after the light subsides."

10

~NAMES TO REMEMBER~

~The light subsided~

"The tomato plants are the size of a tree. Actually, all the vegetable plants are as big as trees," Axle remarked.

"It's the oxygen saturation under pressure. We've conducted experiments that showed these results," Jane answered. "Seeing it on such a grand scale is a bit overwhelming."

"What is Adam doing?" Captain Eli interrupted.

"He's walking in the garden and talking. From his gestures, you would think there was someone standing next to him," Max said.

"My sensors aren't showing anyone at all," Marcella added.

"Could he be having a one-on-one, conversation with God, Himself?"

"Sure looks that way, Max," Marcella said.

"Isn't there a specific format religious people use to talk to God? He doesn't look like he's praying."

"Max, we were all created to enjoy fellowship with God, but *this* level of friendship is astonishing!" Jane replied.

He's even laughing. Does God laugh?" Max questioned.

After a long silence, Doc spoke pensively, "So, if we were created in God's image, then all the emotions we have, *He has?* Including laughter?"

"I would never have imagined God laughing," Marcella said softly.

They remained silent for quite awhile, reflecting upon their own misconceptions of God.

"Does anyone understand what he's saying?" Captain asked, breaking the silence. "Marcella, search the database. Try to find a language match."

"I can't find anything even close, sir," she replied.

"Captain," Doc jumped in, "let me study the recording, I may be able to come up with a loose translation. It may not be totally accurate, since I'm only hearing Adam."

"Did I just hear you say 'hearing Adam'? We are actually hearing Adam's voice!" Jane was awe-struck and unable to control the steady flow of tears.

The moment was surreal. The crew stared in silence.

"I'm reading a multitude of biological life forms converging on the garden. Adam is going to name the animals," Doc spoke up "I may be able to decipher a few words."

Doc, how much time will you need?"

"An hour or so should do it, sir."

"Let me know as soon as you are done. Jane, you scan for the high-oxygen-yielding plants in the garden. I want to get the plants while Adam is still there."

"No need to worry about that, sir," Max exclaimed in astonishment. "He's going to be here for awhile. Look at the parade of creatures! Do you realize the tremendous brain power it takes to name every creature and then remember the names? He also has to learn the characteristics of each plant, as well. His brain capacity is more than all of ours put together, including Marcella's."

They laughed.

"Adam is communicating with the animals!" Doc exclaimed.

"Dr. Doolittle! Tori's favorite story," Jane announced.

Captain Eli laughed, "Now you can tell her where the story came from."

"Sir, all I could get was something about tools," Doc broke in. "Either he is not speaking in complete words, or his conversation is way beyond me. Judging from our historical records, I expected a lot more animals. But, it's apparent what Adam is naming, are all top of the line, superior, prototypes. These animals represent each species. Every variation of animals must have adapted after the climate change. It makes sense, there are no deserts, so there are no camels, at least not yet.

"So what are you trying to say, Doc?" Axle asked.

"I'm saying, Adam is superior to us in every way, and he is the beginning of the entire human race. He is the first of his kind. So then, all *these* animals are the first of *their* kind."

"Let's be sure not underestimate his intelligence," Captain added. "Jane, did you locate the plants we need?"

"I found a large variety of possibilities, sir, but nothing compared to the plants we were unable to reach."

"Have you spotted the two trees yet?"

"Yes, I located both trees. I'm just not sure which is which. They're almost identical."

"Axle, don't approach either one until we are sure," Captain warned.

"Sir," Jane interrupted, "let me use this time to collect fruits and vegetables with the mechanical arm. We'll just have to go back for the plants that we couldn't get to before. But for now, we have the opportunity to bring back uncontaminated, original seed."

"I was assured that we no longer have contaminated seed. Hasn't it all been eradicated?" Captain asked.

"I'm sure that's what everyone believes, but we would know for certain, if we had an original seed to compare it to. Plus, it would be nice to add some fresh fruits and veggies to our dinner tonight," Jane smiled sweetly.

"Okay, direct Axle and get Max to help you with the mechanical arm, if the door still doesn't open."

"Axle, cruise slowly toward the southwest. That's good, land right here. Max, can you give me a hand with the mechanical arm?" Jane asked.

"Don't you want me to try the door?"

"Oh yes! Try the door."

"It won't open. You knew that, didn't you? You're

hiding something," Max chided.

"I just have a theory," she shrugged.

"What theory?" they shouted in unison.

"Okay" she exclaimed. "Look out there. There are no ulterior motives. There's no fear, worry, or selfishness. If we were to go out there, we would bring all that and more, before it's time. We have been given a unique opportunity here; to observe what could have been; to learn from it, and try to make a difference in our world, not just to plot ways to capitalize on the '*white-light*'. That's my theory. So, get over here and give me a hand with this arm."

"Yes, Ma'am," he responded, relinquishing control.

Everyone remained silent. It was obvious they were all doing some soul searching.

Axle realized he had been overtaken by selfish motives. Profiting financially from the w*hite-light* experience was not part of his character. He began this mission with standards and ethics. His intention of turning this into personal gain was now offensive. This time-travel ship, was created for a noble cause; 'to save the world'! *If the temptation is more than I can handle, what would someone driven by desire, without reason, do?* he thought.

11

~THAT FIRST MEETING~

The conference room wall in Partenza Hall, had the ability to be totally transformed into one large monitor, or be reduced to a personal screen that would only be seen by the person seated directly in front of it; similar to the windows on the ship.

Rebecca was seated at the end of the multi-work station, scanning the information on her monitor.

Dom was pacing behind her.

"Dom," she said, "we have tried everything. I don't think communication with the ship will ever be possible. Sending it back is the easy part, but knowing where it goes; impossible! There are a total of eight of us working on it. And, six of them, only have small pieces of the puzzle."

"You know the security protocol as well as I do, they don't need to know," he answered still pacing.

"The fact remains that we don't know *where* or *when* they are," Rebecca said.

"That's why we need a way of tracking them," Dom said, leaning over her shoulder.

"Now, that is something I need to know. Are you holding back on me?"

"You know I would never do that. The idea came to me last night. It won't help with this trip, but it would be to our advantage to have something in place for next time. We need a tracking device built into the ship that would provide a fixed point. Then, we can create a portal that would allow us to deliver an object. We could communicate by sending audio chips. That will also solve the problem of trying to keep a communication line open."

"That just might work, but what about this trip?

Shouldn't they be back already? I hope nothing happened to the ship. This waiting is getting to me, Dom."

"I discussed this with Marcella at great length. She's going to convince Captain Hunter to stay on real time. If they come back early, there is a slight chance it could change our time line, or even start another. We don't want to take that chance."

"I agree. You know, I'm still waiting for the results on the other matter. I'm feeling a little weary. I'm going to my room to lie down. I'll be back later."

Rebecca returned to her quarters with no intentions of lying down. She checked her PWF that inputs thousands of passwords for any given account. She tapped in Oden Zadok's profile. On a whim, she added his negative character traits such as; egotistical, self-centered, arrogant, devious, deceptive, evil, etc. Remarkably, the PWF was able to retrieve his pass-code from these nefarious descriptions.

From there, she had control of his communications and was able to extract an audio file of the conference call made the evening of the lift-off. She copied all his files and made some disturbing discoveries about the group.

Three hours later, she returned to Partenza Hall.

"You were gone quite awhile. Are you alright?" Dom asked concerned.

"Yes, I feel much better. But, I'm starving and I could use some air."

"Let's go out for lunch, I need a break, too. We'll jump a hover shuttle and go to town. Is 'Sal's ' okay?

She nodded.

"I'll call him."

"Great, I love Italian."

Sal, the restaurant owner, knew that when Dom called ahead, he wanted his private room. As soon as they finished talking, Sal made eye contact with his Maitre d' and said "Mr. D's on his way. Prepare the room."

Twenty minutes later, Dom and Rebecca were greeted at the door by Sal, "Your table is ready, Mr. D."

Dom nodded.

Sal ushered them through the private entrance. They turned left into the hallway marked restrooms. About five steps in, just before the ladies room, a door on the left slid open automatically.

As they were walking into the room, Dom put his arm around Rebecca's waist and smiling, pulled her close; giving the appearance of a romantic interlude between lovers, just in case they were followed.

They were seated at an intimate table in the center of the room. Seven larger tables elegantly set, surrounded them. The room was rich in design. The overhead lighting could be controlled from each table. The walls had uniquely crafted lamps that gave off a modest, soft light. There were tapestries and beautiful murals of Venice, Italy; stirring the desire to visit.

"I'll have the steak pizzaiola with a side of your famous stuffed shells. And, my friend will have the spinach manicotti with sausage and meatballs."

Sal smiled, nodded and walked out; the door sliding closed behind him.

"What was that about? I thought you were going to kiss me."

"I just got a little paranoid. If we *are* being watched, it will just look like we're romantically involved."

"That sounds nice," she said with a smile. "How private is this room?"

"As private as you can get. Sal's great grandfather built it, so his friends could hold secret meetings here. It's sound proof. I even helped Sal add a few upgrades. Those wall lamps emit a jamming signal and create the murals. They look real, don't they?"

"They look like authentic paintings, it's a nice touch."

"And, they can be changed on command," Dom boasted, as he demonstrated. "I remember sitting at this very table with Oden Zadok, almost five years ago, presenting my time-travel dream. Getting Sal to let me set up this room for the demonstration wasn't easy. He agreed at first, until he saw the type of equipment I was bringing in. I had to convince him that I wasn't a spy or a terrorist. Or worse yet, someone hired by his ex-wife," he smiled.

Dom pulled a chip from his pocket and slid it into the edge of the table. The tabletop became a monitor.

"I recorded that first meeting. I brought it because I want you to see how our relationship began. Watch this."

Rebecca stared intently at the screen, not being sure of what was to unfold.

"Okay, you got me here. Why are we here and not my office?" Oden Zadok said. He was leaning back in his chair. His arms folded, and a look of disdain on his face.

"Some of my equipment could never get through your building security. So I took the liberty of setting it up here in advance," Dom answered, trying to reassure him.

"Should I be worried?" Zadok asked.

"Worried? You are about to witness the impossible," Dom said confidently.

"I have been around long enough to have seen everything. There is nothing new under the sun, get to the point," Zadok pressed.

"Well, that doesn't apply here. In technology, seeing is... believing," he said with keen expectation, as his eyes trailed to a small metal tray in the center of the table. "Place your ring on the tray," Dom coaxed him.

"Listen, I didn't come to see magic tricks," Zadok responded, a little annoyed.

"Just do it, please."

As Zadok reluctantly placed his ring on the tray, Dom tapped an out-linc and the ring disappeared.

"Am I supposed to be impressed? Where is my ring? It was a gift!" he said angrily.

"Not where, Mr. Zadok. When?" Dom responded.

"When? You're not making sense."

"Let me explain, I've tapped into the time dimension. I just sent your ring back in time."

"I'm here because there was a rumor you were

working on something like this. If this is a con, I'll ruin you," Zadok said intently, leaning in toward Dom.

"Sir, on my life," Dom replied emphatically.

Oden Zadok paled. His body stiffened. He ran the fingers of his left hand through his hair. His right hand tapped the arm of the chair, as he stared blankly off into the distance. His mind appeared to be racing, exploring endless possibilities.

Dom interrupted his thoughts with, "The time dimension is broken into two segments, one segment breaks phase..."

"Whoa!" Zadok shouted, holding up his hand for Dom to stop. It was evident that he was lost when Dom began to explain the scientific details. "Can I send an expert to your lab to verify your findings?"

"The sooner the better. With proper funding, time-travel could become a reality in as little as five years."

"If what I just witnessed, turns out to be accurate, then funding documentation can be signed within 48 hours. I'm looking forward to doing business with you."

The two men shook hands and Oden Zadok exited, forgetting all about his ring. It suddenly had no significance!

The recording ended. Dom extracted the chip from the table and sighed. "Here we are almost five years later, and the dream has become a reality. He has given me all that I have asked for. I owe him everything. And, the fact that we are sitting here now means, you do not have good news."

"You're right, I don't. It seems our boy, Oden Zadok, has a side job. His government job! The Bella Group put him in office. He's their inside man. He funnels the high profit government contracts to The Group through a series of corporations. Maiyorka and her friends sit on all the boards. I was able to recover the conference call from the night of the lift-off. Listen to this."

She removed a chip from her pocket and inserted it into the table and adjusted the volume.

"Congratulations are in order. The Bella project had a successful lift-off today. It's time to get ready for the next phase. I'm getting transfers prepared for all the military personnel that have any knowledge of the project," Oden Zadok said.

"Extremely generous offers are being prepared for the civilian personnel as well," Maiyorka responded. "But, the crew will be a problem. Regretfully, they will have to be eliminated. Marie is already making those arrangements. The next phase is to commence as soon as the ship returns."

Rebecca pulled the chip from the table. "I need to know the date of that first meeting with Oden Zadok."

"Five years ago, October 20th. Can you go back that far?" Dom asked.

"Of course, I just need the time. I'll try to retrieve the visuals of any other conference calls, as well."

"You are way too pretty to be this devious. Why would you know how to do this?"

"I'll tell you someday," Rebecca said, placing her hand on his, reassuringly. "But for now, let's just say... *it's essential*. I'm taking the rest of the day off to contact a friend. I have to do some research."

Dom nodded.

They finished their meal, almost in silence.

Dom returned to the Hangar. Rebecca caught a shuttle to LA.

12

~THE PROTOTYPE~

~*Back on the ship*~

"What Jane said, makes sense," Captain Eli remarked, as he was walking toward the cockpit, sipping from a bag of tomato juice. "Let's stay focused on the mission and put our selfish motives aside. Once the plants are collected, we are free to head back. Mission accomplished! Our obligations would be fulfilled." He paused, now standing at the nose of the ship facing them, "However, I can't help but feel that we are suppose to take back more than just plants. We are experiencing the most unclear and misunderstood parts of history there is. I have the authority to make the decision for us to remain here a little longer to see how things unfold. It would be unfair for me to make that decision *for you*. In order for us to stay, we all have to be in agreement. What say you?"

Axle answered first, "This chance is never going to come around for me, again. I'm in."

"I'm with you, too," Max jumped in.

"Are you kidding me? I could study this place for a lifetime. Count me in," Marcella stated happily.

"You know *I'm* in agreement," Jane added.

"I have nothing back there that compares to this. I'm in," Doc said.

"Thank you, team," Captain Eli said proudly. "I will do everything in my power to keep you from regretting your decision. Now, let's get back to the task at hand." Captain Eli walked to his station, settled in and said, "Jane, the door won't open yet, so we won't attempt to land. Max, I want you to use the mechanical arm, while Axle is hovering. And, Axle, you will have to compensate for the extra weight of the outstretched arm. We will be able to cover more territory, and Max will have a new skill we might need later. Doc, while Max and Jane are retrieving the fruits and vegetable, read what happens next. Just give me the highlights."

"Yes, sir," as she pulled it up on her screen. "**Adam named every living creature; the Lord causes a deep sleep to fall on Adam; took a rib; God made the woman from the rib; showed her to Adam; bone of my bone;**" she paused, looked over at Marcella, winked and said, *"The Wedding Song,"* which caused the girls to giggle.

The Captain cleared his throat loudly.

Doc went back to reading. "Sorry, Captain. Let's see, **'leave parents, become one flesh; they walked naked unashamed'.** Oh my, in chapter three, we meet the serpent!"

"Thanks, Doc. Eve is next."

"I wonder why He didn't create Eve before Adam named all the animals," Doc commented.

Max started laughing.

"What's so funny?"

"Can you imagine naming every animal, with your wife looking over your shoulder, asking you to explain *why* you chose *that* name? God didn't want them to argue on the first day."

The men laughed at that one.

The woman just rolled their eyes.

"Captain, I have the variety of seeds I was looking for," Jane interrupted. "We can all enjoy the fruit, but I better not catch anyone eating a single seed. We'll retrieve the other plants when we can open the door."

"That sounds good. Axle, take us back to Adam. As soon as he's done naming the animals, I want to see the rib become a woman," Captain Eli ordered.

While they were still waiting for Adam to name all the creatures, they had time to relax and enjoy eating the fruit. Each one was sitting at their station with little else to do but observe what was playing on the main screen.

"Have you thought about what you are going to tell

your grandfather when we get back, Axle?" Jane inquired.

"I'm going to tell him that *my* theory was correct about life on Earth."

"What theory is that?"

"That life was placed here by an *'alien'*. Technically, it's true."

"Are you going to tell him that the *'alien'*, also put the Earth, the moon, the sun, and the stars in place? Oh, and let's not forget time and space."

"Not right away. If I did that, he would know I'm talking about God," he laughed.

"Marcella, fast forward until Adam is finished naming all these animals," Captain Eli said, as he was eating a large strawberry.

"I'm moving forward. It's starting."

They watched amazed, as the *white mist* appeared and Adam went to sleep. They quickly stopped eating.

"Marcella! Slow 10 to 1. Max, full screen. He is about to take the rib!" Captain said excitedly.

"That looks like a laser cut, very clean," Doc said impressed. "No blood. His rib is being removed. The entry wound is being sealed, as easily as it was opened. No scar or even redness."

"Why would He take a rib, or any part of Adam, at all?" Axle questioned.

"A rib is the logical choice," Doc answered. "Close to the skin and doesn't affect mobility. The bottom rib is the only bone that will eventually grow back. Bone marrow is a great source of DNA, but I'm not sure why He's using any part of Adam. We know He didn't have to."

"I never thought of this before," Jane spoke up, "but now, they are literally one flesh."

"How does that apply?" Doc asked.

"Don't you see? Being one flesh guarantees they will be attracted to each other. People love themselves more than anybody else. They are literally part of each other; they become one flesh. Bone of my bone."

And they all said in unison, laughing, "*The Wedding Song!*"

"There's Adam's rib on that flat rock," Max cut in. "Here comes the '*white mist*' and it's forming the rib into an entire skeleton. The internal organs are forming."

"She is being created in layers from a single bone! This is truly amazing. This is not a clone being formed; there are very subtle differences," Doc said excitedly.

"You mean like, s*he's a woman?*" Max joked.

"I mean," Doc said emphatically, "she has all the skeletal differences; biceps, forearms, hips, and neck, everything in perfect proportion. She is the perfect female specimen."

"I'll say," he quipped.

We stared in silence, watching the prototype for all women being created.

"She is complete," Doc continued. "Her lungs are filling with air. She's opening her eyes and looking at Adam. Oh, she's smiling! And, she's clothed in light, just like Adam."

"Adam is waking up. Look at how he's admiring *her*," Jane added.

They observed in awe as Adam first laid eyes on a woman created just for him. This is what the creator always intended for *all* men and women. To enjoy a love that would last forever.

Axle glanced over at Jane, just as she was wiping tears from her eyes.

"Neither one of them can stop smiling. Now, that is what I call *love-at-first-sight*," Doc sighed.

"Adam's taking her hand and showing her around the garden," Marcella said in delight.

"Now, he's showing her the animals," Jane added. "He's probably telling her their names. He wants her to know what he knows."

"Marcella, go to real time. Let's stay here awhile and savor the moment," Captain said, while clearing his throat.

Jane glanced Axle's way. He smiled and winked.

The crew became mesmerized, observing Adam and Eve interacting lovingly. Silence blanketed them.

They were witnessing a level of tenderness they never knew existed. Each one felt sadness, yet equally sharing a renewed hope that this is truly possible. This is what was intended from the beginning.

After what seemed like hours, Captain Eli broke the hypnotic trance they were all in. "It's starting to get dark. It's been a long day. Let's get something to eat, and a good nights sleep."

"Great! Who wants an instant dinner and a bag of liquid protein?" Doc joked.

"Yummy," Max laughed, rubbing his stomach.

"I'll make a salad," Jane said. "And, we have plenty of fruit to eat."

"Now *that* sounds *really* yummy." Marcella winked at Max.

While they were eating and rehashing the day, Captain began slowly, "You know, we witnessed some pretty astounding things today."

"*Astounding?*" Axle broke in. "The whole day was *unbelievable.*"

"More like *inconceivable,*" Max added.

"*Amazingly incredible,*" Doc chimed in.

"What about *unthinkable or unphathomable?*" Jane said a bit giddy.

"You mean *unimaginable? A*s in, could *never* have been *imagined,*" Marcella laughed.

"Are you all done?" Captain asked, shaking his head. "The point I am trying to make here, is what do we do with what we've witnessed? I feel that a tremendous responsibility has come with this new found knowledge."

"You're right, Captain." Axle said a bit more subdued. "How do we convey to society what we witnessed?"

"Oh, very carefully," Max added. "Even with the proof that we have, many would still find it hard to believe."

"Max is right," Marcella interjected. "I could never present this to the scientific community. They'd want to commit me to the psych ward."

"Captain," Jane spoke up. "There's an old saying, '*To Thine Own Self Be True*'. It has been my experience that if you remain true to the truth, you will have an undefeatable partner; an ever present help in time of need."

"That's very profound, Jane! Let's hope you're right. Maybe something else will unfold and give us a better handle on the appropriate course of action. But right now, it's late and I am weary. I just want you all to give it some thought," the Captain said while coming to his feet. "We can discuss it at another time. Let's get some sleep." Captain Eli said as he sauntered out of the galley. "Goodnight, all," he called over his shoulder, as he stepped into his cabin.

~ ~ ~

Axle awoke early the next morning. Jane was already busy in the Botany Lab with the plants she collected. Axle went to the galley and returned with two cups of coffee. Smiling, she took one from his hand.

Suddenly, he remembered he had a dream!

"Jane, I know I had a dream last night, but it's vague. I can't seem to recollect all of it."

"Did it have anything to do with a tree?"

"Yes, it did," Axle said nodding. "It was a warning! We are to stay away from the Tree of the Knowledge of Good and Evil. Our presence is being shielded. We are not to compromise our position here."

"That's what I dreamed, too," she replied.

Captain Eli, on his way to his station, stopped briefly at the lab. While sipping his coffee, he peered in and casually announced, "I had a dream last night and the bottom line was to avoid getting too close to the Evil tree. Did anyone else have *that* dream?"

Axle and Jane nodded.

One by one, Captain Eli heard Max, Marcella and Doc reply, "Affirmative, sir.

"Good, we're all on board here, then. Let's take our places," he stated, in his usual nonchalant manner.

Axle and Jane fell in behind the Captain and greeted the crew already in position.

"We still don't know which tree is which, do we?"

"Not yet, sir," Jane said.

"Okay, let's see what Adam and Eve are up to, while I figure out our next move. Max, locate them. Axle, take us there," Captain said, with great expectation.

"Yes, sir," they answered in unison.

"What are they doing now?"

"Sir, it appears Eve is picking fruits and vegetables," Axle reported, "and Adam is walking with a stick that's dangling a leaf, searching for something."

Adam made a wind sock and checked for air-flow. After finding a constant breeze between two trees, he marked the spot by pushing the stick in the ground. He gathered flat rocks and stacked them in precise alignment to the natural-wind tunnel. He built a kiln with an adjustable airflow.

Marcella, scan some of the rocks he didn't use. Is that flint-rock?"

"Yes, and loadstone. How did you know, Max?"

"He needs the flint-rock to start the fire. I'm not sure why he needs the loadstone."

"If I remember correctly from my fifth grade science class, loadstone is magnetic," Axle stated. "My guess is, he's going to be looking for metal."

"Why is he smelling the ground?" Marcella asked. "He's digging and collecting something. I'll analyze it. It's sulfur!"

"Hey, he's looking up in our direction," Max hollered. "Did you touch him with the sensor beam?"

"Just his hand," Marcella said meekly.

"Get it off him, now!" Max yelled.

"He not only knew the beam hit him, but he calculated the direction. That's not even within human capabilities," Jane said, astounded.

"Synesthesia!" Doc exclaimed. "He is equipped with multiple Synesthesia! That explains how he was able to find the rocks and the elements so easily. He has multiple Synesthesia!" she repeated, astonished.

"What is Synesthesia?" Marcella asked.

"Some people have the ability to combine their senses," Doc answered. "I heard of a baseball player that was hit in the head with a ball, and afterward he could remember every day of his life. He could recall a date and then tell you the day of the week and what he was doing on that day. It turned out to be a temporary condition. It manifests itself in other ways, as well. Some people can get a bad taste in their mouth from listening to certain types of music. They say it is hardwired into our brains, but very few people are able to access that ability. This explains a lot."

"I read about a man who saw everything in numbers," Max added. "In his mind, numbers had *color* and *harmony*. He could solve the most complicated math problems in his head by separating the two. I didn't know it had a name. But, if Adam *has* it, we have to be much more careful. He doesn't actually see the beam; the beam breaks the harmony. If he is able to taste music, smell and hear colors, he has a continuous symphony going on."

"Let's not underestimate him again. His intelligence is way out of our league," Captain Eli cautioned.

Adam moved the loadstone close to the ground. He collected fragments of iron ore.

"Marcella, scan the ground around him. Let's see what's there," Max suggested.

"Nearest him, is a rich deposit of iron ore, small pockets of lead, phosphorus, some copper and gold."

"There's gold?" Jane asked astonished.

"And good sized diamonds! Close to the surface," Marcella responded with exuberance.

"Max record where they are," Captain commanded.

"Yes, sir." He answered, almost shouting.

"He's breaking up small branches. He's collecting

phosphorus! How does he know what phosphorus is?" Marcella questioned.

"Didn't they use phosphorus to make hand grenades in the last century?" Axle asked. "Once it catches fire, it burns very hot and can't be put out. It has to *burn* itself out. It even burns underwater."

Adam made a mold from the sand in the bottom of the kiln. He inclined two flat stones across from each other, creating a wedge with a small gap in between. He coated the wood with phosphorus and a small amount of sulfur, to start the fire. Then, he placed the wood on the inclined stones. He placed another flat stone on top, covering half the kiln.

"That stone will probably hold the iron ore, when it melts. It should flow off the top rock, through the fire, through the gap between the two inclined rocks and into the mold below," Axle said.

They continued to watch in amazement, as Adam rolled the iron flakes into green leaves, like long, thin cigars. He lit the fire with the flint-rock and adjusted the airflow. The ore was uniformly wrapped in the leaves. This allowed him to maintain a steady flow. He was safely able to control the speed in which he fed the ore over the top rock and into the fire.

"Incredible! This is amazing," Axle said. "He's letting whatever it is cool. What is that? Max, can you figure it out?"

"Not from this angle. Wait, it looks like an ax-head, complete with a hole big enough to slide a handle through. It even has a flat side that can be used as a hammer. Nice job!"

They watched Adam use the ax-head to cut tree branches of various lengths to craft handles for leverage. He used the ax to cut wood and the hammer to forge other tools. He made a crude table to cut fruits and vegetables.

Over the next several days, the crew monitored their lives and progress. Although several years of Adam and Eve's lives had passed, it only took seventy two hours of real time.

Adam and his wife enjoyed each other. They smiled

and laughed often. They ate six small meals a day together. The interaction with the animals, the level of cooperation, and mutual respect in how they worked together was astonishing. They dug little pools along the side of the river, so all the animals would have still water to drink.

Life was good.

It was Paradise!

13

~ COULD IT GET ANY WORSE ~

Rebecca entered Partenza Hall, late the next morning. Dom was already busy delegating pieces of the Audio Chip-Delivery Project to the rest of the staff.

At this point, Rebecca suspected they were under surveillance. She approached Dom and gently touched his arm.

"Good morning, I'm sorry I'm late. I was working on a few theories that I would like to discuss with you privately."

"You all know what your jobs are," Dom addressed his group, smiling. "I'll be back later."

Within minutes, they were in the hover shuttle.

As soon as Sal ushered them into the private room of his establishment, Dom asked Rebecca, "Well, did it get any worse? As if it could."

"It could and did. This is from that same night of your first meeting with Oden Zadok."

She put a chip in the table, and Oden Zadok's office appeared on the monitor. Sixteen conference call windows surrounded the perimeter of a large monitor. The members who were seated at their own desks began to appear in each window. Whoever was speaking at the time would be moved to the center, filling the large screen. Oden was the first voice heard.

"I have been speaking with several of you for most of the day. I have come to believe that this is what we have been looking for. The possibilities with time-travel are endless."

"Have you determined a price tag?"

"We can't know for sure, Maiyorka, but a rough

estimate would be 200 billion," he replied.

Everyone gasped.

"Do we really want to risk 200 billion on something, as untested as time-travel?" she asked.

"Relax! I knew you would feel that way. A few of us have already devised a plan that would allow us to use capital from the North American Union. We can keep the project top-secret and vague. The country of origin would be disguised," he assured them.

"But, how do we get them to fund a project of this magnitude, without arousing too much attention?"

"I'm glad you asked that, Maiyorka. We have chosen a cause that would appeal to the Environmental Agency. They're the only agency able to spend that amount of money without scrutiny. The crisis this year is the oxygen level of the earth. A presentation is currently being designed to prove that time-travel will be the only effective tool able to end this crisis. An attempt to solve the dilemma will be addressed on the first mission. After all the capabilities are discovered and the flaws are corrected, we will be able to use the vehicle to our advantage; buying stocks, commodities and key properties in the past. We could achieve global domination within seven years; if the mission is successful. We will need to transfer or eliminate anyone that worked directly on the project, and replace them with our own personnel. Our code name for this undertaking, is *Bella.*"

"*Beautiful!*" Maiyorka said amused.

Dom stared at Rebecca in shock. "We need help! I think I can trust Jack Brock. I just won't let him know that *you* are involved. Send him a copy of both calls, informing him that I have back up files that will come to light, if anything happens to me. Let him think it's coming from me; just in case I'm wrong about him."

14

~ THEY WERE ALREADY LIKE GOD ~

"**H**ow much time passes between chapters two and three, Jane?"

"It could be one day or a hundred years, no one knows, sir."

"What happens next?" he asked.

"Chapter 3; **the serpent was more crafty. He said to the woman, "Did God really say, 'You must not eat from any tree in the garden'?" She said, "We may eat from all the trees, God said '<u>You must not eat from the tree in the middle of the garden, and you must</u> not touch it, or you will die.'" "You won't die," said the serpent. "God knows that when you eat from it, your eyes will be opened, and you will be like God, knowing good and evil."**

"Hold it! Go back to chapter two. Did God say anything about touching the tree?" Captain Eli questioned.

"Let's see, no! *Eve* added that," Jane said.

"That's just like my ex-wife," Captain mused, shaking his head. "Every time she would retell a story, she always tried to make it sound better than it was. Continue reading."

"**So the woman saw that the tree was good for food, that it was pleasant to the eyes, and a tree desirable to make one wise, she ate. She also gave to her husband with her, and he ate. Then the eyes of both of them were opened, and they knew they were naked; and they sewed fig leaves together and made themselves coverings.**"

"What a con job!" Max interrupted. "They would *be like* God? They *were already like God;* created in His image, and living forever in paradise! They lacked nothing. What more did they want?"

"We're born knowing good and evil. We like to think

we're smart enough to recognize deception, but we can all be easily deceived," Jane quickly answered. "We only recognize it after the fact." She continued reading, **"And they heard the Lord God walking in the garden in the cool of the day, and Adam and his wife hid themselves. The Lord God called to Adam,** *'Where are you?'"*

"Why would God ask where Adam was? Didn't He know?" Max interrupted.

Jane continued, **"So Adam said, "I heard You in the garden, and I was afraid because I was naked; and I hid myself." And God said, "Who told you that you were naked? Have you eaten from the tree that I commanded you not to eat?" Then the man said, "The woman You gave me, she gave me of the tree and I ate."**

This time Marcella broke in, "Sure, blame her. God *knew* Adam's location. He wanted to know if Adam was going to take responsibility for his actions. The answer to that is *NO*. Sorry, Jane."

She continued, **"And the Lord God said to the woman, "What have you done?"** "Oh, boy, here it comes, Jane added. **"The woman said, "The serpent deceived me, and I ate."**

"Look how fast she put the blame on the serpent," Max interjected with a laugh.

"Shh!" Jane said. "Here comes the curse. **"So the Lord God said to the serpent; "Because you have done this, you are cursed more than all cattle, And more than every beast of the field; And on your belly you shall go, And you shall eat dust, All the days of your life. And I shall make you and the woman enemies, And between your descendants and hers; One of her descendants will crush your head And you will strike his heel."**

"That's why I can't stand snakes! I don't like anything about them!" Marcella winced. "I can't stand to talk about them. I don't even want to think about them!"

"Please, continue reading the curse," Captain said, impatiently.

"To the woman he said, 'I will greatly multiply your sorrow and your conception; In pain you shall bring forth children; Your desire shall be for your husband, And he shall rule over you."

"Desiring your husband is part of the curse?" Captain interrupted. "Now, *I'm* confused."

"That sounds as if women were 'doomed' from the start," Doc laughed.

"How do you explain *my* parents, Jane? They've been happily married for 32 years. My mom doesn't seem *cursed*." Axle questioned.

"I think it makes perfect sense; a woman has an inert desire to love and be loved, and to nurture her husband and her children. It's wonderful, as long as she's involved with a man who respects her and himself. She'll remain faithful and loyal to him. The *curse* is when a woman stays with a man who abuses her."

"Sounds like my cousin," Max said quickly. "She's with this guy for years. He cheats on her, pushes her around, but she always forgives him, and sometimes even supports him. We've tried to talk to her, but she ends up defending him. She just can't seem to break free."

"And that's why it's called *the curse!*" Jane quipped.

"What happens to Adam next, Jane?" Captain asked.

"Then to Adam he said, 'Because you listened to your wife, and disobeyed me, Cursed is the ground for your sake.'

"So, now the ground is cursed, too?" Does anyone understand what *that* means?" Captain asked.

Silence. No one had an answer for that.

Jane continued, **"In toil you shall eat of it all the days of your life. Both thorns and thistles it shall bring forth for you, And you shall eat the herb of the field. In the sweat of your brow you shall eat bread till you return to the ground, For out of it you were taken, For dust you are, And to dust you shall return."**

"So, that's where they get ashes to ashes, dust to

119

dust," Axle commented.

"It's hard to comprehend that they were actually designed to live forever," Marcella added, sadly.

"How much is left?"

"Just a little. Should I finish, Captain?"

"Please do."

"Adam named his wife Eve, because she'd be the mother of all who live. God made clothing from animal skins for them, then God said, "Look, the human beings have become like us, knowing both good & evil and if they eat fruit from the Tree of Life, they will live forever!" So God banished them from the Garden of Eden. He made Adam cultivate the same ground he was made from. And God stationed mighty angels to the east of the Garden and a flaming sword that went back and forth to guard the Tree of Life."

"Captain," Max broke in, "they're walking toward the center of the garden."

"Marcella, go to real time! This could be it. They could be going to the Tree of Life. Jane, can you determine which tree it is, yet?"

"I'm reading a large life form that just appeared at the base of one of the trees, sir," Doc exclaimed.

"Let me guess, a reptile?"

"It's a reptile, Axle, but like none ever recorded,"

"Now we know which one is the Tree of Life. Axle, approach from the other side, we just heard that this serpent is crafty. Let's not underestimate him. Put the Tree of Life right between him and us, and hopefully, it will serve as a shield. Max, get ready to open the door to the mechanical arm. Marcella, take us to minus five seconds. Max, move the arm out slowly, and grab that big branch right there," Captain ordered.

Max swung the arm towards the tree in a smooth arch. It abruptly halted.

"Max, why did you stop? Did the arm malfunction?" Captain asked impatiently.

"It seems I hit something."

Marcella stepped over to the window. Her eyes widened as they fixed on the end of the arm. "Back it up. Quick!" She shouted.

"What's wrong?" Max yelled as he began to swing the arm back over the rear of the ship.

"The tip of the arm is beginning to melt, and with stainless steel, heat transference is complete."

"What does that mean?" Jane asked.

"It means; the temperature at the tip of the arm will transfer to the base of the arm, until the whole arm is the same temperature. And, it was reading well over two thousand degrees," Marcella said panicky.

"Brock said the ship could withstand four thousand degrees," Jane stated.

"Yes, but he was talking about the *outer* hull. The base of the arm is *inside* the outer hull. If two thousand plus degrees were to enter, we would become baked hams in a matter of minutes," Marcella stammered.

"How is the Tree able to survive two thousand plus degrees?" Max questioned.

"I'm not reading heat any more," she said. "I didn't see a glow or air distortion. I was only reading a small hot triangle, approximately a quarter inch thick, and three inches wide by three inches long."

"A triangle! That sounds very much like the point of a sword, and not just any sword. I don't even want to think about the implications of a flaming sword! That temperature can go from two to ten thousand degrees instantly!" Axle declared.

"Okay, let's try another approach. Max, try to get a smaller branch, and Marcella, monitor closely. At the first sign of heat, have Max back off. Okay, now!" Captain ordered.

"I almost have it, just a little closer."

"Max, stop!" Marcella yelled. "I've got serious heat. And, yes, it's a sword, about four feet long!"

Silence fell.

"I am open to suggestions."

"Why don't we ask, sir?"

They all looked at each other, then back at Jane.

"Why don't *you* ask?" Captain Eli suggested.

Jane closed her eyes. "Father in Heaven, You know our needs before we ask."

Seven leaves immediately fell to the ground!

They were awestruck.

Jane broke the silence, almost whispering, "Don't be so shocked. This was part of my dream."

"Max, pick them up slowly, no fast moves," Captain spoke softly.

"Yes, sir," Max said, still in shock.

"Max, be very careful not to bruise them in any way," Jane pleaded.

"I'll do my best."

They watched Max bring them safely aboard.

"Axle, carefully retrieve them. But, don't touch them with your bare hands," Jane instructed, still barely above a whisper.

"Why not?"

"In my dream, God said He was going to give me a leaf for my daughter, and it should not touch any flesh. He said to put it into a sterile container and to make sure it was sealed. When we get back, I am to open the container, let my daughter smell the leaf, and she would be healed. However, if I touched the leaf with my hand, it would disintegrate without leaving a trace."

"Why did you address God as Father, and not just God?" Marcella questioned Jane.

"God is God to all, but He is 'Father' to the believer," Jane smiled with tears in her eyes.

"You talk to Him like a friend. I can't imagine that! When we get back, we have a lot to talk about," Marcella said, her mind racing.

"It would seem God chose to give each of us a leaf.

And then, with *that* leaf, the power to heal one person!" Doc announced.

"How do I decide who gets healed? How do I handle that kind of responsibility? What if I make the wrong choice? What if I waste it by not choosing at all, because I'm afraid of making the wrong choice?" Axle rambled on.

They all looked at him, and there was a sudden outburst of laughter.

"You finally get it," Jane said. "*You* can't decide, at least not on *your* own. The idea of playing God is much different from the reality."

"Here they come!" Max interrupted.

The serpent was walking upright on legs and had a shiny, flexible body. It was mesmerizing to look at. It attempted to engage Adam in conversation; he ignored it.

"Can a snake get any creeper?" Marcella shrieked.

Marcella tracked Adam and Eve at four hours per minute. During the next six hours of their time, they circled the tree twice. Their clothes were now tinted orange.

"They're intrigued!" Doc said. "They're coming back again. That's three times now."

"Marcella, how much of their time has passed?"

"Eight hours total, sir."

"The orange color has intensified," Max stated. "I'm guessing that orange represents curiosity, and it is building fast. They are not going to last much longer."

The serpent was patiently enticing Adam. It's just a matter of time.

"Marcella, drop to real time."

"Yes, sir."

Adam and Eve circled the tree. Now, the serpent is striving to arouse Eve's interest.

She was beguiled.

"Axle, back us away from the Tree of Life. Things are about to heat up!" Captain Eli commanded.

15

~THE FALL~

"Max, zoom in. It's going down now. Eve's eating! And now Adam! This is the beginning of the end!" Captain Eli sadly announced. "Their light covering is gone, and now they're naked. They look lost."

The crew observed in silence. The significance of what they were witnessing was overwhelming.

Adam and Eve's life went from one of tranquility and perfection to instant shame and fear. In a vain attempt to cover their disobedience, they sewed fig leaves together to replace the covering that God had given them. It didn't work, so they hid.

"This is so tragic!" Jane remarked, somberly.

"They think they are going to die today, it must be terrifying," Doc's voice cracked.

"I wish we could tell Adam he is going to live to be 960 years old," Jane declared.

"Marcella, something is happening," Axle broke in.

The colors in the garden began to fade.

"Didn't you say the colors were brighter, because of the way the sun was shining through the canopy?"

"I have no idea what's happening, Axle," she replied.

"Take us straight up to just under the canopy, Axle," Captain commanded. "What's that?"

A dark mist emitting from the Tree of Good and Evil, embraced every tree and plant in its path, including the birds. The animals ran frantically from it, but to no avail.

"The entire planet will be covered in eighty eight days," Max said grimly. "Marcella, what do you get?"

"If the takeover speed remains constant, I get ninety two days. Much faster if it spreads like a wave and picks up speed. It's too soon to tell. But one thing is for sure, nothing can escape it," Marcella added sadly.

"It's the curse! I never thought of it as being visible. The earth is losing its vibrancy. This is what it looks like back home," Jane said fighting back tears.

"It's still beautiful, but not like before. Something is lost," Doc sighed.

"When sin comes in, the innocence is lost," Jane added weeping.

"I bet we can open the door, *now,*" Max broke in. "Although it doesn't have the same appeal as before."

"Axle, take us back down. Let's see what's going on. But not too close," Captain Eli cautioned. "What did we miss?"

"Those creepy legs are gone from the snake," Marcella rejoiced.

"They're dressed in animal skins," Doc added.

"The first death!" Jane said emphatically.

"What does *that* mean?"

"Animals just don't give up their skin, sir."

"I'd rather see them in snake skin," Marcella added.

"That would take a lot of snakes," Max commented.

"Exactly!"

Adam approached the Tree of Life and was stopped by the flaming swords. They were evicted from the Garden Of Eden! They were barred from Paradise.

"I'm reading briers, sand spurs, weeds of every kind," Jane jumped in, "wherever the black mist has touched."

"They look so defeated," Max said sadly. "There's something really different about them. Marcella, hit Adam with the sensor beam again."

"Why?"

"Please, I just want to see something."

"Okay, but what if he locates us?" she said as she complied with his request. "He doesn't know it's hitting him. What happened?"

"Just as I thought," Max said. "Adam was connected to the knowledge of God. His link has been broken!"

"And the serpent was cunning enough to take Eve's focus off *all* they had, and have her focus on the *only* thing they didn't have. Women still battle that today. They see what they *don't* have, instead of what they *do* have. From now on, I am going to look for things to be grateful for," Doc added tearfully.

"Captain, some of the plants are becoming poisonous. If the door opens, we need to go back and get the other plants before the dark veil contaminates them," Jane interrupted. "*They* could be what we came for. Max, how long do we have?"

"Less than a day, it's hard to tell."

"Axle, take us there. Marcella, put us in 1/10 phase. Max, as soon as we get there, try the door," Captain Eli commanded.

Everyone was moving quickly. Axle landed the ship down in the clearing just like before.

"Sir, the door opened," Max yelled back to the bridge.

"Everyone, grab your gear, quickly. Axle, you're first," Captain Eli said with excitement in his voice.

"Stretching my legs and inhaling fresh air sounds appealing," Axle exclaimed.

They all eagerly bounded out of the ship, except for Marcella. They had to persuade her, promising they would be right by her side.

"Breathing seems different!" Axle exclaimed. "It's very easy to inhale. This is almost like breathing from a scuba tank."

"It's the oxygen saturation, Axle," Doc responded. "It might make us a little dizzy at first. Our brains never get this much oxygen. It might take a moment for us to become acclimated. Also, the oxygen is going to cause some life forms to grow a little larger than we're used to seeing."

"You don't mean snakes, do you?" Marcella asked apprehensively.

"Well," Doc warned, "maybe a little."

Captain Eli yelled, "What the heck are *they*? Don't

tell me *they're* bugs? They're way too big to step on!"

"That's the life form I was talking about," Doc answered quickly. "Insects breathe through their skin, so the higher the oxygen level, the bigger the insects. Because the oxygen level at home is so low, the insects are real small."

"I never looked at the bugs at home as being real small. But, thank God we don't have anything like this!" Marcella squealed.

"Max, scan that one. How big is it?" Doc asked.

" It's just over twenty two inches."

"And I thought the snake with legs was creepy! I won't be spending too much time outside the ship," Marcella said squeamishly.

"They're not aggressive, they won't hurt you," Jane said trying to comfort her.

"Just looking at bugs this big is *killing* me," she responded.

"This does explain a lot," Doc interjected. "I saw a fossil of a dragon-fly with a four foot wing span."

"Four feet? That would make the mosquito big enough to drink directly from your heart," Max laughed.

"Oh, Max, that's so disgusting," Doc yelled.

"Please, God, don't let me see anything like that," Marcella pleaded.

"I didn't know you prayed, Marcella," Max teased.

"I never felt a need to pray... until now," she said, sounding terrified.

"Everyone, keep your communicators on. I'll let you know if this is it. Axle, come with me, please," Jane said excitedly.

"No one move," Doc whispered with slight panic in her voice. "I thought I saw something move in the bushes."

They froze!

"Oh snap, it's a lion. He's coming toward us!" Doc exclaimed.

Marcella screamed!

"Be calm! Animals aren't aggressive until after the

flood," Jane remarked. "Here boy!"

"Are you crazy?" Max yelled at her. "We don't know for sure he won't attack!"

"By the way she's petting him, my guess is, he's docile!" Axle added, amazed.

"His coat is so soft. Come on guys, let him know we're friendly," Jane coaxed.

"No thanks," Marcella stated as she took a few steps back. "I can be friendly from over here."

"Axle, let's go," Jane said, taking the lead through the oversized jungle.

As his foot went through the thick mass of overgrown vegetation, he worried if he would be disturbing creatures, bugs, and snakes. The strange, thunderous, crunching noise surrounding them added to his level of dread. What happened to Paradise?

"Axle, come quick, over here," Jane announced, excitedly, as she scanned the area with her tricorder. "I'm not sure what plants these are, but they have an incredibly high oxygen-yield. Get the pots. I want as many plants, and as much soil as we can carry."

"Come in, Captain. We're coming back for the rest of the equipment. Since the mechanical arm only reaches sixty feet, we'll use the carts," Axle said.

"We'll pull out the tools," Captain responded.

As they reached the ship, Axle asked, "Where's Marcella?"

"See that spider web?" Captain Eli laughed.

"Yeah, why is it so thick?"

"Well, the spider that made it; looks like something out of an old time horror movie. Consequently, Marcella is inside and is not coming out. She will be guarding the ship and monitoring the progress of the dark veil. Load up the carts, let's get moving," Captain Eli said chuckling again.

"I'll take one, follow me," Axle said. "The weight of the cart will create a path for us to walk on."

While they were digging, Captain Eli called over to

Max, "Come here and scan this. Is it silver?"

"Yes, sir. It's metal."

"What kind?" Captain Eli asked impatiently.

"Just a second, it's not silver, it's platinum!" Max exclaimed, loudly. *"It's platinum!"*

"How much is there?"

"It's all over the place," Max yelled, while scanning frantically. "There is a heavy concentration right here, about eight pounds."

"Jane, I need a pot over here. Doc and Max, separate as much platinum as you can," Captain Eli commanded. He could not contain his excitement. No one could!

"Captain, tell us that we're keeping this? I once heard of platinum *credit*; but, we'll have *actual platinum!*" Max shouted.

"We were all promised a large reward to take this mission, but I say we hold on to this for backup, just in case someone changes their mind," Captain stated.

"I agree, sir. I agree! Does that mean we'll be going back for the diamonds?" Max exclaimed, unable to hide his excitement.

"Absolutely! Marcella, how much time do we have?"

"Just a few hours at most, sir, the veil is approaching rapidly."

"I have a surprise for you, Marcella," Max added.

"Does it involve the platinum and diamonds? I was just calculating the exchange rate," she replied joyfully.

"How did you know?" he asked.

"Your scanner is tied into the ships scanner. Oh, and I already deleted it out of the scanner log, so don't scan it again," she laughed.

"Yes Ma'am! Out!" Max answered her. "I really like the way she thinks," he said to Axle. "The more I get to know her, the more I like her."

"I hate to spoil the moment, but we are running out of time," Captain interjected.

"Max, can you load the pots onto the ship with the

mechanical arm, if we get them within reach?" Axle asked.

"No problem. I've spent so many hours in virtual reality halls; I could probably put them right on the shelves."

"Excellent. You girls load and the Captain and I will bring the carts to Max, and he'll unload. Okay, sir?"

"It's alright with me, Axle.

Even with the assembly line, they barely finished loading the plants before the dark veil reached them. Everyone was dirty and sweaty, except for Marcella. If it weren't for the oxygen saturation, they'd be totally worn out.

"We cut that one awfully close," Marcella said.

"It would have gone faster with a little more help, Marcella," Captain Eli chided her.

"I was helping Max load the pots. See?" she said, holding out her dirty hands.

He gave her a wink and said, "Just joking. How about we let the ladies shower first?"

"Captain, why not go for a swim in the ocean? We could pick up the diamonds along the way? Max asked.

"Sir, now that we have the plants on board, we're on the clock. They won't survive more than a week," Jane said concerned.

"This might be our last chance to get some water samples and do some buoyancy tests. Let's take two hours to pick up the diamonds and go for a quick swim. Not a minute longer. Axle, take us up, and make sure Adam and Eve aren't near the diamonds." He paused, "I can't believe I just said that!" Captain Eli stared at his crew and chuckled, "I'm talking about *diamonds and* the real *Adam and Eve!"*

16

~ WHERE'S DOC ~

"It's clear. I'm taking us down, sir," Axle reported.

As soon as they landed, Max jumped out of the ship with the controls to the mechanical arm. He had the diamonds out of the ground before the shovels were unloaded. They were on their way in less than six minutes.

"We don't have any swimsuits," Doc exclaimed.

"Me neither," Axle said smiling.

"Wear shorts, Axle. I brought my snorkeling gear and an extra snorkel," Max replied, exuberantly. "Brock said no scuba tanks, but our emergency kits have watertight goggles."

"We *still* don't have swimsuits!" Doc said firmly, her hands on her hips.

"You can wear shorts, too, and I'll give you some of my black t-shirts," Captain Eli suggested. "Max, do you have any place in mind?"

"I don't see any beaches," Marcella interrupted, "and the jungle goes right into the water. I can put the ship in buoyancy mode, and we can swim right off the ship, if that's okay with you, Max?"

"That sounds good to me."

"Oh, I'm going to look just great in goggles and a black t-shirt down to my ankles," Jane laughed.

"Don't worry; you'll still be one of the four most beautiful women on earth," Axle winked.

"Oh, that's so sweet."

"You better watch him, Jane," Marcella warned.

"Oh, I am," she answered, winking back at Axle. "Max, will you show me how to snorkel?"

"I'd love to, Marcella."

"I hate to interrupt this joyous occasion," Captain Eli said with a hint of sarcasm, "but no one goes in until the water is analyzed. Max, get a sample."

"Yes, sir. Here, Marcella, how safe is the water?"

"It's fresh water. It's drinkable! It's not salty. That's why it has so much plant life. But, how could this much water reach the current salt level in just six thousand years?" she pondered.

"I'm registering thousands of unknown species that never made it to our time," Doc added.

"Suit up, let's go," commanded Captain Eli.

"It was my idea, I'm first!" Max said pushing himself past everyone, just like a child. He was in the water before he finished getting the words out of his mouth. "It's beautiful! Axle, toss my mask and fins. The water feels so good."

"Give me a pair of goggles, please. I'm next," Doc said, excitedly.

Marcella jumped in with Max's extra snorkel.

"You go, Captain, I'll wait for Jane," Axle coaxed.

It took Axle a minute to convince Jane that she looked fine. The truth was, all the women looked so ridiculous it was hard to keep a straight face. The Captain's black t-shirts covered most of their arms and fell well below their shins. With the goggles and wet hair, they looked hilarious.

"Marcella, you picked up snorkeling pretty quickly for someone who has never done it before; and who lives in Hawaii!" Jane chided.

"That's because he's a wonderful teacher," Marcella smiled at Max. She was actually playful!

Max was a happy man!

The ocean floor was thick with plant life. Even with the goggles, it was hard to see the bottom. For the next few minutes, they played like kids. Swimming, snorkeling, splashing and truly enjoying themselves.

Suddenly, they realized . . . Doc was missing!

"Doc? Doc?" They yelled frantically.

When she didn't answer, they searched underwater.

Axle saw something that made his heart sink. Tangled in seaweed on the ocean floor, was a pale leg sticking out from under a black t-shirt.

"Down here!" Axle quickly dove toward Doc, with Max at his heels. Captain Eli was right at his side when they reached her.

Captain Eli grabbed her arm. Max and Axle quickly untangled her. They were in a panic. They immediately sensed deep down, that it was already too late.

Even underwater, behind the goggles, Axle could feel his eyes filling up with tears.

They rushed her to the surface and dragged her into the ship and onto the floor. Captain Eli began CPR immediately while Max quickly ran to the Captain's station. He slid a lever and unfolded a table six foot long, from the back of his chair.

"Is she going to be alright?" Jane asked terrified.

Axle looked at her and tried to speak. No words would come. When she saw his tears, she began crying uncontrollably. Marcella began crying. Max and Captain Eli were trying to hold back their tears.

Everyone was frantic, and yelling out suggestions to Captain Eli. Marcella found a respirator and gave it to him. He put it on her, and it began breathing for her. It cleared the water from her lungs, but she still wasn't moving. She wasn't breathing on her own.

She was comatose! Max and Marcella downloaded the manuals for the medical equipment, so they could hook up the brain activity monitor. Max yelled for them to bring her over. Captain Eli and Axle carefully lifted Doc from the floor and laid her on the table. Jane was carrying the respirator.

"Max, connect the leads to her temples," Marcella pleaded. "I don't see anything happening! I'm sure everything is connected correctly. Max, put the leads on your temples, so we can see if it's working," Marcella said in despair. "Oh, no, it *is* working! Captain, she has no brain activity. What are we going to do?"

He didn't say anything. He couldn't. He just stared down at Doc.

Jane, trying frantically to compose herself, suddenly yelled, "Wait, the leaves!" She took off towards the lab, while shouting, "Max, put on rubber gloves!" She was back almost instantly and handed the container to Max. "Be very careful with it," she warned.

"How do we get her to breathe it? She's not breathing on her own?" the Captain pleaded.

"Axle, turn off the respirator and give me the mask when I'm ready," Max demanded. "I need to quickly lodge the leaf in the respirator mask, without touching her skin. Okay, I'm ready. There, I have it wedged in. Turn it on."

They were holding their breath!

The respirator's lights and pump whirled to life. Air began to flow through the hose into the face mask, and passed over the leaf; bringing its healing powers directly into Doc's lungs.

They watched intently as Doc's chest began to rise, and then fall with each deep breath the machine pumped into her.

"What happened?" Jane gasped. "The leaf is gone."

"The air from the respirator must have blown the leaf onto her skin," Max cried.

"She must have gotten a partial breath. She has a weak pulse and is breathing slightly on her own now," Marcella cried.

"Is she going to be alright?" Jane pleaded.

"No brain activity," Max said shaking his head.

"Jane, get another leaf. Now that she's breathing on her own, it might work," Axle yelled.

"The chances are very slim. Her brain waves have been dormant for a long time," Marcella wailed.

"*Get it*! Max," Captain Eli yelled. "Axle, help me turn her over. Let's put her on her knees and lift her shoulders to keep the pressure off her chest."

"Captain, I'll put the leaf in a cup, so we can put it right over her nose. The cup is deep enough, so the leaf won't touch her flesh," Jane said sobbing uncontrollably again.

"Do it quickly, she's barely breathing," Captain Eli shouted. "Marcella, is there any change?"

"There is still no brain activity, sir. How long do we keep it up?" she said weeping.

"For as long as it takes, so help me, God," he cried out, panicked.

"Captain, her breathing is getting stronger," Marcella yelled excitedly. "Her brain activity is starting to register. Her involuntary systems are being activated one by one. But, no voluntary motor skills, yet."

Axle whispered to Jane, "She started to come back right after the Captain said, 'so help me, God'. Could that have been construed as a prayer?"

She nodded, tears kept her from speaking.

"But, he barely got the words out," Axle added.

Jane still couldn't respond.

"She's moving, turn her over!" Marcella shouted.

They were all still crying as they gently turned her over on her back. Doc opened her eyes. She looked up to see them all staring down at her.

They looked distraught! Their eyes were red, their faces moist with tears. Their expressions were of disbelief and shock.

Doc looked up at them and said, hesitantly, "What's going on?"

Everyone began cheering. Marcella was still weeping. They hugged each other tightly.

Captain Eli, wiping his eyes, leaned down and softly said "Welcome back, Patricia."

"What do you mean, 'welcome back'?"

"You were gone!" his voice cracked.

"Gone? I was just swimming. I went down to get a closer look at a water lizard. I remember getting tangled in seaweed, and I couldn't breath. Then, I felt a hand on my arm and suddenly, I was at peace. How long was I unconscious?"

"A respirator was doing your breathing. You were not unconscious! You were brain dead for more than twenty minutes," Max choked.

"That's impossible!" Doc snapped back.

"We used two leaves from the Tree on you," Captain Eli replied, his words barely audible.

"I only had one leaf. Who supplied the other one?"

"I did," they all said simultaneously.

They looked at each other, sensing a shift in their relationship. Realizing, they were becoming a family.

Doc smiling, reached up to hug Captain Eli. His strong arms encircled her as he kissed her hair.

"Please, help me up," she whispered.

"I want you to rest," Eli said emphatically.

"Our time is important. We're on a once in a lifetime journey, and I don't want to miss any of it. I want to see what changed the earth from a perfectly balanced environment, where mammals could live for a thousand years, to a planet that is winding down and running out of time. And according to Jane, we have less than one week to find out," she said, all in one breath, as he helped her to her feet.

"Did you take another college course for the half hour you were gone?" Axle asked, smiling, while wiping the tears from his face.

"I feel energized and totally refreshed," she grinned.

"Thank God, Patricia. However, I'm not letting you out of my sight for the rest of this trip," Captain Eli promised. Then shifting gears, he commanded, "Okay, Max, flush out the systems and fill the water tanks. We have a lot to accomplish, and *we have less than a week*," he reiterated, winking at Doc. "Let's wrap it up here!"

17

~ LAVIA-THING ~

"Captain, the systems are flushing, and it will take another ten minutes for the water to fill," Max reported.

"Good. Let's have a brain-storming session to address a real challenge. We need to compile a list of scientific events that we want to record. The challenge *is*, we don't know what the events are, as of yet, *or* when they're going to happen. Marcella, let's start with you; you have the most knowledge about the sensor capabilities."

"Captain, we should set the sensors to pickup on specific categories; like population levels," she responded.

"Will they pick up unusual biological life forms?" Doc asked.

"That depends. If you program in a specific, unusual trait, it will pick up on all the life forms with *that* trait, Doc."

"I'll work on a list."

"I want to know about all the major geological and climate changes," Max said, "and I want to know where Cane's wife came from!"

"He married his sister," Doc said, emphatically.

"His sister? I'm sorry I asked. Wouldn't their children have deformities?"

"Their gene pool would be pristine. Gene deficiencies won't become evident for several thousand years."

"There isn't a law against intermarriage until the time of Moses," Jane interjected.

"Can the sensors still track Adam and Eve?"

"Yes, Doc," Marcella answered.

"Jane, how much time before the flood hits? We *have* to be out of here before that happens," Captain interrupted.

"About 1600 years, sir. Marcella, the Ark is made of gopher wood, and it took 120 years to build; so we'll have a good idea of when the flood will begin."

Marcella set the sensors to bring the ship to 1/10 phase, and jumped 150 years. After a full sensor sweep, they located Eve; she had at least twenty children. Another camp was being populated to the east.

There was a significant growth in the size of reptiles. Lizards now resembled smaller versions of dinosaurs.

They jumped in one hundred year increments. The population grew rapidly. There were cities and commerce, people living in tents, as well as wood and stone dwellings. More sophisticated tools were crafted from bronze and iron. Drums, crude wind, and string instruments were created.

"One of those musical instruments would be worth a fortune today," Max quipped.

"Antique dealers would scramble for any item from the pre-flood era," Doc joked.

"Can we get out and look around?" Jane asked.

"We can't interact. The slightest thing could change history," Marcella broke in.

"Wait a minute, if the whole world is going to be destroyed in the flood, how can we change history by interacting now?" Axle mused.

"That's the thing about changing history," Max said. You won't know until it's too late. What if we did something that caused one more person to get on the Ark? That's all it would take."

"Forget it, they would know we don't belong. Except for maybe the Captain," Doc said, with a bit of humor.

"Why?" they asked, almost in unison.

"Most of the adults are between seven and eight feet tall. Not to mention, it looks like slave trade is already taking place. Our size would make us easy targets."

"End of discussion! Marcella, go forward another hundred years," Captain Eli ordered.

"How could there already be millions of people, in

less than four hundred years?" Marcella asked, astonished.

"Don't forget, almost no one has died, and women that are four hundred years old are *still* having babies," Doc said incredulously, "and *most* of the women *are* pregnant. The population is really going to take off now."

"Marcella, take us ahead another five hundred years and find Adam. I want to see what a nine hundred year old man looks like."

"Yes, sir. This might take a minute, there are already billions of people," she responded.

The frightening wonder of seeing fully matured dinosaurs had the crew captivated. They were clearly the strongest, most powerful and frightening creatures on Earth. Their sharp claws and teeth could instantly shred man or beast. Their mighty tails were the size of cedar trees, and had the ability to topple a structure with a single sweep. However, instead of wreaking havoc, and people screaming and running from them, they were being utilized as work-animals.

"How did they accomplish that?" Doc asked.

"Nothing on the planet eats meat yet," Jane said.

"I thought dinosaurs were carnivorous," Axle said.

"Obviously, that was pure speculation," Max joked.

Marcella interrupted their banter with, "I've located Adam! He looks like a cave man right out of a textbook. What happened?"

"The bone under your eyebrow keeps growing very slowly, as well as your ears and nose," Doc informed them.

"So, it appears that *cavemen* came from *man*, and *not the other way around!*" Axle said shocked.

"That would explain why we can't find transitional links to man, or any other animal, for that matter. The theory for evolution seemed to be so logical, too," Marcella added, shaking her head.

"The only problem I had with *that* theory, was that every scientific fact that stood against it, was written off as a mystery of science," Max added.

"Any theory can be proven if you write off everything that *can't* be explained," Marcella quipped.

"My grandfather always joked that if scientist's left out enough facts, they could prove parking tickets grew on windshields," Axle laughed.

"I like how he thinks," Jane said.

"So, now we're watching men and dinosaurs living at the same time."

"Evidence of *that* was discovered in Texas, Max, years ago," Jane jumped in. "I remember studying that they found footprints."

"I've heard that story, too. Never believed it, until now. People are certainly going to struggle with the fact that dinosaurs are nothing more than nine hundred year old lizards. It's funny how I've *never had a* problem believing that dinosaurs came from a single cell," Max laughed. "The absurdity bypasses the ridiculous."

"Max, zoom in on the waters edge right over there," Doc interrupted. "I have never seen a species like *that* recorded! Axle, take us closer to the water. It's hidden by those trees, and I want a better angle."

"Just say when."

"That's good, right there." Doc paused and then shouted. "Is that what I think it is? It bares a strong resemblance to a mid-evil dragon!"

"Complete with wings," Axle uttered loudly.

They could hear Marcella muffling her screams.

"They're water wings. Thank God it can't fly!" Doc interjected. "What's it doing? Axle, move in closer. We're still *out of phase;* it can't see us. Get closer. It looks like it's eating something."

"It's not eating!" Captain Eli shouted. "That's not food, they're eggs. It's a *nest*! Axle, get us out of here!"

"Too late!" Axle cried. "Brace yourselves!"

The creature stood up. It was horrifying and over sixty feet tall. It turned toward the ship. A giant claw hit the side of the ship and spun it in circles. They were hit with a ball of fire! Then another!

"Hang on!" Axle yelled as he lunged the ship out of the creature's reach, while they were still spinning. "We're on fire. How can that be?"

"It's chemical," Doc shouted back.

The ship stopped spinning.

"Hang on!" Axle yelled again and steered the ship toward the water.

"Its chemical! Water won't put it out," Captain yelled.

Max quickly grabbed the remote and repelled the fire from the windows. The ship hit the water and swiftly descended to the bottom of the ocean.

Axle slowly dragged the right and underside of the ship on the muddy ocean floor, until the fire went out. Then swiftly maneuvered the ship up and out of the water, flying sideways!

"I can't steer, the motors on the right side are damaged. I'm trying to compensate, but we have to land."

Axle was visibly shaken. He looked at their faces, and their expressions of horror matched his own.

"It's over! You can get up now, Marcella," Max said helping her to her feet.

"My heart is beating so fast, I'm dizzy," she said.

"Max, find a safe place to land where we can survey the damage. Axle, just keep us up a little longer. Max, we need that safe place, now!"

"Captain, we're okay," Axle reassured him.

"No we're not! Max, I said *now*! We're angled down and flying sideways!" Captain demanded.

"Sir, I got this. We won't crash, I can hold this till we find a safe place," Axle said with a nervous laugh.

"Okay, Axle, I'm going to trust you on this." He now turned his gaze to Max. "What's so funny?" he asked, clearly angered.

"We really put on a show for the locals. They will be telling that story for hundreds of years," Max said laughing.

"Doc, what *was* that and how did it breathe fire? " Captain asked, now gaining composure.

"Leviathan!" Jane said horrified.

"What is a Leviathan?"

"It's an invincible creature, sir, described at the end of the book of Job. There has always been a lot of controversy whether or not God was talking about a literal, fire-breathing dragon," Jane answered, almost breathless.

"Well, I pronounce *that* controversy officially over!" Captain Eli declared.

"*That thing* was able to pin-point our location while we were out of phase," Marcella shrieked.

"Which means, being invisible is not necessarily hiding. I just want to know how *that thing* was able to breathe fire?" Max questioned.

"I haven't got a clue," Jane said astonished, shaking her head.

"Doc, how did you know it was a chemical fire?" Captain Eli asked. "Are you all right?"

"I'm okay, sir. I'm just unnerved. I'm having a hard time believing this myself. It must work on the same principle as the bomb-a-deer beetle."

"Which is?"

"Two sacks, each filled with a harmless chemical, that is, until they are mixed together. Once mixed, the chemical reaction is a very hot fire."

"How would a scientist explain 'that' creature evolving, Max?" Axle asked.

"Easy, it's a mystery of science. It doesn't look like much of a mystery any more. Captain, I think we found an uninhabited place to land," Max said. "I mean, there aren't any people, but there *are* animals and thick plant life."

"You mean dinosaurs?" he asked.

"Yes, I do."

"The animals shouldn't be aggressive yet," Jane stated, trying to calm them.

"Oh really, then how come no one told that *Lavia-*

thing?" Captain Eli chided.

"We just got a little too close to her nest. There are no signs of a nest here, so this is as safe as it gets," Doc said, assuring him.

"Captain, we don't have a choice, now," Axle broke in. "The ship is not handling properly. I have to realign the motors on the starboard side."

"I'm having real difficulty with the deep phase control," Marcella added, "and I need to run a few tests."

"I can dust the area with steam to chase the giant insects and animals from the landing site," Max said.

Marcella groaned.

"Alright, we land. But I want the sensors pointed in all directions, as to alert us if anything bigger than a house cat gets within a fifty-foot radius. Doc, you watch the sensors for anything that might be able to harm us. Axle, take us down," Captain Eli commanded.

18

~ WHY DID I HAVE TO SEE THAT ~

Axle landed the ship, and everyone but Marcella climbed out. She was testing the phase control.

"The two starboard motors are damaged. Max, can we cannibalize this one and use the parts to rebuild that one?" Axle asked.

"Yes, I think we can. Let's get started," Max replied as he was searching for the right tools.

"Captain," Doc called with concern in her voice, "I'm reading an extremely large bird circling around us. It's a pterodactyl!"

"I see it," he responded. "It looks harmless. It's not a pterodactyl, it has feathers."

"Science must have taken away the feathers to make it look scarier," Doc said.

"It's landing on the ship," Captain said loudly.

Marcella's voice came across the communicator, with incredible enthusiasm. "I can send an electric charge through the hull. Just say the word!"

"Not yet," Captain Eli cautioned. "He seems more curious than anything else, and he's eating the giant bugs around the ship. However, I will grab a taser just in case he gets hostel."

As he came aboard to retrieve the taser, Marcella pulled him aside and whispered, "Sir, I'm not able to fix the deep phase control. I can barely reach minus 1/10, which makes the autopilot useless."

"Which also means, from this point forward, we'll be vulnerable to anything flying through the air?" he questioned.

"Correct."

"That shouldn't be a problem until we are jumping through the 19th Century. We can avoid all the known flight paths. We'll just have to take our chances that small aircraft and rockets, and God knows what else, won't hit us," he responded.

"I was more concerned with the flood, sir."

"Why? It's just rain, and we know it's the water canopy falling. We should be able to jump right through it."

"Sir, something causes the canopy to fall."

"Care to speculate?"

"We can't speculate. The entire earth is going to flood. We have to find out what makes the canopy fall. And, we have to know in advance, so we can prepare," Marcella warned.

"You figure out what the cause is and let me worry about being prepared."

"Captain, the Earth gets knocked on its axis. We might have to be in real time responding manually, with no cushion for error. With one starboard motor gone, I don't think we'll be able to pull it off," Marcella said, concerned.

"No, you don't think *Axle* can pull it off, do you?" he quizzed. "I am convinced, if it can be done, he's the man for the job."

They both stood there staring at Axle, watching him and Max repair the motor.

"Logic dictates we find out what causes the flood, so we can speculate what the conditions will be," Captain Eli responded over his shoulder, as he stepped outside the ship.

"Max, how are you making out over there? How much longer? This bird is beginning to make me nervous. I think he's starting to see me as a bug," Captain shouted over.

"We're wrapping it up now, sir," Axle answered, while putting the tools away. He and Max quickly boarded the ship.

"We need to move forward and find out what causes the flood. Jane, what is the time frame of the Ark?"

"Approximately seven hundred years, sir."

" Marcella, find Noah. Axle, take off immediately!"

"Trying, Captain. I'm having real difficulty gaining

altitude. It's the weight from that bird outside the ship."

"Marcella, zap him but don't hurt him. Don't get him mad."

"Yes, sir, I'll zap him slowly, until he gets off." She was smiling.

She ran her index finger along the glass pane in front of her. The display responded, indicating the increasing amount of voltage coursing through the hull exterior. Marcella's finger was nearly at the right end of the scale.

"He isn't moving, and I'm almost at full charge! What now?" she asked, smile gone, a little panicked.

"Turn off the power and hit him with a full charge, all at once."

The bird let out a hideous squawk as the sudden jolt of electricity made contact with its feet, launching it nearly five feet into the air, before it even began to flap its wings. They could see a little smoke coming from its feet.

"It worked. He moved," she said relieved.

"Oh no, he's coming back," Jane yelled. "And he's attacking!"

"Axle, help, he's coming back," Marcella screamed.

"Marcella, I'll take him up, when I start a rapid descent, zap him again. When he's far enough away, jump the ship forward in time. Just a little higher. Zap it now!"

Marcella followed his orders and zapped it, just as Axle dropped the ship downward.

"That did it!" he breathed a sigh. "It's all yours."

Marcella exhaled loudly. "The sensors are set to stop us when the Ark is located." She paused, then said, "Thank you, Axle."

"For what?"

"For being able to handle every situation that we've faced so far."

Why do I get the feeling I'm missing something, Axle thought.

"Captain, this could be it. The sensors just brought us to real time. I'm detecting a large quantity of gopher wood,"

Marcella said.

"Max, six panels, zoom in. See if this is it," Captain Eli requested.

"It looks like a boat in the beginning stages. Jane, how long did you say the Ark is going to take to build?"

"120 years, Max."

"Who starts a project that's takes 120 years to finish? And builds a ship in the middle of nowhere?"

"It isn't that long, if you live over 900 years. Having to endure the people laughing and mocking, for a hundred years, was the hard part. God told Noah a flood was coming, and to build an Ark. He believed God and followed His instructions to the letter. That's why you and I are able to be here having this conversation right now," Jane added.

Max quickly changed the subject. "Captain, I'll compare the sensor readings to the time we just left. I want to know what changes occurred in the last 600 years."

Max analyzed his data readouts rapidly. "Wow, the planet is geologically the same, not even the slightest hint of any type of natural disaster and zero changes geologically. Jane was right. It seems the Earth was designed to last forever."

"Why do you and Marcella seem so shocked?" Captain asked, noticing their expressions.

"With less than one hundred years before the whole Earth is destroyed by a world-wide flood; there should be some signs," Marcella said.

"The climate is still constant; the entire planet is still a tropical forest," Max added. "The trees at the North Pole have grown to over three hundred feet tall. The earth still has no tilt. The magnetic pole shows no sign of decay. In our time, the magnetic pole has become considerably weaker. It decayed 10% in just the last 400 years."

"The pressure under the earth's crust has increased considerably, but that would tend to happen naturally over time. I don't see anything that might indicate a cause for a world wide-flood," Marcella reiterated.

"Is there anything different with the other planets?" Axle asked.

"The moon hasn't changed. Wait a minute; I don't know how I missed this before. Saturn has no rings, and it has two extra moons! That's it! Our moon still doesn't have craters; in fact, none of the planets have craters!" Max exclaimed.

"So what?" Axle asked.

"I can't *even think* of anything that could make all the craters on the planets in our solar system, without totally destroying the earth," Marcella added.

"According to the Genesis chip, the Earth is totally destroyed; except for the Ark," Jane interjected.

"It sounds like an asteroid hit the earth hard enough to knock it on its axis. It could have created a dust cloud that blotted out the sunlight long enough, to form the ice age. Jane, what does the chip say?" Marcella asked.

"Let's see, it's right here in Chapter 7, '**On the second month, the 17th day, all the fountains of the great deep were broken open. And the windows of Heaven were opened and the rain was on the earth forty days and forty nights.**'

"Well there goes the dust cloud theory. An asteroid obviously hit the ocean, cracking the earths crust, releasing the water under pressure," Marcella said. "And then, with the water canopy falling, any dust cloud would have been localized and short lived. That explains the flood, the ocean trenches and the mountains. But when is the ice age?"

"We're going to have to wait and see," Max said.

"*Wait and see,* is not the best course of action," Captain Eli spoke up. "Marcella tells me that the deep phase control is damaged, and we won't even reach minus one second. That's not long enough for the automatic pilot to respond. Because we don't have enough rocket fuel to leave Earth's atmosphere, we'll have to go through the upcoming disaster using manual control."

"Can't we jump through it?" Doc questioned.

"The autopilot uses the time delay to dodge anything that might destroy the ship. Without it, we can only jump where we think there won't be anything in the way. Even then, we take a chance. But to try jump through something like this, would be suicide." Marcella responded.

"Axle, I assured Marcella that you could handle it. And, I know I wasn't mistaken!" Captain said, confidently.

She doubted my ability. It's gratifying to know her opinion of me has changed for the better. That's why the thank you! Axle thought.

"Captain, I could most likely avoid what is coming at us, if Max could tap into my monitor. I need his help with providing coordinates on the fly, for safe places to hide. What do you think, Max?" Axle asked.

"I think we can pull it off for a while, but not for forty days and nights. Marcella, if you can manipulate the time to get us through as quickly as possible, then I think we have a chance," Max responded.

"I can do it, but it would be easier if we knew exactly what we were dealing with," she replied.

"There is not going to be any room for error, we can't allow even one mistake. Start scanning outer space. Find out what is out there, so we can prepare. Meanwhile, Doc, you do the biological scans," Captain Eli ordered.

"Yes, sir. Max, show me how to work the zoom again," she said.

Max demonstrated, "Out, in, focus and number of panels."

"Let's see if anything has changed. *Who* is that?" Doc gasped.

"That is one cruel looking individual," Max stated. "Put him up on nine panels."

"That's not what I mean!" Doc winced as they viewed the top half of a bare-chested man. She zoomed out.

They all gasped!

"How tall *is* he?" Jane asked.

"The men next to him are between seven and eight

feet tall," Doc continued. "The sensors put him at just over four meters. He's over thirteen feet tall!"

"He's twice my size! Where did *he* come from?" Captain Eli exclaimed.

"I think he came from hell, sir, "Jane said. "In chapter six, it says, '**And in those days and even after wards, when the evil beings from the spirit world became involved with human women, their children became giants, of whom so many legends are told.**' He is the offspring of a fallen angel and a woman. So technically, his father came from hell."

"Look behind him. He has a throne. He must be like a god to these people," Doc said in disgust.

"Doc, may I take over the visuals?" Max broke in. "I want a closer look at what's going on down there."

"Please do" she said eagerly.

Max focused on a city being built. There was clearly two classes of people. Those that ruled and carried clubs and those that were enslaved, some in chains.

"The men working without chains all have the same limp. Does that mean......"

Doc cut him off, her voice trembling, "Yes, Max, it does. The Achilles tendon on their right foot has been strategically damaged. They can work, but they can't run. It appears the animals were maimed as well, to enslave them. The ones in chains must be waiting to be maimed, and those in cages must be his prisoners."

"Prisoners? Not a chance. This guy wouldn't take prisoners," Captain said in disdain.

They watched in horror as men were released from their constraints, one at a time, and speared for target practice, as they ran for their lives!

"*They* are his entertainment! This is terrifying!" Marcella shrieked.

"That one man is really fast. He might just make it. Can you believe he dodged that spear? He actually got away." Max yelled, in complete shock.

No one could have predicted what was to happen next. The guard who missed his target was summoned. He approached trembling, as if knowing what was to be his fate. This evil, dreadful ruler, then placed his over-sized hands around the man's head, locked his fingers and squeezed, crushing his skull with his bare hands!

The crew watched in horror. Doc screamed in disgust, almost gagging, "Oh, God, why did I have to see that! I didn't even think that was possible."

"It seems the brutality of this era has no limit," Marcella said, putting her hands over her mouth.

"What does the Genesis Chip say about this period of time?" Captain Eli inquired, repulsed by what he had just seen.

Jane responded, scrolling quickly, **"People began multiplying, and daughters were born to them, the sons of God saw that they were fair; and they took wives for themselves of all that they chose. Then the Lord said, "My spirit shall not abide in mortals forever, for they are flesh; their days shall be one hundred twenty years. The Nephilim were on the earth in those days—and also afterward—when the sons of God went in to the daughters of humans, who bore children to them. These were the warriors of old. The LORD saw that the wickedness of humankind was great, and that every inclination of the thoughts of their hearts was only evil continually. And the LORD was sorry that he had made humankind, and it grieved him to his heart. So the LORD said, "I will blot out from the earth the human beings I have created—people together with animals and creeping things and birds of the air, for I am sorry that I have made them." But Noah found favor in the sight of the LORD."**

"Why isn't there more detailed description about what was actually happening?" Captain Eli questioned.

"There has always been a lot of speculation about these giants," Jane answered, still shaken. "They took any and all the women they wanted, had large harems and were continually plotting to kill and control. My thinking is that God didn't want the new world to begin with that much knowledge of evil. They would have it soon enough."

"This is the only camp we've seen. Axle take us up, do a 360 degree sweep in a 100 mile radius. Max, Marcella, Doc and Jane, scan the ground in four different directions. Take four panels each. Find some more camps."

After examining five other camps, it was easy to see why the details were left out. The brutality was unimaginable. Literally, they could never have imagined this!

An entirely different race of people were emerging; enslaving man and beast, and exalting savage rulers, as if they were gods. The entire population was contaminated. In a quest for favor and power, they were killing and brutalizing each other. This was a heartless generation. Such immorality and perversion! This was a perfect world. Now life is cheap, a bloody, lawless ghetto, run by twisted tyrants.

They were sorry they watched.

"God, help me get these images out of my mind," Axle begged.

"Max, did you record that?" Captain Eli grimaced.

"I deleted it. There is no reason anyone should ever have to see that!"

"Thank you. That is one decision I'm glad I did not have to make."

"That's why God changed the life span," Jane said.

"What do you mean?" Doc questioned.

"People seem to mellow and make personality changes the older they get. But imagine being arrogant, selfish, evil and corrupt for hundreds of years? Living without consequences and making your own laws without fear; caused the brutality and corruption to be out of control."

"Now we know for sure, why God started the world over. Man's mind being continually on evil, was putting it mildly. No values or standards, no ethics, no compassion or empathy, just selfish insanity. Oh God, help me get those images out of my mind!" Now, it was Jane pleading. "They had everything in such overwhelming abundance; oxygen, food, water, no viruses or disease, a lifespan ten times longer than ours. They were not satisfied with what God had given them."

"When that protective canopy falls, viruses and disease will run rampant," Doc said, angered. "In the 19th century, one worldwide outbreak of influenza took out 100 million people. The plague killed 1/3rd of the population of medieval Europe. And, we *were* losing three million people annually to Malaria; until we finally developed a vaccine five years ago. More than half of all natural disasters took place during the last century. Millions died during the numerous famines caused by droughts and climate changes."

"So let me get this straight, from what I'm hearing, all the natural disasters started here and really *are* an act of God? The repercussions of this one judgment of God, still impacts the Earth, 4,500 years later?" Captain Eli asked, shocked. "

"The Earth at this time is environmentally stable, no fault lines, there's no chance of a river overflowing since it hasn't even rained yet, and it's been 1,500 years," Marcella answered. "So, essentially, you're correct, sir."

"Everything is perfectly balanced," Max added. "The theory can be formulated that what ever it is that knocks the Earth on its axis, is what also causes all major geological events from this point forward. Volcanic eruptions, earthquakes, giant sinkholes, even meteorological events like typhoons and hurricanes, are all aftershocks of this one catastrophic event."

"Captain, I think we should move forward," Marcella interrupted. "Our scans aren't showing anything yet."

"Move on, but keep an eye on the Ark. We have to plan a strategy before the animals start arriving, or it will be too late."

"It would help if we knew in what general direction the asteroid was coming from," Max said.

"Well, we know that Saturn takes a monumental hit.

Can you calculate where Saturn will be?" Jane asked.

"That's it!" Max announced, excitedly. "We know where all the craters are! Marcella, separate and align what gets hit. We'll know the direction and exact time, in a matter of minutes."

19

~ GAME OVER ~

"I calculate thirty two years, seven months. But the cause of the impact is still too far out to scan. I'll push us forward thirty two years; we should see something then. The asteroid should be coming on the screen now. Oh, no! This is much worse than I thought," Marcella shouted.

"It's a comet! Game over!" Max yelled.

"Why is a comet worse than an asteroid?" Jane asked panicky.

"Size, for one thing," Max answered. "If it were an asteroid, it would be a lot smaller. Then we would just have to dodge the initial impact and aftermath. The magnitude of which, we can't even begin to speculate about."

They remained silent.

"A comet could easily be the size of the earth," Max continued. "And it has a tale consisting of ice and rock that will greatly prolong the impact and add to the aftermath."

"What's our plan of action?" Axle asked. "Is there going to be any place safe enough to hide? Can we stay on the other side and keep the earth between us and the comet?"

"Easier said than done," Max shot back. "The earth is spinning at about twelve hundred MPH. We would have to maintain that speed, for who knows how long; at the same time dodge the debris that the earth's gravity will catch and sling at us, and keep the freezing ice from sticking to the hull. Like I said 'game over'!"

Captain Eli clearly annoyed by this talk, jumped in and sternly said, "Max, It's *not* a game, and it's *not* over! I've been in a lot of tough spots, and one thing I've learned is; there are always several ways out of every situation. Some are better than others, but they all lead out. I realize we have a lot working against us, but we have to believe that we can figure out what will work for us. As long as we return with our lives and the plants, everything else can be sacrificed. If necessary, even the plants can be sacrificed. At this point, we have no choice but to wing it. If it can be done, this crew will do it. Marcella, move us forward, now!"

"We're moving forward, Captain. Oh no!" she yelled in dismay. "It's almost the size of earth. Mostly ice, so now we know where the Ice Age came from. I am reading rocks the size of Texas. If *they* hit, it *will* be game over!"

Captain Eli snapped back, "Marcella, again, it's *not* over! History tells us what gets hit."

"Antarctica takes a serious blow, and we know where it takes place," Max interjected. "Maybe we can avoid it."

"Max, I'm reading a direct hit; almost dead center," Marcella yelled.

"That's about a million to one shot," he groaned.

"Much more than that," she snapped back. "It appears the earth is the target; and the comet is aimed directly at it."

Marcella looked at Jane and pleaded, "Jane, *He* knows we're still here, right? Do you think *He* will help us?"

"I have no reason to believe *He* won't!" Jane said, confidently.

"I wish I could believe that. I just don't have that much confidence in myself, let alone someone else."

"The comet is approaching Saturn," Max said fearfully. "We'll get a glimpse of what we're in for. Saturn's two extra moons have just been pulverized! All the moons are taking a serious beating."

"The rings are forming." Marcella interrupted. "How can something this scary be so beautiful? Everything without an atmosphere is getting pummeled. If I didn't know better, I would think all the meteors and asteroids that could cause irreparable damage are purposely being filtered out. There are just too many coincidences for it to be luck. The gravity of Jupiter is pulling in debris. And its rings are forming."

"Jupiter has rings?" Jane asked.

"Yes, Jupiter *and* Uranus both have rings. Only they aren't as big and visible. Mars just took a hit that would have turned the Earth to dust," Max yelled.

"Marcella, speed things up, move forward, let's get this over with," Captain Eli ordered.

"Yes, sir. I'll slow down just before contact."

"How cold is the ice, Max?" Doc inquired.

"Roughly 300 degrees below zero."

Doc exclaimed, "Now, that explains another mystery of science concerning woolly mammoths that were frozen standing upright, near the North Pole."

"So, what's the mystery?" Max asked.

"Well, the way their blood and internal organs were cracked, and the food still in their mouths; they would have had to freeze in less than five hours. I researched and learned that it would take a temperature of almost three hundred degrees below zero to freeze a fully-grown elephant in less than five hours. No one could come up with a scenario that could drop the temperature from tropical to three hundred degrees below zero instantly."

"Until today," Max quipped.

"Why didn't our scientists discover this, Max?"

He replied shaking his head, "Don't be too hard on them, Doc. It's only obvious to us now, because we're seeing it. I studied all the theories. It turns out they were all futile speculations. It never occurred to me to read the Book of Controversy. But now that I know how the book got *that* name, I'm getting myself a chip, *if* we get back in one piece."

"Here it comes!" Marcella yelled, frantically. "Our moon is now getting hammered. Debris is flying! The comet appears to be almost all ice now!"

"Everyone get into position. This is it!" Captain Eli commanded loudly, and proceeded to shout orders. "Axle, take us around to the other side of the planet. Max, link your monitor to Axle's. Marcella, continue to explain what we are seeing, so we can take evasive action."

"Yes, sir. The comet is beginning to hit the earth now;

it punched a vast hole in the water canopy and the canopy is starting to fall. When the canopy comes down we might lose visual on the other side. Wait a minute, the comet is splintering in the atmosphere! I might be able to bounce a signal off the ice. There, I got it. I'll put it up on 12 panels."

"Marcella, clear the bottom row of panels. It's too distracting for me to pilot," Axle yelled.

"Oh, thank God! The poles of the earth are attracting the magnetic properties in the ice. The north and south polls are taking the brunt of the impact!" Marcella reported.

"Axle, I'm reading the ice at over 300 degrees below zero," Max jumped in. "Don't let it bury us."

"I found a safe place for now, down by the equator, on the back side. The ship is stable for now!" Axle shouted.

"I'm going to check the lab, and secure the plants," Jane said as she unfastened her seat belt.

"I'm reading an open solar panel cover. I have to close it manually," Max yelled.

"You stay! I'll get it," Captain Eli said, following right behind Jane.

"The ice is piling up like a snow cone at the poles. The North Pole seems to be taking most of the impact. The tropical forest now has several thousand feet of freezing ice, and still rising!" Max yelled.

"All life surrounding the North and South Poles, is being destroyed instantly; all plants, animals, fish and people. The earth is becoming top heavy; the ice is moving down and pushing everything in its path. *This certainly is the ice age!"* Marcella exclaimed.

"The asteroid just hit Antarctica! Oh my God, I can't believe what I'm seeing. It's causing the earth to wobble erratically! Between that hit and the weight at the North Pole, the earth is moving in an irregular rocking motion, from side to side. The crust of the earth has a hairline crack, like an egg." Max uttered loudly, panic in his voice.

"Axle, move us up, the pressure is tremendous, it could shoot up several thousand feet," Marcella shouted.

Max, yelling again, "The cracks are spreading fast; one is forming directly below us. Axle, north-northeast, two hundred kilometers, full throttle. Go!"

"Here it comes. Max, turn off the outside microphones, and make sure we're sound proof," Marcella screamed.

"I'm ready!" Axle yelled.

A wall of hot water with steam bellowing out of it shot straight up passed the ship. It was followed by the most deafening noise that anyone has ever heard. It was unbearable! Their hands automatically covered their ears. It didn't help. Marcella motioned to Max, to deaden the sound, by running her finger across her throat. Max nodded that he already did.

The ship shook violently!

Max and Axle were the only ones still strapped in. Everyone else was knocked to the floor; face down. They couldn't let go of their ears. If the ship wasn't sound proof, the noise would have killed them.

The wind tossed the ship around like a cork in the ocean during a storm. Finally, the noise died down. They were able to remove their hands from their ringing ears.

Axle quickly grabbed the controls and moved the ship further away from the gushing water. The turbulence subsided a little. The wind from the water blast was pushing away the freezing ice from the comet. It created a small, safe zone. He moved the ship in and held it there.

"We'll be safe here, for a while," Axle said as he looked back to see how everyone was.

The floor was covered with debris. Dirt from the plants, half eaten snacks and open bags of liquid protein, were scattered everywhere. What a mess!

"Is everyone alright?" Axle yelled.

"Over here!" Marcella shouted. She was covered in blood.

Axle looked frantically for Doc. She was wedged between her chair and her console. He grabbed her arm and pulled her to her feet. They rushed to Marcella. It looked pretty grim. She had blood on her head, neck, stomach and ankle. Doc searched the area to see what could cause that much injury; there didn't seem to be anything sharp.

Max pushed his way through, "Doc, she looks like she's been cut badly. Is she alright?"

Doc put her finger in the blood, looked at it closely and then licked her finger. Marcella was speechless.

"What are you doing?" Max yelled.

"It's the Captain's bag of tomato juice," Doc said smiling, as she pulled the torn juice bag from under Marcella.

They tried not to laugh, but just couldn't help it. Marcella was embarrassed but laughed with them. Axle looked around still laughing, and suddenly noticed Captain Eli and Jane lying in the hallway.

They weren't laughing.

"Doc, over there!" he yelled.

Doc ran over to Captain Eli, first. Axle went to Jane.

Jane was lying face down. Her arms straight out; hands balled into fists, she was moaning.

"Jane, what's wrong?" he asked, kneeling by her side.

She could barely lift her head, tears streaming down her face. She couldn't talk. She was in considerable pain.

Axle examined her head then gently squeezed her shoulders and arms. When he touched her right leg, she yelled in anguish. It was broken.

"Doc!" Axle shouted, "Jane's leg. I think it's broken."

Doc came quickly and whispered, "Jane, this is something for the pain; I'll examine your leg in a minute. I have to see if Eli is hurt. Axle, stay with her. See that she doesn't move her leg."

"I won't leave her side," he said, comforting her.

The shot took effect quickly.

"Ever?" Jane said softly, as she drifted.

"Doc, what was in that?" Axle asked.

"I gave it to *her*, why are *you* smiling?" she said as she was moving rapidly toward the Captain.

"Marcella, get the table open. Max, help me get the Captain on it."

"I'll open it" Axle yelled.

Captain Eli was lying on his back, in the doorway of the Botany Lab. His long legs extended into the hallway. His head was twisted and wedged between a wall and a metal table leg. A rapidly growing pool of blood was forming under his head.

"We can't move him, his neck looks broken," Doc wailed.

"Is he still....?" Max choked.

Doc cut him off quickly, "Yes," as she removed her fingers from the Captains neck. "His vitals are weak, his pulse is almost gone. We need to bring him to, and fast! Axle, you make sure we don't crash, we can handle this." She frantically yelled out orders.

"I'm monitoring the autopilot right from here. I'm staying." Axle stood by helplessly.

Doc was in full panic, "I can't stop the bleeding. His blood pressure is dropping. He's bleeding out, he's not going to make it."

She looked up Max; he was already running to the back of the lab.

Marcella whispered in Doc's ear, "We have to lift his head."

"We can't, he'll die," Doc cried.

"We have no choice."

Seconds later Max returned with a leaf.

"Max, help me lift his head," Marcella demanded. "Get the cup over his nose; don't let the leaf touch his skin."

"Oh, God," Doc begged. "Don't let it be too late."

They had difficulty getting the leaf close to his nose, in the position that he was in. The cup was too far away, and his breathing was too shallow. They tried frantically to rearrange their stance, but to no avail. The blood from his head was now pooling around their knees.

It was taking way too long. He was declining rapidly.

Doc looked at Max and Axle. Her eyes were begging them to do something!

Marcella's head was shaking from side to side. She was crying.

Max was sobbing loudly. "Doc, he's gone," he cried.

"No!" A piercing scream erupted from her. She wedged her hands around the cup and Eli's nose, trying to get a better seal, and began to plead. "Come on, Eli. Breathe! Just one breath! Please!"

Nothing happened.

She repeated it again and again!

"Breathe, Eli, breathe!"

Suddenly, his chest expanded ever so slightly.

Doc leaned in closely and whispered in his ear, "Eli, just a few more breaths. His vitals are getting stronger," she shouted to Max. "The bleeding just stopped."

Doc sobbed. Her body went limp; her shoulders now slumped, head hanging down. Her hair was dripping with sweat. She kept repeating, "Thank you, God. Thank you, God."

Before they realized what was happening, the pool of blood they were kneeling in quickly shrank, until it totally disappeared. Without leaving a trace anywhere.

Max promptly handed the cup to Axle. He quickly ran to Jane. Suddenly, the ship shook violently again and knocked the leaf and Axle to the floor. They watched in dismay as it disintegrated.

Captain's eyes opened slowly.

"I feel really great. Well rested and extremely alert, relaxed and revitalized. So tell me, why am I lying here on the floor, wedged against the wall?" Captain asked, dumbfounded.

Max and Marcella shook their heads, too drained to laugh or answer.

Doc relieved, whispered, "All is well, now, Eli." She took a breath and said, "Max, help the Captain up while I go set Jane's broken leg.

"Jane's broken leg? What did *I* miss?" Captain asked, shocked, his concern now shifting to his crew.

"Doc, should I get another leaf for Jane?" Max interrupted.

Jane lifted her head and mumbled, "Only if I'm dying," then drifted off again.

"Another leaf? You used a leaf on *me*?" Captain asked, stunned, as he rose to his feet.

They nodded.

"Was I dying?"

"Yes," Doc answered softly, tears welling in her eyes.

"Thank God, that water blast wasn't a direct hit." Axle added. "It would have sliced the ship in half like a loaf of bread. I still can't believe what I'm seeing. It's a wall of water; like a slit in a fire hose, stretching out like a fan, as far as the eye can see."

"I'm reading that the initial blast reached over twenty miles high. We were almost pulverized!" Max jumped in.

"Twenty miles, that's three times higher than Mt. Everest," Marcella said, sounding exhausted. "That's impossible. Let me see that data. Our situation is going to change drastically in just a few minutes."

"More drastic than this?" Doc asked as she was tending to Jane. Now fear in her voice.

"Axle, watch closely. That water going up is coming down as ice. Most will remain in space, but what falls down could easily crush us," Marcella yelled. "Max, calculate which side of the geyser the ice will fall."

"How do I do that?" he snapped back.

"Da utter shide," Jane blurted, slurring her words.

"What?" Max laughed.

"I shaid, da utter shide. Da ishe will fall on da utter shide," she repeated.

"Don't listen to her," Max quipped, laughing again. "She's high from that shot. She's not making any sense."

"Max, lighten up. How do you know that, Jane?" Axle asked.

"Becaushe, it hash to. If it doeshn't, we all die," she said giggling. "Ishn't dat right, Marshella?"

"I wasn't going to say anything, because I calculate a 2% chance that we will make it, if the ice falls on this side," Marcella said, suppressing a laugh.

"2%? You were keeping a 98% chance of us *not* surviving, to yourself?" Captain Eli said in disbelief!

"Because, Captain, I *know* the ice *will* fall on the other side, as well." After a pause, she added, "I just don't know *how* I know it. But, how do *you* know it, Jane?"

"Dat dream! Daughter running, shkipping. Healed wit da leaf. Shooooo, we *are* going back. We jush have to do our part!" she said, almost singing her words. Jane then closed her eyes and drifted off to sleep again.

"What's *our* part?" Captain Eli asked the crew.

"Now that's a good question," Axle muttered.

"I don't know for sure, but my guess is, to keep alert and look for safe places. From the dream, we know that one will be provided for us," Doc added.

"That's it? A dream? Great! We're going to make it *because Jane* had a dream! Does anyone have anything a little more substantial than, *Jane had a dream?*" Max yelled, frustrated.

"Max, get a grip," Marcella said trying to calm him. "I'm reading the ice falling on the other side. It's because of the direction that the earth is spinning."

They all looked at Max and could tell he felt a little foolish.

He quickly recovered. "Well, as long as we have confirmation."

"I've been slowly pushing us forward," Marcella added. "The geyser has calmed down considerably. We need to look for another safe place."

"I have an idea. Can you locate the Ark, Max? We know it survives." Axle said.

"I'll try. Marcella, give me a hand. There's so much floating debris, this is not going to be easy," he replied.

"I've located the Ark," Doc exclaimed, with tears in her eyes.

"How did you do that so quickly? And why the tears, Doc?" Max asked.

"I just set the biological sensors to pick up life outside our ship. I'm detecting a small amount of humans and animals in a confined area."

Silence fell.

Doc continued, speaking softly, as she wept. "That's it? That's all that's left? All those billions of people and animals are just *gone.*"

They stood together in silence.

Finally, Captain Eli spoke, touching her arm tenderly, "Doc, we knew this was coming, but right now we have to make sure we don't join them. We'll talk about it later."

"Captain, getting to the Ark is another story. It's on the other side of the geyser," Max interrupted.

"Can't we go around the earth the other way, Max?"

"Sir, this exact thing is happening at every fault line on earth. We have to cross here and, we have to cross now!" Marcella added, with panic in her voice.

"What if we stay here until the geyser dissipates?" Captain asked.

"That's not an option, sir!" she shot back quickly. "The ice and snow from the comet are already breaking through the wind. It's beginning to pelt us now."

"This is *your* expertise, Captain. We need a strategy," Axle pleaded.

"We can start near the source of the geyser, and accelerate upward. We enter and let the geyser push us, as we work our way through it. We'll be getting pelted with debris the entire time. We must get through as quickly as possible, to keep the damage to a minimum." Captain Eli, in total command, continued, "Axle, are you able to avoid the sheets of ice that are falling, after we get through?"

"I don't think I can concentrate on the controls *and* plot a course through falling debris at the same time, sir. If

Max can help navigate, we'll have a much better chance."

"Well, Max, can you handle it?" Captain asked.

"Is there any other way?"

"I don't see one."

"Then I can handle it," Max said assuring him.

"We have to go, now!" Marcella interrupted, with urgency in her voice.

"Give me one more minute. I'm assembling ear protection," Doc broke in. "It's going to be loud at the source of the geyser. Just so you know; we won't be able to hear each other."

"We won't be able to hear each other, *with or without* ear protection. Max, you and Axle work out hand signals," Captain Eli demanded.

"You mean like crane signals, or umpire, or how about referee signals?" Max asked, nervously; knowing their lives were depending on him. He flailed his arms around mimicking each signal; crane up, you're out and field goal arm movements.

"Just keep it simple," Captain Eli yelled back shaking his head. "Marcella, please help them."

"Yes, sir. Easy left, hard right, up, down, slow and stop," she said with hand gestures. "You got it?"

"We were just about to do that!" Max said sheepishly. "A few more seconds and we would have gotten it!"

Marcella rolled her eyes a little and said, "Just remember, our lives depend on it."

"That's what I'm afraid of," Max said under his breath.

"Okay, so it was, hard left, back, sharp right, stop and go.....right?" Axle whispered to Max.

"No, no, no. It was soft left, hard right, full forward, down, and stop," Max replied, just as confused.

Doc walked over to them, tapped them on the shoulder and said, "Here." as she handed them the inserts for their ears. "It's easy left, hard right, up, down, slow and stop. Got it?" She whispered, through clenched teeth, as she demonstrated the hand signals.

"Yep," They both reassured her.

"Are you ready, Max?" Axle asked.

"I'm ready. Put in your ear protection and get close."

Max counted down from five on his fingers. Axle took off. Max was putting his entire body into his signals. He looked like a dancing orchestra leader, and was remarkably easy to follow.

After accelerating, Axle entered near the base of the geyser and was passing through very quickly. So far, things were going according to plan. After they emerged, the visibility was still zero. A thick gray coating covered the entire ship. Max was still leading; following the sensors. Axle was following Max. From some of the maneuvers the ship was making, it's a good thing no one could see.

Captain Eli picked up the remote and cleared the windows. Axle could hardly stay focused on Max, with all the gasping and screeching in the background. They couldn't believe what they were seeing! They were dodging immense sheets of ice and rocks being hurled at them from every direction. Chunks of gray mud were sticking to the windows. Max, being a true gamer, never took his eyes off the screen, thank God!

Max motioned for the others to remove their ear protection. "We've cleared the falling sheets of ice," he said, sounding concerned. "However, shards of ice are becoming imbedded in the mud that's coating the ship. We will be immobilized in less than two minutes!"

"Axle, hit the water below," Captain Eli ordered.

"Here we go, sir. Hang on!"

As they looked down, upon the once crystal clear, blue ocean, they were horrified to see it was now shades of gray and black. White caps were now tinged brown with dirt. The surface was thick with floating debris, mixed with large chunks of ice. They could see uprooted trees, animal carcasses, and dead bodies. The sight sickened them, but there was no other option.

Axle plunged the craft into the water, creating a path through the debris. They were below the floating ice, with zero visibility. The dense plant life and seaweed were becoming entangled in the motors.

Axle needed to surface quickly. He could see daylight breaking through the water, just a few feet above.

Suddenly, the temperature inside the ship dropped drastically in a matter of seconds. The controls were becoming sluggish from the cold. Axle could barely hold on, his fingers were numb from gripping the controls so tightly.

The crew was in a panic.

Axle whispered, "God help us!"

As the ship shot out of the dark ocean into the light, Captain Eli shouted, "Head for the Ark. Full speed ahead!"

The ice began to dissipate, as they drew closer to the Ark. They blasted the heat inside the ship. Marcella was sending out a constant electrical charge, keeping the ice from collecting on the hull.

"Thank God, we made it! And, thank you, Axle," Marcella said weeping.

"Axle, it's an honor to work alongside of you," Max said breathlessly.

"You all deserve medals for getting us through *that,*" Captain Eli stated gratefully. "Marcella, what is all that gray material that's being shot out of the earth?"

"I'm reading billions of tons of sand, mud, shell and eroded rock. I'm also reading diatoms," she answered.

"What's a diatom?" Axle asked, calming down a bit.

"It's a one-celled animal that's used in everything; from swimming pool filters, to non-toxic insecticides. It's also found in many other products, too numerous to mention. They're necessary to create the fossil records."

"And now we know why there are *no* fossil records, just fossils all created at the same time," Max added emphatically.

"How long before we reach the Ark?" Doc asked.

"Just a few more minutes," Max answered.

"Doc, how's Jane?" Axle asked.

"Her leg has a small fracture, I already set it. Her mobility won't even be affected. She's awake but still a little groggy."

"I'm alright, now," Jane whispered. "I really want to see the Ark. Can you help me adjust the back of my chair, so I can sit up?"

"The Ark is coming up on the port side," Max said.

"So, what side am *I* on again?" she asked, as she randomly looked around the ship through the glass, including straight down.

Captain Eli said smiling, "you're on the port side, Jane. Max, put it up on nine panels for her."

"Oh my goodness," she said, sounding like a child. "It's really Noah's Ark. Is it supposed to sit that low in the water?"

"It's impossible to capsize," Captain Eli said.

"It's hardly rocking," Doc added.

"A perfect design," Captain Eli stated, as he stared in amazement. "Do you know that the design for all the ships that ever sailed the seas came from this Ark? No one has ever been able to improve its perfect six to one ratio. Take us in closer."

"Captain, the ice and snow from the comet are almost non existent here. Other than the torrential rain, tornado force gusting winds, freezing temperatures and extremely high seas, this is the safest place on earth!" Marcella said chuckling a bit at her own observations.

"Why am I not surprised?" Max said laughing.

"Axle, hover above the Ark. Try to stay close, while Marcella pushes us forward in time, until things calm down and we are out of danger. Is that possible?" Captain asked.

Not without a tractor beam from a sci-fi movie, Axle thought.

"We can coordinate with Marcella to slow us down, if the Ark drifts more than a mile," Max suggested.

"How long will it take?"

"That depends on how fast the Ark drifts. We won't know till we start, sir."

"Make it happen."

"Axle, follow my coordinates," Max ordered. "Marcella, begin slowly, if the Ark does drift more than a mile, hold until we catch up. Let's do it!"

"Here's four hours a minute," Marcella replied.

"Keep picking up the pace, until I tell you to stop," Max replied.

"Okay, eight hours per minute," she paused, "now sixteen," pausing again, "thirty two. Are you keeping up, Max?"

"Yes, the Ark hasn't drifted more than a mile. It's calm out there. Marcella, it's all yours."

"Something is keeping the Ark in this area. I've got a feeling we'll be safe here and for the record, if we ever come back, let's just stay with the Ark to begin with. From this location, I'll be able to take us all the way back to our time," Marcella said.

"Then do it." Captain Eli ordered.

"But, Captain, we need to stay longer. There are so many more theories that need verifying," she pleaded.

"How much time do you need?"

"I guess a year is too much to ask," she said meekly.

"We have to get the plants back, sir," Jane said, finally coming out of her fog.

Captain Eli shot Marcella a look and said, "I can give you eight hours."

She stared back at him in disbelief.

He reiterated, "I said eight hours! That's it."

"Max, Doc, please help me. I need a strategy. I have to do the impossible, *in eight hours,*" Marcella mimicked.

20

~ ARE THESE THE GOOD GUYS ~

Jack Brock found Dom Brothers in Partenza Hall, checking instrument panels.

"Dom, we need to discuss maintenance priorities in my office. Is now a good time?"

He nodded and immediately followed Jack back to his office. He studied the room without saying a word, while Jack shut and locked the door behind him. "It's safe to talk here," he assured him. "I just swept the office for bugs and turned on the jammer."

"What options do we have?" Dom asked.

"In order to derail Zadok's plans, the ship would have to be significantly damaged or destroyed. Both would be horribly regrettable," he answered with sadness in his voice.

"Is it *possible* to significantly damage the ship, without harming the crew?"

"That would be a long shot. The Coalter D security laser grid is the only available means I have of damaging the ship. I have a colleague in that department, but without being able to pinpoint their return; the chances of him being there, at *that* exact time, are only 20%. The only thing I was able to do so far, is render their security grid code useless."

"Marcella is like a daughter to me," Dom said wiping tears from his eyes with his handkerchief.

"I know, Dom. I'm close to Eli Hunter, as well. Let's not forget, Zadok's group already has them marked for death. They're ruthless people. They have to be stopped, at all cost!"

"Well, if the crew is hurt, or worse; *it most certainly will be,* at all cost," Dom said angrily.

"If by some miracle, my friend is able to help and some of the crew does survive, I have to convince Zadok, that they are worth more alive than dead; without revealing that I know his plan. That's our short-term solution. But, if your source can retrieve more of the group's conference calls, or expose any other illegal activities, we can turn them over to a colleague in the Justice Department."

"Does he have a good track record?" Dom asked.

"Oh yeah, this guy lives to investigate high-profile crimes. If he can get a foothold, he'll put this group out of business within the next few years. But, if our plan fails and the Bella group is able to commandeer the ship and go back in time, *they will alter history*! They'll gain global dominance and achieve world power! They *will be* an unstoppable force!" Jack said sternly. "The well being of the many, will outweigh the well being of the few."

Dom rose slowly to his feet. It was apparent that this conversation weighed heavily on him. He left without saying a word.

As soon as Dom returned to Partenza Hall, he made eye contact with Rebecca. She knew instinctively that he was troubled. She excused herself from her colleagues and left the room, ignoring him. He stayed fifteen minutes longer, chatting. He pardoned himself and said, "I need to check on some things. I'll be back later."

Rebecca was already seated at Sal's, waiting patiently for his arrival.

"Well, how did it go with Jack?" she asked, greatly concerned.

"He has a friend in the Justice Department that can shut the Bella Group down in time; if my anonymous source can get more information on them."

"How much time will he need?"

"Two years."

"Are you kidding me? You know the damage they can do in one day with a time-travel ship! They just have to take off once, and it's over."

"We discussed that. Brock has implemented a plan that will damage the ship, so we would have to rebuild it. That should buy us enough time."

"And just how does he plan on damaging the ship? We don't know where, or even when, it is."

"He has a friend in Global Security…"

She cut him off, "That idiot canceled their laser grid codes, didn't he? Isn't that like swatting a fly with a sledge hammer? He just condemned the whole crew to death! Marcella, Max, our friends?" She was angry.

"He said his friend might be able to help," Dom said, hopefully.

"*Might*, is right. Did he tell you there is only a 20% chance his friend will be there? And even if he is, there's only a 40% chance he will stop one, maybe two blasts. I helped design the Coalter D Security system; it's the most secure in the world. It changes strategies every six seconds. The optimum word here is "S-e-c-u-r-i-t-y". They're as good as dead!"

"He said there was a reasonable chance of that, but the well being…"

She cut him off again, "I know the well being cliché."

"If you have another option, I'll take it to Jack." Dom sounded more and more defeated.

"Let me think." She paused for a minute, shaking her head. "There must be another way. He can't be right. I can't live with that, Dom!"

"I"m afraid we don't have a choice," he said, regrettably.

"We do! It's time for another course of action. It's time for me to step in!" she said.

"You? What can *you* do?" he questioned, shocked at her statement.

"Dom, what do you really know about me?"

"I know that you are a computer genius. You're able to transform my theories into practical application, and that you are closer to me than anyone has ever been. And, you don't like to talk about your past. I have respected that for the past five years, hoping some day you'll open up."

"Is today good for you?"

"Today's great," Dom replied, startled. Almost afraid of what he was about to hear.

"I started out as a banker with a policemen friend in the fraud department. I would spot a scam, alert my friend and clean out the scammer's personal account return the money to his victims just before he was arrested. I made a routine inquiry on an account that traced back to an organized crime figure that came after me. I changed my identity, drained his bosses account and made it look like he was stealing from his boss. I became an anonymous organized crime informant to IGS and CHASE. A CHASE agent tracked me down and made me aware of an IGS agent after a 20 million dollar bounty on my head. I was recruited by CHASE as freelance so I didn't have rules to follow. We were recruiting agents at the science fair in Hawaii 5 years ago when you approached Marcella I read you as an unselfish honest man. We checked you out and found you were issued a 180 billion dollar grant. We realized your grant was about to be jumped, the giver would clam non-performance have their shell company come in steal your idea and force you to work for them to fulfill your contract. I couldn't let that happen. I told CHASE I was taking 5 years off and got you to hire me. I thought Oden was after the money, I should have known he was after the ship.

Now, Dom came to life. That's why you purchased this abandon air base and got me to hire Brock on your first day. You knew I had to show performance. But why didn't you tell me about Oden?

I couldn't, I love being with you because you have no deception and my gift of knowing when people are lying is at peace with you. Trying to hide the fact that you knew what Oden was up to would have been exhausting and hindered your progress on the mission. I'm telling you now because I think you are ready to handle it.

"Wow! What's the next move?"

My specialty is finding the weaknesses in organizations, like the Bella Group. I will find who they have on the inside. I designed surveillance equipment for IGS, CHASE, and other agencies. Bugs work both ways. Let's go. I have bugs to find and bad guys to manipulate."

~~~

As soon as they arrived at Partenza Hall, Rebecca went to work creating a bug sweeper that was able to detect both visual and audio equipment. She built it in plain sight, without arousing suspicion. It was designed to vibrate in her lab coat pocket to avoid detection.

The next morning; Rebecca approached Dom in the hall Zëo-pad in hand.

"I found 6 audio-visual high quality bugs, and narrowed our inside candidates down to Powell and Nadia."

"Why them, I thought it was Carlos."

They both have impeccable references and their qualifications fit their job descriptions too perfectly. Carlos had a few false references and overstated his qualifications. Brandon and Albert never get here early or work late. I sent their profiles to my contact in CHASE and none of them were ever field agents, so they must be freelance. We have to mislead them into thinking we are on the verge of building a time portal that will make the ship obsolete. I want you to call a meeting in the conference room this morning; I'll hand out the time portal assignments. Hopefully Tom and Nadia will let the group know a time portal will make the ship obsolete.

21

~Mr. Right~

"First, move forward until the rain subsides," Doc suggested.

"Not yet, I want to measure the liquefaction," Marcella pleaded.

"What is liquefaction?" Axle asked.

"The water gushing out of the earth, is stirring the dirt and animal carcasses. The theory states; they will be sorted by density; the dirt will separate and form layers of rock. The animals will separate, and mix with the layers. Making it appear, as if the animals on the bottom layer died first. In reality, we now know they all died at the same time. The heaviest animals buried, were pressed into oil, along with humans. The plants turned to coal. And a little bit of everything became petrified," Marcella stated, with absolute confidence in her theory.

While she was chattering away, Axle was observing Jane. She was gazing down at the muddy water that covered the entire planet. Her leg was outstretched and elevated, her hair still tousled. She looked lost in thought. She looked beautiful!

There's something so different about her. She intrigues me, Axle thought. *For the first time, I could actually see myself spending the rest of my life with one woman, maybe this woman.*

He glanced away, then realized that Doc had been watching *him*, the entire time. She was smiling. She seemed to sense what he was thinking. Doc got up from her station and headed for the galley. Axle set the autopilot, and leaned over to Max. "I could use a break. Can you handle things until I get back?"

Max just nodded as he listened to Marcella trail on incessantly, about the scientific properties of the liquefaction, or *'whatever that is'!*

Axle headed back towards the galley. He glanced quickly over his shoulder, making sure the Captain wasn't following. He wanted to talk with Doc privately.

Doc had already filled a mug of hot coffee for herself, and was pouring one for Axle when he walked in.

He laughed. "How did you know?"

"It's all over your face," she smiled back. "What do you want to know?"

"How long have you known Jane?"

"We go back a very long time," she said, still smiling.

Doc was slowly sipping her coffee, her eyes never leaving Axle's. She was enjoying this.

"Help me out here," he said a bit embarrassed. "I'd just like to know a little more about her; like what her social life is like."

"You mean, does she date?" Doc asked, with a laugh." Well I can safely tell you, that I arranged to have her meet two eligible men, after her daughter's father died. Before the end of each date, she managed to have an emergency arise, so she could suddenly leave. Her standards are high. She told me she would never settle again. She was willing to trust God for *Mr. Right;* whatever that means! And that she would know him, when he showed up. Apparently, the men I tried to fix her up with, weren't *him!* I never interfered again. Anything else you'd like to know?" she said, as she made her way over to the table to sit.

"Yes, you used the term 'her daughter's father'. She uses that term too. Were they ever married?"

"Of course they were married, Axle! She just doesn't ever want to forget that he was *never* a husband. Come to think of it, he wasn't ever really much of a father to Tori, either. So, why all the questions about Jane?" she pressed.

"I've grown very fond of her, and I hardly know her. I've never felt this way about anyone before. Do you think *I* might have a chance with her?"

"It's possible," Doc laughed. "And judging from that comment that I pretended not to hear; you could be *him*. I can't believe what we're talking about. I haven't had a conversation like this since high school. Besides, if it turns out you *are* the man that she's been waiting for, and you hurt her; I know sixteen, maybe seventeen, ways that you could die of *natural causes*," she said laughing.

"Thanks for the warning. But as far as being the right guy, I can only hope."

"Just be yourself, Axle. Either you *are him,* or your not," she said emphatically, as she turned away smiling.

Axle followed her back to the front of the ship, with coffee in hand. He couldn't get the smile off his face!

"Max, record at high speed, I'm moving us forward." Marcella suddenly went into action. "Axle, the forty days are almost over. Get ready to move as soon as it's calm. Take us up fifteen miles; we need to be elevated, so I can determine just where on earth we are."

"How will you be able to do that? Axle asked. "There's water and ice everywhere."

"It's calm. Take us up now and I'll show you. See?" Marcella said, pointing down. "That's the North Pole. We know the ice came down as far as Ohio." Does anyone know where the Ark lands?"

"The Ark landed on Mt. Ararat," Jane said, fully coherent.

They all looked at her with gratitude that she was back.

"How are you doing, Jane?" Captain Eli asked.

"Just a little painful, but please, no more shots."

"Axle, stay over the Ark," Marcella interrupted, "until it lands on the mountain. Max, start overlaying the earth's fault lines, so we'll be able to pinpoint our exact location through the flood waters. I'll push forward a few months till the mud settles."

"Good thinking," Max said to her. "I'll have it in a

few minutes."

They were in awe, watching Marcella flow in her element.

"When all the pressure is released, voids will form under the earth," she said. "As soon as all the water is pushed out, Dr. Browns Hydro-plate theory, should take effect. The pressure will push dirt up through the cracks, lifting the crust of the earth. It will then slide away from the cracks, and we will watch the mountains form. It will look like wrinkles in a rug, that's been pushed up against a wall."

The crust began to buckle, and the mountains were formed. The Ark was pushed up, safely out of the way. The crust also buckled downward, forming the ocean trenches. The sun broke through the clouds. The perfect environment was gone!

"Max, tint the windows, it's already getting hot in here," Axle said, a bit saddened.

Marcella interjected, "Only one year has passed now, I need to pick up the pace, and move us forward. Now that the underground pressure has been released, the weight of the water is filling the voids. The mountains will continue to rise for another thousand years, or so. We know the highest mountain only reaches six miles high."

"Only? Six miles *is* high, Marcella!" Jane said.

"No, not really. The Earth is eight thousand miles in diameter. If the mountains and valleys were drawn to scale, six miles would be a flat line. The Earth is still wobbling and won't stabilize to its tilt, for a few thousand years. The continents are forming and growing to size. Now it's beginning to look like the Earth we know. That took less than 100 years."

"Wait, what's going on? The continents are growing even larger. How can that be, Marcella?"

"Actually, this explains a lot, Axle. You can see how you could walk to Australia, or any of the continents, for that matter. This explains how the animals got there. Jane, you said the animals didn't become aggressive until after the flood, right? So the aggressive animals have forced the passive animals to other regions. That explains why kangaroos and other species are only found in specific locations; yet their bones and fossils are found all over the world."

"How profound!" Axle said. "And I thought my grandfather was borderline crazy."

"I doubt if anybody's crazy in your family, Axle," Jane said sweetly.

Axle quickly glanced at Doc, just in time to see her suppress a giggle and roll her eyes.

Things are looking promising for *"Mr Right!"*

22

~ Blood Soaked Arrows~

"**J**ane, are you well enough to skim read the next part?"

"Yes, Captain." Jane said softly. She pulled up the text from the Genesis Chip, on the screen in front of her.

"**God tells Noah to come out of the Ark. Noah builds an Alter; God says he will never again curse the ground for man's sake, or destroy every living thing. The seasons start; seed, time and harvest, cold and heat, winter and summer, day and night will not stop. God blesses Noah and his sons, be fruitful and multiply. God puts the dread of man in the animals and tells Noah that everything that moves, everything alive, is his for food. Don't eat blood; He demands the life of any animal that kills a person, and any person that kills another person, because human beings were made in his image.**"

"What happened to *Thou shall not kill?*" Max interrupted.

"The real translation of that is, **'Thou shall not murder.'** And His law said if you murder someone, the family of the victim has not only the right, but also the duty, to kill you." She went on to read, "**Then he promises never to flood the earth again and signs it with a rainbow.**"

"Look, Utah has a great lake and it's bigger than all the other lakes combined," Doc exclaimed, in amazement.

"Watch it closely, Max, and let me know when the water starts to drain off. Oh, there is too much to watch. I need months!" Marcella pleaded.

"We only have hours, do your best," Captain Eli reminded her.

"I'm picking up the pace, Captain," Marcella said apologetically.

"From the looks of the animal migration patterns, there are animals all over the world," Doc reported. "But I'm reading thousands of people living in a small area. Axle, take us back to Mt. Ararat."

"Marcella, set the controls to cycle at ten days per minute, and eliminate the nights, and Max, zoom in on that structure and put it up on sixteen panels." Captain ordered, without taking a breath.

"It's the beginning of a city with walls being built on the first piece of flatland that Noah's descendants could find." Max answered.

"If they are the only people alive now, why do they need walls?" Doc asked. "And, when did they start making bricks? Everything was made from stone."

"Before the flood, the sun coming through the canopy wasn't hot enough to bake bricks, and they didn't have the right kind of soil then, either. All that has changed. Judging from the foundation, the structure they're building, is going to be enormous. Marcella, speed things up. Wow, it's already over two miles high, and the people are working frantically, even the pregnant women are making bricks. This is really a magnificent feat of engineering. I wish I could go inside to see why the weight of the building isn't crushing the lower bricks?" Max stated.

"Nimrod!" Jane interrupted.

"Who are you calling a Nimrod?" Max questioned defensively.

The crew began to laugh hysterically.

"Not you," she said, laughing herself. "This is the city of Babylon, and that is the Tower of Babel. Nimrod is Noah's great-grandson. He's a tyrant that built all of the great cities of his day."

"So there was really a man named Nimrod?" Max joked.

"Another tyrant? *Already*?" Captain Eli cut him off. "We are only three generations from Noah. How long does *this* one live?"

"It is said, Nimrod lived well over four hundred years," Jane continued, "and he wanted to defy God and not populate the Earth. He wanted to be worshiped instead of God. So, he convinced the people to build a city, and a tower that reached to the Heavens, to display their greatness. Now, they would have no need for God. Nimrod perpetuated a myth that from the top of the tower, arrows could be shot into the Heavens, and they would come back dripping blood. As if, actually waging war on God."

"Waging war on God? Does God crush him to dust?" Captain asked incredulously.

"It just says, **God confuses the language, they stopped building and are scattered throughout the earth.**" Jane stated.

"Nimrod, must mean FOOL!" Captain said in disgust.

"Something's happening, I'm slowing sir, the wind is really picking up, and the ground is beginning to tremble," Marcella interrupted. "The tower is still stable, but all the work has abruptly come to a halt."

"Max, keep full screen, and add audio."

"It's all garbled, sir. The sensors are picking up people yelling in frustration, in 72 different languages!"

The crew watched this generation's glory, turn to shame in a single afternoon! No longer being able to communicate, brought total chaos. They left the city, in disgrace, and spread out in every direction.

"Marcella, move forward, one hundred and fifty years. Let's get out of here. I've seen enough of this!"

"I agree, sir." Marcella made the jump with the touch of her screen. "I am showing pockets of people, spread out all over the Earth now."

23

~WILLINGLY IGNORANT~

"It seems the skin pigmentation of those living in colder climates, have already started to fade; becoming lighter, with *this* generation. We truly are all one race," Doc said pensively.

"Marcella, slow down. The water is draining off Utah," Max said with enthusiasm.

"Oh, my goodness, are we watching the Grand Canyon being formed right before our eyes?" Jane announced loudly.

The sheer power of the gushing water washed through the deep valley, carrying out the sediment, still soft from the flood waters. It then added layer upon layer of brilliantly colored silt, that hardened into rock forming the breathtaking Grand Canyon.

Everyone watched in awe, speechless. A magnificent movie was unfolding; and they were the audience. No one wanted this to end.

"How much real time did *that* take?" Max asked, breaking the moment.

"Just a few weeks. No one is going to believe the flood caused all this," Marcella said, astonished.

"I thought the flood was a myth, I refused to see all the signs. The Sahara Desert, the Great Barrier Reef, the amount of mud in the ocean, even the world population, all dates back 4,500 years," Max interjected.

"I'm amazed over the magnitude of destruction the flood caused, and is *still* causing *4,500 years* later. It is beyond comprehension," Captain added. "God has the power to do anything! Couldn't He have just stop everybody's heart? Why cause a flood, with this level of destruction?"

"God used the flood, because it would leave a preponderance of evidence and shorten man's life span. He wanted to let us know how much He hated man's inhumanity to man. Didn't we just read that **men were selfish and continually plotting evil?**" Jane reminded them.

"Oh boy! That sounds a lot like today." Max added.

"People are *willingly-ignorant* of the flood, because the flood is the dividing line," Doc pondered. "Those that want to believe in the old Earth theories have to deny the flood ever happened; even in the face of overwhelming evidence. But, that *will* change when we get back, with the actual proof. We now know that every natural disaster is proof of the flood!"

"Don't bet on it. Just like you said, people are *willingly-ignorant!*" Max said, arms folded, head nodding.

"This makes me wonder what lengths someone would go, to suppress the truth."

"What are you getting at, Captain?" Doc asked.

"Maybe we need to be a little cautious about all our findings. Our records have suddenly become very valuable. I think it might be wise to safe guard what we've recorded."

"Aren't you being just a little paranoid, Captain?" Max asked.

"Why take the chance? Max, make copies of all the records. It's possible we could have all our findings confiscated and destroyed. We could easily be discredited without proof. If that were to happen, our careers and compensation could be jeopardized. Marcella, is there a place on the ship where we can hide everything, without it being discovered?"

"I don't think so, sir."

"Do you really think we would be *searched*?" Doc asked, shocked.

"I can't be sure," Captain replied. "Marcella, adjust your sensors to sweep for surveillance equipment."

They adjusted their sensors and joined Marcella sweeping the ship. Doc began sweeping overhead bins, in the galley, cabins and lab; scanning all the contents. Axle was making a futile attempt, but didn't honestly believe they would discover anything.

Nothing was found.

Max and Marcella decided to link their scanners to boost its detection capabilities.

Max yelled first, "A light on my sensor just lit. I'm getting a reading. Everyone, adjust your scanners to .166.

Immediately, all their sensors lit.

"I never trusted Brock, this must be *his* doing," Max said angrily.

"Max, you're wrong!" Captain Eli snapped at him. "I know him well. This is *not* his style."

"Who else could it be?" Max asked frustrated.

"Well, *I* can vouch for Dom and Rebecca. It's not them," Marcella said emphatically, defending her friends.

"Well obviously, someone working for them is *not* who they say they are," Captain stressed.

"I have an audio bug here," Max broke in.

"I have two visuals here," Marcella added. "Very advanced equipment, expertly concealed. They've recorded everything we've done and said!"

"Can you and Max edit everything?"

"Not without them knowing it, sir." After a pause, Marcella glanced over at Max, and he winked. Smiling, she said, "Max, what are you thinking?"

Max used his scanner to trace the signal to a small panel under the mechanical arm. He popped the cover.

"Over here. It's a single control device. Gotcha!"

They both laughed.

"What are you two laughing about?" Captain asked, wanting in on the joke.

"We don't have to edit anything. All the cameras and listening devices are routed to a single piece of equipment. We can cause the device to malfunction, *on its own,*" Marcella announced happily. "It will scramble any surveillance they have on us."

"There, that should do it," Max said proudly, after crossing a few wires.

"Won't they know it was sabotaged, Max?"

"They might suspect, Jane."

"If they *do* suspect," Captain Eli interjected, "they *will* search until they find everything. Not just the duplicate records, but the platinum, the diamonds, and the leaves."

Jane's voice revealed her anxiety as she pleaded, "We can't let them find the leaves. I can do without the platinum and diamonds, but not the leaves!

"What if we hide all of it, *off* the ship?" Marcella asked.

"Like where?" Doc questioned.

"More, like *when*? The Coalter D Security defense system has been online twenty five years. It would have to be before then. Any time after that, *we* would be detected and destroyed," Max added.

"We need a place that hasn't changed, that no one knows about, and that hasn't been affected by natural disasters," Jane said excitedly.

"You mean something like a mausoleum, or a cemetery?" Doc suggested.

"I would prefer somewhere indoors," Captain stated.

"I have just the place," Axle said exuberantly. "My grandfather's house, it's been in my family for almost a hundred years. It's on two acres of land and sits on a lake. So, landing, *out of phase*, wouldn't be a problem. I had a lot of great times there when I was a kid."

Captain Eli remarked, with sarcasm in his voice, "Oh, how nice; but keep focused. How would we hide something there that *you* wouldn't eventually find?"

"As a child, I discovered a crawl space in the basement. That's where *I* hid things."

"Again, if we hide our stuff there, you will find it as a child; and you would probably change history, and screw up the future," Captain Eli responded, sarcastically, with a half smile.

"The crawl space was big, and there was a section I was afraid to explore. I thought it was haunted. I wouldn't go near it. It's perfect!" Axle persisted.

"Does anyone have a *better* idea?" Captain asked.

Silence.

"Again, does anyone else have another idea? Anyone?"

Silence.

"Okay," he said. "We'll do it, but I think it's absurd!"

"It sounds exciting!" Jane squealed.

"Max, Marcella, work out the timing, Axle, give them the location. Let's just get this over with!" Captain said, with great reluctance.

24

~ NOSEY OLD LADY NEXT DOOR ~

"**I**'m adding five years to my calculations, Captain. We can't be certain that the laser technology wasn't being tested before it was officially installed and announced."

"Good thinking, Marcella," Max said encouragingly. "When we get back, *we're* going to be a team!"

Marcella said with a grin, "If you mean partners, I'd *love* to be your partner, Max."

Captain Eli said, clearing his throat, "Could we stay focused here, please?"

"Marcella, can you add three years to that and make it August 10th?" Axle asked her.

"Okay, we're on our way, but why *that* day?"

"My grandmother use to tell a story, about my dad. It was three years before I was born, even before he was married. My father was testing the prototype LTF Surveillance Glider, the ejection seat didn't work, and it crashed with him in it. He was airlifted to the hospital and was not expected to live. The entire family, their friends and most of their neighbors stayed at the hospital for days praying. They said it was a miracle he survived. But, what I'm getting at is; no one is at home!"

"That will work." Marcella responded. "Let's do it. Max, seal everything in a pneumatic container. We're almost there."

"Doc, please help Max *carefully* pack the container," Captain commanded.

So, this is what my town looked like before I was born, pretty rural. I don't see the high-speed transport tube, or the 10- level merchant complex, no hover shuttles, Axle thought, as he guided the craft approaching the house he knew so well.

"There's my grandfather's bass boat. Right there on the lake. He still has that today. And that bench swing looks brand new. They still love to sit and watch the sunset on that," Axle said out loud as he reminisced.

"I want to see it," Jane said excitedly. "I'd love to go out on the lake."

"What? Are we on vacation? Set the ship down, Axle," Captain Eli said impatiently.

"I'll land the ship around back, between the porch and the lake; so no one sees me stepping out of an invisible ship!"

"Sensors show we're clear," Marcella said. "Go, Axle."

"Is anyone else coming?"

"Can I go?" Jane asked quickly.

"Actually, you could use the exercise, Jane," Doc answered. "Is that alright, Captain?"

"Why not, it's your plan! Can it get any worse?" the Captain said, annoyed.

"Axle, help her," Doc said, smiling.

The door of the ship opened, the stairs dropped down. Jane picked up the container; Axle picked up Jane and carried her carefully down the stairs.

Axle and Jane could hear the crew laughing behind them as they strode across the back lawn. They also heard the Captain yell, "Don't make me regret this!"

The spare key was still where it's always been, in the antique hide-a-key rock! Axle carefully set Jane down, as he opened the door. They were entering the house through the back.

Axle looked around in amazement. The room was the same; except for the plastic that was now covering the couches. They must be brand new. All the family pictures on the mantle, that Axle always looked at as a child, were not there, except for one of his grandparents. But, the room still had that same peaceful atmosphere.

"Jane, you wait here in the den, while I take the container down to the basement."

"Here, put it in this burlap bag. It'll be easier to carry."

"Look real paper!" Axle point to a pad on the counter. "I better leave a note of warning not to open the container, just in case someone finds it," he said as an afterthought.

While Axle was writing the note, he glanced over and saw Jane staring at a wedding picture of his grandparents.

She ran her fingers over the picture, looked over at him and said, "I love your grandmother's wedding dress."

"My mom is going to wear that same dress next year, when she marries my dad. It's always been my mom's wish to pass it down. It's still in her closet today."

"Do you have any sisters?"

"No, just a brother. He's married now."

"Did his wife wear it?"

"No. She hated it."

They both laughed. Then she said softly, "Well, I think it's beautiful."

"You know, we can hear you," Captain interrupted, over the communicator.

Is she picturing herself in my grandmother's wedding dress? Axle thought. *Because I am!*

Suddenly, there was a knock at the door. They froze, not sure of what to do. Axle peeked out the window and said, "It's the 'nosey old lady' from next door."

"Don't answer!" Captain Eli yelled.

"She already saw us through the curtains. She's carrying a covered dish. How am I going to get rid of her?"

"I'll help. Open the door," Jane said.

Axle hid the container beside the chair and reached for the door. "Hello, you must be Lucy. Aunt Grace said you might stop by. I'm Foster's cousin, from New York City. This is Jane, my fiancé," he said rambling.

Jane reached out to shake Miss Lucy's hand. She then quickly put her left arm around Axle's waist and pulled herself close to him, blocking the door. She gazed into his eyes. Axle almost forgot where he was.

"Why you look enough like Foster, to be his brother," Lucy said, eyes squinting to get a better look. "Grace never mentioned any relatives from New York City."

Jane said, interrupting her, "Darling, we promised your aunt that we would be right back."

"Well, then, don't let me keep you," Lucy responded, taking the hint. "I just brought over some chicken and dumplings. How's Foster doing?"

"He'll be fine," Axle said abruptly, not wanting to engage her further in conversation.

"Okay then, I'll let you two-love bird's get on your way."

"Thanks again," Axle said, while closing the door.

They both said in unison "Love birds?"

"She's not an old lady," Jane said.

"She will be the next time *we* see her."

"We?" she said, as Axle turned, and headed toward the basement.

"Yeah, *we,*" he repeated under his breath.

"Axle," Captain Eli broke in again, "hide the canister before anything else happens!"

"I'm on my way, sir." He could hear Max and Marcella laughing again.

Axle went down to the crawl space. It was a lot tighter now that he was an adult. *It doesn't look scary. Why was I so afraid to go back there?* He thought. Puzzled, he grabbed the canister and placed it out of sight. He climbed out and looked back. That's when he saw it! The burlap bag was casting a frightening shadow.

"That's the 'haunted place!' Oh, no one is ever going to believe this story!" he said astonished, as he was climbing the stairs back to Jane.

"Won't Miss Lucy tell your grandparents about us?"

"Probably, but no one ever believes her crazy stories. However, we should take the evidence with us," he winked.

"If you're talking about the food, I agree." She picked up the casserole and held it tightly.

They slipped out the back door. Axle scooped her up, as if he had done that many times before, and walked briskly down the back steps toward the ship.

Before they could even climb in, Max stuck his head out. "I smell real food. Let me help you," Max said eagerly.

Jane handed the platter to Axle and stretched out her hand for Max to assist her. Instead, Max jerked the platter from Axle's hand, leaving Jane with an outstretched arm.

Axle and Jane stood there laughing!

"We heard you had company, you both handled it well," Doc said with a giggle, complimenting them, as they climbed aboard.

"I *knew* it was going to get complicated," Captain Eli complained. "You were seen, and you talked to someone. You better not have changed history."

"Captain, the container is hidden, and I can assure you it will *not* be found!" Axle said confidently.

"Max, transfer the food into this container," Marcella yelled, as she came running from the galley. "If we take that dish back with us, they'll know we stopped somewhere."

"At least someone is thinking clearly," Captain Eli remarked.

Axle tossed the empty platter onto the ground close to the back porch, hoping Miss Lucy would find it before his family returns home.

"Let's eat. I'm starving," Captain ordered.

"Yes, sir."

"This is fitting; our last meal together is home-cooked, just like our first!" Max said while reaching for a dumpling.

"Remember, we can't leave any evidence," Doc added.

"What happened to *not traveling through time,* on a full stomach?" Marcella asked.

"I guess we'll just have to risk it," Max joked.

They all enjoyed their time together; and ate until there wasn't a trace of food left.

Pulling away from the table and rising to his feet, Captain Eli raised his glass, looked at his crew and said, "We have accomplished what we were commissioned to do. Job well done."

They cheered, hugged and cried as they toasted their Captain and each other, taking a few minutes to recap their events with tears and laughter.

"Marcella," Captain Eli Hunter commanded, "lock in the code. Let's go home!"

25

~ CRASH THE LASER GRID ~

Marcella sent the defense grid coordinates to Axle's screen. "Don't deviate."

"I travel through the Coalter D all the time. I'll keep us safe. I've even designed simulations to crash through the grid," Axle assured her.

"Like *that's* possible," Max laughed.

"I'm ready, the coordinates are locked in. Hangar 14 is right below on the other side of the laser grid. You can move forward any time, Marcella," Axle said confidently.

"Captain, I'm going to calculate the time we were gone, and add it to the time we left, down to the second. Dom and I are convinced that returning even a minute sooner could start a new time line." Marcella announced, smiling.

"Good thinking, I wouldn't want the feeling of living in the past."

"Captain," Axle interrupted, "if we get separated during our debriefing and are unable to communicate; let's plan to meet back at my grandfather's home, at 1700 hours tomorrow. Agreed?"

They all nodded.

"We are almost at the right time," Marcella announced, excitedly. "I'm bringing the ship *in phase*, so we can communicate with the ground. Three, two, one, now!"

"**XODIS** to Jack Brock," Captain Eli called.

There was a loud noise. The ship shook.

"We're under laser fire!" Captain Eli shouted. "Take the ship *out of phase,* Marcella! Axle, evasive maneuvers!"

"Captain, that shot took out the phase control. Why are they firing at us?" Marcella screamed.

"It's automated! **XODIS** to ground - stop the lasers!

Stop the lasers!" Captain yelled.

"Sir, I can't out-maneuver the lasers in this ship. I'm going to play dead."

A final strike from the laser jolted the ship before Axle was able to turn off the engines. They began to free-fall.

"If you're wrong, we won't have to *play* dead! The ship won't take much more of this," Captain shouted to Axle.

"Marcella, this could be my only chance to ask, if we survive, can I take you to dinner?" Max yelled.

"Axle, please tell me that Max and I will see our first date!" Marcella pleaded loudly.

"If I can't pull the nose up enough to change direction before we crash, I want you all to know that it has been a real honor serving with you." Axle uttered loudly, his voice cracking. He cleared his throat, and then quickly added, "We are going way too fast, and if I start the engines, it will attract more laser fire."

"Axle, please, my daughter is waiting for me. Just do your part. All you can do!" Jane pleaded.

Axle then hit the booster rockets. The speed was decreasing. The heat immediately attracted laser fire. In an instant, both rockets were gone! Another laser blast hit the ship and took out most of the starboard side.

Doc screamed! She was being pulled toward the vast hull breach.

With a single motion, the Captain had his seat belt undone and his left foot hooked in the footrest of his station. He stretched across the isle and with his right hand, grasped and stabilized her chair. His left hand undid her seat belt. He snatched her by her clothing; jerking her out of her seat like a rag doll. He pulled her across the isle, without her feet ever touching the ground. He stuffed her in his seat as he let go of her chair.

Immediately, her entire station flew out the gaping hole in the side of the ship! He pulled himself back into his seat, half sitting on Doc, wedging her in. He pulled the harness across both of them and locked it. Doc was clinging to him with her face buried in his chest, muffling her screams; her body trembling.

"Axle, if you are going to pull the ship up, now is the time!" Captain yelled.

"The blast helped slow us down! It even pushed up the nose of the ship. Just a few more seconds and we're under the grid, sir," he shouted excitedly.

Axle started the engines, the ship slowed down, but not enough. "I'm moving the ship forward, but I can't pull us up. We need a miracle! We are going to crash!" Axle yelled, warning them.

"There's a lake on the other side of those trees!" Max called back.

"Hold on, I'm going for it! I'm not able to avoid the trees. We're going down."

The ship crashed through the treetops along the riverbank, slowing down their descent considerably. The craft, now on an angle, slid across the water in the shallow part of the lake, dragging on the soft, muddy bottom. They gradually came to a halt, where the water was only two feet deep. Any deeper the ship would have come apart; any shallower, it would have crumbled.

"Is everyone alright?" Captain Eli questioned, stunned, as he unfastened the seat belt and stood up, leaving Doc sitting in the chair; dazed.

Max then immediately raised the ship to the top of the water on its telescopic pads. The muddy water was draining out of the gaping hole next to where Doc's station use to be. Max, wiping sweat from his brow, looked over at Marcella, winked and said, "We have a date!"

As they looked out, they realized they were in the middle of a residential area!

Max quickly tinted the windows.

"Axle, I don't know how you were able to pull it off, but the next mission I take, you're coming," Captain Eli said gratefully.

Axle was visibly shaken. "Are you kidding me? A

laser blast that just happened slowed us down, lifting the nose enough for us to move forward. The sloping treetops, shallow water, and soft mud! It wasn't me, sir!"

"You did your part, Axle, and God did his part" Captain Eli remarked. "I finally get it," he said under his breath.

"Look, there are people coming out of their homes, and they're running toward the ship," Marcella exclaimed.

"I'll handle it," Captain said.

He then spoke sternly over the outside speakers, "For your own safety, remain fifty yards from the craft to avoid contamination."

The spectators stopped dead in their tracks, looked around at each other and then took several steps back and retreated into their homes. The crew began laughing.

"You really know how to break up a crowd," Max said smiling.

They heard sirens in the distance.

"I have to call Brock and. . . ," but before the Captain could finish his sentence, they heard a hover shuttle directly overhead. "That would be Jack now."

"Remember 1700 hours, tomorrow," Axle added.

26

~ THE DEBRIEFING ~

The crew looked up and could see Medical Evacuation Units and a hover shuttle, followed by a helo-lift, of extraordinary size; descending rapidly. It looked to be over one hundred feet long and fifty feet wide. It hovered over the craft.

One MEU landed in the water alongside the ship.

There was a brushing sound on the door.

Max was the first to stand.

"Sit down!" Captain yelled. "Cover your faces! Do it, now!"

They immediately did as he commanded.

Suddenly, they heard two rapid explosions. The exit door to the **XODIS** was blasted off. It splintered into pieces and disappeared into the water. The smoke from the explosions lingered in the hallway.

A medic in an orange jacket, suddenly appeared in the fog, yelling, "I'm in."

"Why did you blast the door, you could have killed us?" Max shouted.

The medic, whose badge read, David M. Corena, tapped his earpiece and said excitedly, "We have a survivor." He stopped in his tracks, stunned. The others quickly stood to their feet coughing and choking from the smoke.

Max was angry. His fist was in a ball, and he was ready to swing. Captain Eli intercepted and grabbed his arm firmly and said, "Calm down, Max."

Doc stood, choking, eyes tearing. "I'm a medical doctor, and we *were* all fine, until *you* tried to kill us."

"Evac Unit to M U, no fatalities," the medic spoke, in a hushed tone.

"Morgue Unit? They thought we were dead!" Axle said astonished.

"Dead?" Captain's eyes glanced around the ship, "We should have been!"

"I count six alive and well," the medic spoke again quietly.

"From up here, that doesn't seem possible. Are they in shock?" the voice from the MU asked.

"No, I am!"

Doc and Marcella looked up through the tinted panels, just in time to see the Morgue Unit take off.

"Sir, I'm sorry." David M. said.

"And, I apologize for my crew being so harsh. As you can see, we've been through a lot. You were just acting according to protocol. You did the right thing!"

"From the looks of the ship, I wasn't expecting survivors." David M. Corena, now at ease said "You must have done something right!"

"Not yet, but that's about to change," Max responded, as he withdrew the Genesis Chip from Jane's station, and held it high between his thumb and forefinger, before dropping it safely in his pocket.

"How did you know the door was going to blow, Captain?"

"We should have opened the door immediately, Axle. Standard procedure for a medic, is to assume that we were unable to open the door, so they blow it, and rush to survivors. Again, he did the right thing."

The hover shuttle had landed on the opposite side of the EU. The doors were already down, creating walkways between the three crafts.

As Brock entered the E U, he stepped aside allowing a maintenance engineer to pass, whose uniform bore the name of "Piper" above the left shirt pocket. He was the same man that helped roll **XODIS** out of Hangar 14. Except this time, he had suction cups on both knees and one in each hand. He slipped through the small opening between the EU and the ship. Using the suction cups, he effortlessly climbed to the top of **XODIS**, directly above their heads.

With their eyes still on him, they exited the ship and entered the EU. They watched Piper as he popped a small cover from the top of the craft, revealing a cross bar. He stood upright and directed the helo-lift, as it lowered a canvas tarp, covering him and the entire ship. Suddenly, he appeared through a hole in the top of the tarp. He grabbed the main cable that lowered the canvas, and hooked it to the cross bar. A cable seat was lowered. Piper sat on it, and while he was still being raised up, the helo-lift quickly took off. The green tarp was flying through the air; hiding the **XODIS**. In minutes, the ship was gone.

Brock greeted them saying, "Thank God you're all alive," as he ushered them into his shuttle, from the Evac Unit.

As soon as they boarded, Captain Eli saluted him, "Mission accomplished, sir." He then abruptly grabbed Jack by the front of his shirt, lifting him off the ground, and yelled, "God we thank, but where were you?"

"Let me go, I had nothing to do with this, Eli," Jack yelled back.

Captain Eli released his hold.

Trying to remain professional, Jack Brock readjusted his tie and said calmly, "Somehow, there was an error in your code. I have already initiated an investigation. Because the ship is an unknown, one-of-a-kind craft, it registered as a weapon. We did everything in our power to combat the lasers. We knew it was coded for 'destruction'. You were to be annihilated!"

Captain Hunter replied, still angered, "I need a better explanation than that, Jack!"

"I'm working on it, but first I have to explain to the TMA, why their one hundred billion dollar, time-travel ship, is pretty much toast. Then I have to explain to Coalter D Security, how my ship was able to get through *their* security grid. *That* maneuver has *never* been accomplished! And, all without letting them know it's a time-travel ship!" Brock snapped back.

"We almost died, Jack, it's a miracle we're alive," Captain Eli yelled, still agitated.

"You all appear to be fine," Brock, said gratefully. "No one's even hurt. I see Miss Doe's leg is in a cast, but I guess I'll learn more about that when I examine the ships log. That's if, there's anything left of it."

After several minutes, the two men finally calmed down. Brock leaned back, folded his arms across his chest and said in a softer tone, "So tell me what was the world like 20,000 years ago?"

Everyone started talking at once, each one saying something different. It was total chaos.

"The Earth is about 6,000 years old," Eli stated.

Max was saying at the same time, "the Earth was created with a very different environment."

"The Livia-thing was terrifying," Doc grimaced.

"Evil giants, Adam and Eve," Jane broke in.

"Disgusting bugs, snakes," Marcella said shivering.

"The flood was caused by an ice comet," Axle joined in, excitedly. "Noah's Ark! Adam named the animals."

"Did someone say 'Noah's Ark?" Jack shot back not believing the bits and pieces of information his ears were picking up.

"Yes, the real Noah's Ark. Flood and all!" Marcella said, breathlessly. "Thank God we had a Genesis Chip on board."

"Knowing what was going to happen in advance, spared our lives more than once," Doc said excitedly.

"We recorded the six days of creation, in every incredible detail." Max beamed.

They were all talking over each other!

"STOP! Quiet, one at a time, please. I can't believe what I'm hearing. You all witnessed this and have proof?"

Now they were all silent, just nodding their heads and grinning.

Jack fell silent, as well.

"This is too controversial to discuss at this time," Jack said shaking his head, now standing and wanting to pace. "I have to get to those records before they fall into the wrong hands. You did make copies, didn't you?" he asked, very concerned.

Marcella spoke up quickly before anyone could answer. "No. We didn't think there *were* wrong hands!"

"There are always wrong hands, Marcella. How do you think people get into positions of power? When they have knowledge that can put them there, that's how!" he answered anxiously.

"What will *your* hands do with them, Jack?" Captain Eli asked, questioning Jack's motives.

"I know their true value. I'll protect them. They'll remain with me until the right time. I'm not sure who I can trust. So, I need you to keep this experience to yourselves for the time being." He paused briefly. "I have to talk to the pilot. I'll be right back." Jack abruptly turned and made his way into the cockpit.

Max leaned forward and whispered to Captain Eli, "Can Brock be trusted?"

Captain Eli nodded, "I'll vouch for him. It's agreed then, we tell no one."

They all nodded and remained silent.

Jack Brock, still in the cockpit, was now on a call with Oden Zadok.

"Oden, we have the plants, but the ship has been severely damaged. We'll be at the Hangar shortly to assess the damage. At this point, I don't think we can retrieve much."

"Did anyone survive?" Oden asked.

"Miraculously.... All of them."

"How long before we rebuild?"

"With the help of the crew, possibly three years," he answered.

"How do we ensure their allegiance for that length of

time?" Oden questioned.

"I'm glad you asked. With the proper compensation, we can guarantee their silence. It will be contingent on their non-disclosure agreements."

"But, how can we be assured that they'll help rebuild the ship?"

"Because, I have a feeling, they'll want to take another trip back." He paused, took a breath, then continued, "I need a grant, a large one!"

"I can reward the Botanist with developing the plants, $110 million."

"Do better!" Jack said firmly.

"I can also pull a "rare disease" grant for the Doctor."

"How much?" Jack asked directly. He was tapping his zeo-pad as he waited for Zadok to reply. He smiled, "Good, get it."

Brock returned to the crew. "There will be a team of experts at the Hangar to handle the plants. Jane, are you well enough to inform them of any pertinent information?"

"Yes, with Doc's help."

"Good, I need the rest of you to help do a quick evaluation of the ship today. Starting tomorrow, you'll get a week or so off. I was able to finalize your compensation. Jane will be accredited with developing the high oxygen-yielding plants; and Doc will be awarded for her work in rare disease. The research grants will be tax free and split between all of you. Your non-disclosures will remain active. You cannot reveal that you went back in time. You all know the repercussions if the agreement is violated."

They stared in silence, no one asking the question they were all thinking.

After landing at Hangar 14, Jack Brock stood up to emerge from the shuttle first. He stopped, turned back to the crew and said, "Marcella, how quickly can you divide 336 by 6?" When he got to the bottom of the stairs, he shouted back, "That's in millions!"

Jane grabbed Axle's hand and squeezed tightly. Max

hugged Marcella and Captain Eli scooped up Doc, and they were laughing. It took them a few minutes to compose themselves, so they could exit the shuttle, but not before hugging and embracing each other. It was as if they completely forgot, they still have platinum and diamonds waiting for them.

Jane and Doc were ushered into a warehouse, adjacent to Hangar 14. Doc readily agreed to assist Jane in debriefing the group. Several men and women from the "Green House Project" were anxiously awaiting their arrival, including Franklin St. Marten. The ground crew quickly retrieved a few plants from the **XODIS,** to satisfy the curiosity of the environmentalists.

Together, the women explained the filtered sunlight, the 25+ PSI air pressure, and the mist watering system. Jane was allowed to expand on the oxygen saturation discoveries.

The experts that were seated listened intently. However, they seemed somewhat skeptical of what was being presented. When they began to question the whereabouts of the location of the plants, Mr. Brock abruptly took over the session, explaining that the crew needed to be debriefed and then have a period of rest; adding that Jane's leg needed tending to. He assured them that they would be back within an hour, to answer all their questions.

The girls smiled knowing that would never happen.

Mr. Brock then ushered the invited guests into the mess hall, for a luncheon that was quickly prepared for them.

The **XODIS** had already been pulled back into Partenza Hall. The tarp was being lifted by Piper and his team. Captain Eli quickly surveyed the structural damage done to the craft. There wasn't much left of it. "Everything was hit but us."

"Look at this" Max pointed out. The lab and plants are untouched. The blast that took out Doc's station, also took out the mechanical arm and the internal surveillance equipment." Max whispered with a smile."

Axle stated, "The lasers cut off the booster rockets off

clean. If they were hit we would not have survived the explosion. The motors didn't survive being dragged across the trees, the mud and water. No wonder they thought we were dead."

Max & Marcella had just retrieved the recordings for Jack, as Dom and Rebecca entered Partenza Hall. Marcella's face lit up. "Its Dom!" she exclaimed, as she ran to him.

He briskly made his way to her and hugged her tightly, with tears streaming down his face. "I'm so glad to see you alive."

She was now crying. "The ship didn't make it, Dom."

He put his hands on her cheeks and replied, "But you did!"

He took a step back and began to survey the craft. He folded his arms, looked back at Marcella and said, "Did I forget to mention that I wanted it back it one piece?"

They hugged again, crying and laughing.

"We can rebuild it, even better," Dom whispered.

Jack interrupted them and asked Dom if he could have a moment with him alone. As they walked away, Brock put his arm on Dom's shoulder. They were speaking in hushed tones. "Dom, I convinced Oden Zadok that the crew is vital in rebuilding the ship. I also persuaded him to highly compensate them. Their grant is more than they could have ever imagined. This insures their loyalty and their silence."

"Well, having something to lose always guarantees cooperation," Dom agreed. "And being faithful to the project should keep them alive!" After a pause, he added, "My source has been securing more incriminating evidence for you to pass on to your man in the Justice Department. Hopefully, it will put the "Bella Project" group, not just out of business; but give most of them indefinite jail time. Your *man* can begin his investigation, as soon as the funding to rebuild the project, is in place."

"And the crew is compensated," Jack added. He nodded, and then turned to leave.

Dom quickly grabbed his arm, saying, "Good work,

Jack, on destroying the ship and sparing the crew. From the looks of the ship, that was an incredible accomplishment."

"I only took care of the ship. *Something else,* took care of the crew!"

Dom and Jack both turned and stared at the crew in amazement.

"I wonder what really took place," Dom said.

"God only knows!" Jack Brock replied.

27

~33 YEAR OLD SECRET~

"Hello, Grandpa. I'm back, and you are not going to believe where I've been!"

"Axle! So happy to hear your voice. I told your father you would be fine, and there was nothing to worry about. How are you, my boy? When did you get back?"

"Last night."

"Was your mission a success?"

"More than I could have ever imagined."

"Wonderful. I am so glad to hear that. Come over and see us as soon as you can."

"That's actually why I'm calling. I was trying to get a hold of Mom and Dad, but I can't reach them. I want to have a little get together."

"You mother dragged your father on an Alaskan excursion, and they won't be home till next week sometime. What about Saturday night would that be okay?"

"Here's the thing, Grandpa. It has to be at 5 PM today, and it has to be at your house. There will be six of us. Tell Grandma I arraigned to have Sherazzada's deliver a feast; lobster, champagne, the works! I'll explain everything when I get there, okay?"

"Sounds great. I've been looking forward to meeting Jane."

"How do you know about Jane?"

"I'll explain when you get here. Gotta go," Grandpa laughed and clicked off.

Axle's mind was racing. *Did he tamper with the container? Did he accidentally destroy the leaves? Did he find the platinum and diamonds? What am I going to tell the Captain? What am I going to tell Jane? God help me!*

He arrived at his grandfather's house, just seconds before the crew. He lost his window of opportunity to speak to him alone.

Doc and Jane came together, along with her daughter. Tori was in a high-tech motorized chair. She looked thin and terribly pale, yet so pretty, just like her mother.

The others arrived at the same time.

Axle's grandfather, hearing them pull up, bounded out of the house and down the stairs. In his usual boisterous tone, he yelled, "Welcome, I'm Vinny Kade, Axle's grandfather." He made his way to Jane first and said, "Hi, Jane, I've been looking forward to meeting you."

Doc gave Jane a puzzled look and said, "How does he know about you?"

"Grandpa, *this* is the team," Axle said as he hugged him, trying to hide his apprehension. "This is Captain Eli Hunter."

Vinny snapped to attention, saluted him and then shook his hand and said, "It's an honor to meet you, sir."

"This is Max Grant and Marcella Qui, our brilliant Science Officers. And this is Dr. Patricia Lucas."

They embraced and exchanged pleasantries.

"This is Jane Doe, our foremost Botanist, and Jane's daughter, whom I haven't had the pleasure of meeting yet myself," Axle said with a smile.

"I'm Tori, very pleased to meet you," she said so sweetly, as she put out her frail hand.

"I'm Vinny, and I'm very pleased to meet you, too. How old are you?"

"I'm seven and a half. How old are you?"

"How old do I look?"

"A hundred!"

"Not quite," he said laughing, as he motioned everyone to come inside.

Axle lifted Tori and carried her up the stairs in his arms. Max and Captain Eli carried the chair.

Tori looked at Axle, smiling, "I think I like you."

Axle kissed her head as he set her down.

The girls made their way into the kitchen to introduce themselves to Grandma Grace, who was busy setting up the dining room table; complete with china. She was so hospitable, never letting on to the pain that was surging through her body. Years of arthritis had taken its toll on her hands, neck and knees.

"Hi, Grandma," Axle said, while giving her a loving hug.

She whispered in his ear, "We have been waiting a long time for this day."

Axle groaned. *They both know!*

Grandpa Vinny cut in "Axle, why don't you go down and retrieve your container from the crawl space, while I talk to Jane."

"How do you know about the container? Did you open it?" Axle whispered, petrified of the answer.

"Of course not," he replied. "I read the note. Why do you think I didn't question you, when you told me you were going back in time? I've been waiting thirty three years for this day."

Axle let out a sigh of relief, and said, *"Thank You, God!"*

Vinny pulled a folded piece paper out of his wallet, opened it and let it fall from his hand to the table.

Grandpa,

Do not open this container. And if I find it, don't let me open it. I will be back for it when I'm 30. I will explain then.   Axle

Captain Eli and Max quickly followed Axle down the stairs, to the crawl space. Marcella and Doc were still helping Grace in the dining room.

Vinny, finding himself alone in the kitchen with Jane, said, "Jane, you are so much more than I expected."

"Than you expected?" she asked puzzled. "Why

would you expect *me*?"

"Lucy," he replied with a wink.

"Axle said you would never believe your neighbor."

"Ordinarily, I wouldn't have. My son was pronounced brain dead that day. I asked God for a miracle. But there was no change. We knew our stay at the hospital would be a long one, so we returned home briefly that night to pick up some things. As soon as we pulled in, Lucy came running over to tell us this crazy story about relatives from New York City having a big celebration because Foster was going to be fine'. I asked her how she knew that, and she said, 'because your nephew and his friend Jane, told me'. I knew it was a sign. I grilled Lucy for every detail," Grandpa said with tears in his eyes. "She said he looked enough like Foster to be his brother and asked if we enjoyed the tray of dumpling. After she left. I looked around and saw that nothing was missing, but a burlap bag. I was looking at the lake through the window when I saw a tray on the ground. I then noticed the note pad was moved. I saw an impression on the note pad. do not open this container, so I searched until I found it and the note. The note said everything to me. Foster was going to live and have a son, and his name would be Axle. I would be a part of his life. He would trust me, and I would live to see this day! That's the main reason I kept the house."

"So you knew me by the cast on my leg?" she smiled.

"No, I knew you by the look in your eyes."

Jane put her finger to her lips, motioning him to say no more, as the men came up the stairs.

Vinny ushered them into the living room and told them to place the canister on the coffee table. Axle carefully set it down. They all gave Marcella the honor of opening it.

Vinny broke the silence. "I've been waiting thirty three years to see what's in there," he remarked excitedly.

"Grandpa, you will *not* be disappointed."

"Axle, you have never disappointed me," he said, while looking over at Jane.

"Everything seems to be just as we left it," Marcella broke in.

"That's a miracle," Eli quipped.

Everyone watched as she carefully emptied the container on the table. Jane immediately reached for the clear plastic receptacles that housed the leaves.

"You hid leaves, stones, and dirt? For thirty three years? Are these computer chips?" Vinny asked shocked.

"These stones are diamonds, the dirt is platinum, and the leaves are from the Tree of Life, in the Garden of Eden."

Axle put his arm around his shoulder and said, "Grandpa, watch this!"

Jane's hands were shaking as she held the open container under Tori's nose. She said softly, "Breathe."

They watched in amazement as Tori took her first breath. They could actually see pink coming to her cheeks. A milky haze lifted, exposing bright, clear blue eyes. She sat up straighter in her chair.

Jane whispered again, her voice cracking, "Breathe, honey."

Vinny took a seat; he could hardly believe what he was seeing. Grace was crying. They were all sobbing.

Tori leaned forward, braced her hands on the arms of the chair and rose to her feet - for the first time in five years.

Jane, still speaking softly said, "Walk, Tori."

Doc was monitoring Tori's vital signs with her scanner. "Strength is returning to her bones."

"Tori, take a few more deep breaths," Jane said.

"Tori, you are in perfect health," Doc sobbed.

Jane handed the container to Doc, as she hugged her daughter, both crying.

Doc looked at Axle, and he nodded yes. She quickly went over to Grandma Grace and said, "Breathe."

They watched as she took her first breath. Her fingers, horribly crippled for years, immediately straightened. She was able to arch her back and she stood erect; she seemed to be taller, by several inches.

Doc handed the container to Axle and said, "You do the honors."

He approached his grandfather, who was now slumped in his chair, reduced to tears, as he stared lovingly at his wife of more than fifty years.

Axle said, "You're turn, Grandpa." He took a few breaths, and they watched the leaf disintegrate. The air had contaminated it, but not before restoring his grandfather's health. It was several minutes before anyone could utter a word.

Vinny spoke first, in a hushed tone. "Tell me *every* detail of your trip!"

Max and Axle immediately looked at Captain Eli, for approval, knowing this could jeopardize their non-disclosure. He stared at Vinny for a moment and said, "Anyone that can have a container for thirty three years without opening it, has no problem keeping a secret. Tell him everything."

Max opened the small plastic container and inserted a computer chip into the wall monitor.

"Grandpa, we can do better than that. We can show you," Axle said excitedly.

For the next several hours, they all watched in amazement, as if seeing it for the first time again.

The Creation of the Universe!

Vinny had so many questions. He had them pause and rewind over and over, and explain in detail just what he was seeing. It took all night.

They ate, laughed, cried and just enjoyed themselves!

Grace was teaching Tori how to dance!

"What are you going to do with the diamonds and platinum?" Vinny asked.

"We haven't discussed it yet. Why? Don't tell me you know people in the international diamond and precious metal industry?" Axle said chuckling.

"I know that if you try to sell them, they will probably be confiscated. My good friend, Nathan, was a diamond cutter for many years, before his company forced him to retire. He lives at Sunset Lakes, behind the merchant complex. He has been making jewelry with a friend of his, to supplement his income. Don't do anything until I talk to him, and don't worry, I can be very discreet."

"I don't doubt that for a minute," Captain Eli said. "Go ahead, Vinny. At least find out what our next step is."

It was morning, when the doorbell rang. Grace jumped up with a new vitality and answered the door with a big smile, "Good morning, Lucy."

Jane and Axle looked at each other as Lucy entered the room. She politely greeted everyone and was following Grandma Grace into the kitchen, when she suddenly turned around and stared at Jane. She glanced down at the cast on Jane's leg and said, "Have we met before, dear? Do I know you?"

"I don't think so," Jane replied casually.

Lucy shrugged and left the room, before hearing Jane add, "Not unless you've been to New York City."

They laughed till they cried!

28

~ THE GOOD NEWS ~

Several days after the debriefing, Marcella was chosen to make the call.

After an exchange of niceties, she said, "Dom, the crew elected me to contact you, concerning our compensation. Could you inquire as to when we can expect payment?"

"Sure thing, Marcella, it's probably too late today, I'll call tomorrow. I have to speak with Zadok about funding the **XODIS II** project anyway."

"Okay, but please don't put it off. And remember, be as direct as possible. Don't let him be evasive as to how soon. You are going to handle it, right?"

"Yes, I said I would. I'll handle it. I give you my word." He clicked off, saying aloud, "I *really* dislike handling this."

The next morning Dom approached Brock.

"Jack, I need to find out about funding for the new project and the crews compensation."

"Okay, Zadok should be in by now. Let's call him from my office."

As soon as the men entered, Jack wasted no time reaching Oden. "Mr. Zadok, this is Jack Brock. Dom Brothers is here, as well. We are assembling a construction schedule and need to know when we might expect the funding for the **XODIS II** project?"

"The cost for **XODIS** was estimated at one hundred eighty six billion," Zadok replied. "The actual cost was only one hundred nine billion. So, I was able to run **XODIS II** as a continuation of the same project. I already increased the estimated cost by 35%. I know there are some upgrades Dom wanted to make. That will give him a twenty one billion dollar cushion. The advantage is, the funding will not be interrupted."

"Excellent! Thank you," Dom said.

"While I have you," Jack continued, "when might the crew expect their compensation?"

"Actually, I put that in the works this morning. It will be three days at the latest. I want them to know we can be trusted to do our part," he said with expectancy in his voice.

"Good! Because the crew is anxiously waiting *to do their* part," knowing that's what Oden Zadok wanted to hear.

"Great! Feel free to call if there is anything else I can do." Zadok clicked off.

"Amazing," Dom said gratefully. "That went a hundred times smoother than I thought. I had a sleepless night dreading that call. Thank you for making it for me. You have a real gift for getting right to the point."

Jack chuckled without smiling. "*I'll* make calls. *You* build time-travel ships."

"It's a deal."

"Before you go, I want you to listen in while I call Simon. He's a good friend of mine who is willing to investigate the Bella Group."

Dom nodded and gave him the go-ahead.

"Simon, Jack here."

"I was hoping you would call. What kind of operation are you running at the TMA? The only thing I was able to find out, is the letters stand for Time Management Agency."

"Around here," Jack laughed, "the TMA stands for Top Secret-Don't Ask."

"Same old Jack."

"Listen, I need you to hold off investigating the Bella Group, for three days, until all funding is secured."

"About that, I did some preliminaries, nothing that would arouse suspicion. I have to tell you, this is a real challenge. They are better connected than most heads of state and have more money than some countries. Their lawyers could tie this up for five hundred years."

"I'm sending the rest of the intel I have."

"Jack, the challenge is knowing who I can trust. But I can get a case together in less than two years."

"Simon, there's no one better than you." Jack clicked off.

"Two years, Jack?" Dom asked with skepticism.

"Let's just trust him," he replied.

Dom left his office to look for Rebecca. He found her in Partenza Hall, making a list of anything that might be salvaged from the ship.

"Rebecca, I have news, not all of it good. I spoke with Oden Zadok, the funding never stopped. The crew will be paid in three days or less."

"What's the bad news?"

"Jack let me sit in on a call to his investigator, Simon."

"I know who Simon is. He's a good man; he can't be bought," Rebecca commented.

"He basically said the Bella Group is well connected and highly funded. It might take about two years to get the case to court."

"Dom, two years is too long, they could be in jeopardy *now!*" she said, fearfully.

"Rebecca, the crew is necessary for the rebuilding of the ship," Dom said reassuringly. "We have time."

"I hope you're right," she replied handing him her report. "This is a partial list of what can be salvaged."

"Let's see," Dom said as he scanned. "Four stations, five counting the Captain's chair, two kitchen appliances, three beds and the Botany lab. How much of the lab was spared?"

"*All of it!* It was virtually untouched."

"Every plant made it back? What are the chances of that happening?" Dom questioned in amazement.

"Take a closer look, the lasers hit every part of the ship; except the lab and exactly where they were sitting.

Doc's station wasn't hit directly. She had time to get to safety. This goes way beyond chance or luck. No one has ever been able to design a ship that could crash the laser grid. What really went on up there?" Rebecca asked, without expecting an answer.

~ ~ ~

Later that same day, Marcella called Dom to remind him to contact Zadok. His reply shocked her.

"Of course, I made the call. I said I would handle it. You'll be paid in three days or less, and the project funding never stopped."

"Thanks so much, Dom. I know it must have been uncomfortable for you. I'm so proud of you. Thanks again."

Dom was grinning from ear to ear.

Marcella quickly began calling the others.

"Max, I just talked to Dom, and we will be getting paid in three days. More importantly, why haven't you called me about our dinner date?"

"I thought you might have needed a few more days. Is tonight too soon?"

"Tonight's fine. What time?"

"I'll come for you in thirty minutes."

"Max, it's still afternoon. Make it an hour," she said laughing. "I still have to call the rest of the crew and then get ready,"

Marcella called Doc. She was ecstatic. And she insisted on relieving Marcella of the burden of calling Captain Eli. Marcella wasn't surprised.

Axle was next. When she gave him the good news, she expected the same reaction as the Doc; that he would want to call Jane himself. Instead, she heard Axle say, "Jane did you hear that?"

Jane, in the background, shouted, "Woohoo!"

"Marcella, while I have you. My grandfather has been persistent about scheduling a meeting between us and his friend Nathan; concerning the dirt and rocks. I've been putting him off. But in light of this good news, maybe now is a good time. We still have a few more days off."

"Maybe check with the Captain, before you set up a meeting."

"Good idea. I'll call him right now."

"You better get him before Doc gets a hold of him," she laughed, and they clicked off.

"Hi, Captain."

"Axle, I just got the news from Doc."

"I know, this is about my grandfather wanting us to meet with Nathan. They have a business plan."

"Does he know who we are?"

"He told him we are the "Eden Group.""

"Tell Vinny, I love the name. At some point, we'll meet with Nathan, just not yet. Vinny can begin by finding out how much start up capital is needed and what our cut would be. Then let him put 15% of the material in Nathan's hands. If he does well, we'll give him more. If he doesn't have all the material, we stay in control. But knowing there's more to come will motivate him to do well. Your grandfather will be our paid emissary," After a brief pause, Eli added, "Listen, I am putting together a leadership training course."

Axle cut him off. "Count me in. Thanks"

Eli laughed, and then clicked off.

Axle relayed the info to his grandfather. Vinny was ecstatic to be a part of the team.

"Axle, Nathan only needs a small investment for legal documents and equipment upgrades. Your cut would be 50%, on a very long term business. Much more lucrative then selling it as raw material outright."

"Thanks, I'll tell the others." Axle replied.

29

~ VINCENT, THE EMISSARY ~

"How's your lobster, Tori? Your mom told me that it's your favorite.

"Really good, thanks, Axle."

"How's yours, Jane?

"Delicious! This is such a beautiful place, Axle. Very peaceful, the cool breeze coming off the water, the colored fountain in the middle of the lake, the soft music. I've always wanted to come to Sherazzada's, but just never did. I'm glad my first time is with you. Thank you, Axle."

"Can I ask you a question?"

He reached into his pocket and pulled out a small velvet box. He dropped down on one knee, opened the box and stretched out his arm in her direction.

"Will you marry me?"

Jane was caught rather off-guard. A smile spread across her face. She thought he would ask someday. But today, in front of Tori, she wanted to say yes, but glanced at Tori first. Her daughter had a big open-mouthed smile on her face.

The long pause seemed like an eternity to Axle.

Tori giggled, "See, Axle, I told you I could keep a secret. Mom, answer him."

When Jane realized Tori was in on it, and was obviously excited about it, she said crying and laughing at the same time, "Of course, I will marry you. We love you, Axle."

They spent the rest of the evening talking, laughing and enjoying the richness of their surroundings, etching this day forever in their memory.

The next morning, Axle slept in. He, Jane and Tori

lingered at the restaurant for hours the night before, no one wanting the evening to end. He awoke abruptly, remembering that his parents were now back in town.

"Hi, Dad, I want your advice on something, and I have some news. Is now a good time to come over?"

"Son, so happy to hear you're back. Actually, this is a great time. We arrived home to find your grandfather waiting for us at our door. For the past two hours, he's been telling me some far-fetched stories about you. Please, get yourself over here, right now," he begged with a touch of apprehension in his voice.

Axle arrived to find his father and grandfather patiently waiting for him on the front porch. Foster bounded down the porch steps to quickly embrace his son. They both turned to look at Vinny, standing at the top step, briefcase in hand, very fashionably dressed.

Foster pulled his son close to him again, and whispered in his ear, "What the heck happened to my father?"

Axle was laughing, as Vinny strode down the stairs and handed him his business card.

The Eden Group
Vincent Kade, Chief Emissary

"It was a toss up between The Eden Crew or Group. Which one do you like? Because I can change it," he said excitedly.

"They're both fine, Grandpa."

He's now Vincent? What have we done? Axle thought.

"Dad, whatever Grandpa told you, is true."

"Do you *know* what he told me?"

"Yes, I do. The experience cannot be exaggerated. We recorded the entire event. The only recording we didn't get, was crashing the laser grid."

"Crashing the laser grid? That's impossible!"

"That's what I always thought, but I'm here!"

"What happened to the ship?"

"Dad, the craft took so many hits, it was totally destroyed. We crash landed, but all six of us walked away, unharmed."

"That's a miracle son," his dad said, shaking his head.

Oh my God! It was a miracle. Not just the laser grid; but the whole thing. The other dimensions, Leviathan, the flood, the leaves. We should have all died several times. We didn't somehow make it back! We were brought back!

Axle's father interrupted his thoughts. "Son, you said you have some news."

"Oh yeah, I'm getting married and I'm meeting her parents tonight. How do I make a good impression on her father?"

"What? You're getting married? I didn't even know you were dating. Who is she?"

"Jane!" Grandpa answered.

"Who's Jane?"

"The Botanist," Grandpa broke in. "Oh, and you're getting the sweetest, little seven year old granddaughter you have ever seen."

"I went on a seven day cruise, and its like ten years have passed," Axle's dad responded in shock.

"Relax, Dad, you'll meet her. So what do I do?"

Grandpa answered instead, "Axle, ask to speak to her father alone. Ask him for his daughter's hand. Promise him you will love her and take care of her and Tori. Remember alone, and man to man. Look him right in the eye."

"Do you know how old fashioned that is? Men don't do that anymore," Foster laughed.

Vincent cut him off, "Axle, it will work, because it's the truth. Trust me. I am the Chief Emissary."

Axle took another look at his grandfather. Well dressed, clear thinking, sharp as a tack, confident, and full of purpose.

Axle left his fathers house after a late lunch and many more questions from both men. He stopped home to clean up.

He couldn't wait to see Jane. He was prompt, arriving at her parent's home exactly at 7 pm.

Tori was waiting for him by the window and flew out the door, and into his arms within seconds of his arrival.

Jane came running out right after, with her parents following behind.

"Mom, Dad, this is Axle Kade."

"Hello, Mrs. Doe. I've been looking forward to meeting you."

"Please, call me Ann. I've heard so much about you," she said as she politely hugged him. "Honey, come meet Axle," she turned just in time to see her husband extending his hand.

"I'm, Mr. Jeremy Doe," he said solemnly.

"It's a pleasure to meet you, sir," Axle replied a bit unnerved.

Dinner was awkward.

Jane, her mother and Tori, did all the talking. Axle answered a few questions, but her father hardly spoke and didn't even make eye contact with Axle.

Finally, looking directly at Axle, Jeremy said, "So, you two met about a month ago. Is that correct?"

"Yes, sir, that's correct. I know it doesn't sound like a long time, but I can assure you, we have already shared a lifetime of experiences."

The girls took their cue to begin clearing the table. All except Tori, she was just enjoying everyone being together. She was going to have a father, and she loved that idea.

Jane entered the dining room again, and asked if Tori would help put the dessert out.

Jeremy continued questioning Axle. He felt more uncomfortable with each passing minute. His heart began pounding; he knew he had to do what his grandfather told him.

He cleared his throat and then boldly interrupted Jeremy. "Excuse me, sir. May I have a word with you in private?"

Mr. Doe rose to his feet. Axle followed him into his study. Jeremy motioned for him to sit. Axle's hands were trembling; he hoped Jane's father didn't notice.

Axle cleared his throat again, looked Jeremy right in the eye and confidently said, "Sir, I love your daughter and Tori. I don't take marriage vows lightly. I've been waiting my whole life for her. I promise to always honor and cherish them. It is very important to both of us, to the *three* of us, that we have your blessing."

Jeremy's countenance began to soften a bit. He looked down at the floor for what seemed like an eternity, and then softly replied, "I trust my daughter, and she is very much in love with you. It's obvious that Tori adores you, as well. So yes, Axle, you have my blessing. And, I *will* hold you to your promise," Jeremy said with a hint of a smile.

Axle exhaled. He hadn't realized that he had been holding his breath the entire time. This was right up there with crashing the laser grid! All he could mutter was, "Thank you, sir."

"Now let's go back to the women and enjoy some dessert," Jeremy said, putting Axle at ease.

Tori, was outside the study door, peeking in, when she saw the men not only shake hands, but actually embrace. She ran giggling with delight back to the kitchen, to tell her mom the good news. "Gramps likes Axle!"

The remainder of the evening was remarkably pleasant. They talked and laughed and truly got to know each other.

Several hours passed; finally it was time to leave. Jane wanted to stay and continue talking with her parents. She was so excited that things went so well.

When Axle got up to leave, Jane's dad rose to his feet, stretch out his hand to Axle, and said, "Please, call me Jeremy, son."

Jane walked Axle out and whispered, "What did you say to my dad? I can't believe he hugged you."

"I followed great advice from a wise old man. I told him the truth."

Axle arrived home late and couldn't stop smiling. He was lying in bed trying to sleep, with the events of the evening replaying in his head. Things could not be going any better. His thoughts were interrupted by an incoming call.

"Marcella, is everything alright?"

"Everything is terrific. I have great news that can't wait until morning," she squealed with joy. "We are officially rich! The money is in our account. I can't wait to wake everyone up. Plus, I sent the venture capital, requested by Vinny. Oh, excuse me, I mean," she giggled,

"Vincent Kade, Chief Emissary."

30

~THE VAPOR~

"Dom, the way I figure it, we have about two months, maybe less, before Patricia is in jeopardy," Rebecca said, as she burst into Dom's office.

He was seated at his desk, calculating the cost of new upgrades. He immediately rose to greet Rebecca.

"You caught me in the middle of something. What are you talking about?" Dom quizzed.

"The crew! At some point, Oden Zadok is going to eliminate and replace them with his own people. He will start with the most nonessential to the project. I am trying to compile a list. I'm not sure if Doc will be first. It seems that Eli Hunter and Jack will be targeted around the same time."

"Are you certain about this?"

"Dom, I am positive. Axle will probably follow Jack. Jane is safe, for awhile because the grant is in her name. Max, Marcella, you and I, will not be harmed until the very end. But have no misconceptions, we are on the list, as well." Rebecca reported.

Dom staggered back to his chair. "This is so hard to comprehend."

Rebecca continued, "I informed my contact from CHASE. They'll keep an eye on Doc. I need you to inform Jack that he's in the cross-hairs."

Dom was sweating. "Why Jack?"

"Because, the Mission Director is the one who approves the new personnel. They'll want him eliminated quickly. I'll continue monitoring their communication and will keep you informed, as things progress."

"I don't know what I'd do without you!" Dom said. He turned his back on Rebecca and faced the wall behind him. He did not want her to see the fear in his eyes.

~ ~ ~

"More calls?" Jack asked as Dom stepped into his office. Dom just shook his head no, his expression was grim.

Jack switched on his jamming device. "Close the door, you can talk now."

"My contact says the group will start replacing the crew in about two months."

"Any idea who will be first?"

"Yes, Dr. Patricia. And then the one who approves the replacements."

"That's me!" Jack exclaimed.

"I know. My contact will monitor the group's communications and warn us when things are being arranged."

"Like accidents?" Jack asked.

Dom nodded his head again. He attempted to reassure him, saying, "I trust my source will able to intervene at the right time."

"Let's hope so. I figured out who your contact is."

"What? Who?" Dom questioned.

"It can only be one person, The Vapor. I thought he was a myth. The stories that have been circulating throughout the Government agencies are incredible. Do you know him personally? Will he expose the group? Simon's two year plan is not going to help us now. Let's just hope the Vapor can intervene, I don't like putting all my hope in just one person. Especially, someone I don't even know," Jack stated.

"He's working on it," Dom said, then quickly left Jack's office. He suppressed a sigh of relief that Jack hadn't calculated the contact was Rebecca.

~ ~ ~

"Jack ascertained who my contact is."

"I *thought* we might be underestimating him, Dom. What did he say?" Rebecca inquired.

"He said, he was grateful to have you on our side and that he's hoping you will expose the Bella Group, before anyone dies. I told him you were working on it. Then he asked if I knew, the *'Vapor',* personally. Had I ever seen *him*? Apparently, you are thought to be a myth, and a man," Dom said with a halfhearted grin.

"The Vapor! Now there's a name I haven't heard for a while," Rebecca smiled.

31

~ THE NEXT SIX WEEKS ~

Axle's parents set up a dinner to meet Jeremy, Ann, Jane and Tori.

Foster and Eva immediately fell in love with Jane and her daughter. After all these years, they were going to be grandparents. The two families came together, as if they were always one.

"Your grandfather told me that you both were very well compensated for this mission. Are you planning on having an extravagant wedding?" Foster asked his son, while they were all enjoying dinner.

"I don't know. I thought I would leave that up to Jane," Axle said as he reached for her hand.

"Smart move, son."

"Tell them what you want, Jane," her mother coaxed.

"I would like to invite all our friends and family, of course. And I want to keep it simple enough, so everyone has a great time. Most of all, I don't want anything to interfere with our celebration; like non-stop, posed pictures."

They laughed, obviously remembering their own weddings.

"Oh, and I scheduled premarital counseling classes, for Axle and I. I want the focus to be on the marriage, not just on the wedding day. The only thing that *will* be priceless - is my wedding dress!"

"You already picked it out?" Ann and Eva asked, almost simultaneously.

"Yes, it's been waiting for me for years, in your upstairs closet," she said looking at Eva.

Axle's parents were in awe of what they were hearing. Eva's eyes welled quickly. She rose to embrace her soon-to-be '*daughter-in-love*.'

"Oh, just wait until Grace hears this!" Eva cried.

"Axle, do you know how rare she is? She is what your mother and I have been praying for. And Tori, is just God smiling down on us!" Foster said, a little teary eyed himself.

Their gaze went to that precious little girl, oblivious to this conversation, now stuffing her face with cheesecake. They all laughed till they cried, including Tori.

The three women quickly cleared the dishes, so they could begin planning the wedding. The men knew it was their time to retire to the study to discuss more 'manly' things. As they were exiting the dining room, Axle looked over to Jane, winked and said, "Six weeks, right?"

She assured her future husband, that with her mother and Eva, and the help of Doc and Marcella, they could arrange a beautiful wedding, in just six weeks. For the next several hours, they planned.

~ ~ ~

Three days later, the crew was called to attend a short conference at Hangar 14. Oden Zadok, Jack Brock, two government financiers and several men and woman from the EPA, would be in attendance, as well.

This was the crew's first reunion, since the gathering at Vincent's house. They embraced each other and were busy chatting, when Jack Brock called the meeting to order. He was direct and to the point, as was his style. The crew was asked to assist in building the new ship. They would be recruited again for the next mission on **XODIS II**. They readily agreed and signed all necessary documents.

Jack Brock was pleased to report that the **XODIS II** project has now officially begun. All the product venders are already in place. The molds for the clear panels have been fabricated. The crew's stations, including suggested upgrades, were in the process of being built. The project was due to come in way under budget and in less than half the allotted time. Soon they would see another mission.

Jack dismissed the crew. He took time answering questions from the remaining guest, and discussing budget allocations.

All six left, relieved and thankful to Jack, that their presence wasn't mandatory for that. Axle suggested they go to Sherazzada's for lobster, and it was unanimously agreed upon, by all.

~ ~ ~

Over the next several weeks, the crew stayed busy.

Max and Marcella were now steadily dating and studying the Genesis chip together. She had so many questions but hesitated to call Jane; she did not want to distract her from the wedding plans. Jane reassured her friend, that she would always make time for her. Marcella didn't ask easy questions. She was developing a keen understanding and remarkable insight.

Max and Marcella also, were back working with Dom and Rebecca, on the construction of the ship. Their new found wisdom gave them the intuitiveness to develop systems within systems. Max was also getting assistance from Axle to help improve his motor designs.

Captain Eli remained focused on each system to maximize its performance. He was the principal consultant for their next endeavor; all the while developing a leadership training course. He was pleased that Axle would be his first enrolled, after the wedding.

The six weeks were flying by. Jane still had not settled on a venue for the wedding. The list kept outgrowing each banquet room they chose.

She told Marcella that Sherazzada's would have been the perfect place, since that's where Axle proposed and their menu is exceptional; but they just cannot accommodate weddings.

Max and Marcella were now a force to be reckoned with. They had a new-found boldness and decided to petition the owner. He reluctantly met with them.

He was a large, burly, man. He gave the impression

of not being inclined to satisfying anyone's needs but his own. He listened intently, the entire time remaining stoic. Sometimes even saying, "Absolutely not!"

Max persisted. The owner stated emphatically that he was pleased with the success of his restaurant, and it was fully booked for the next month.

Max then showed him the list of technological upgrades that could become a reality in his establishment. The owner's expression was beginning to soften, his pupils dilated. He was now intrigued. However, he remained unmovable. It was out of the question.

Until Max said, "We will pay for every upgrade. I guarantee that it will be done efficiently and in rapid time."

Seeing the profit potential of future weddings, the owner now became their new best friend. He was suddenly in agreement with all the changes. He even made suggestions of his own. He would give them free reign; even close the restaurant, if needed. Max assured him that wasn't necessary.

The owner said it will be an honor to have Axle and Jane become his first couple to be married in his new establishment. He only had one condition; can his family be invited? They laughed and even embraced.

Max and Marcella were able to accomplish the impossible. It was their wedding present to their friends.

Jane's wedding list just grew by four!

32

~MARCH 7TH, THE BIG DAY~

The wedding day was now here. Axle was nervous. The restaurant was filled to capacity with friends and family.

"Dad, I pray I am ready for the responsibility of a wife and a child."

"Axle, no man is ever *totally* ready. That's why women set a date. Marriage is on the job training. Just act like you're ready and ask God to make you look good. Worked for me!" Foster said, reassuringly.

~ ~ ~

Suddenly, the Hallelujah Chorus began to play. It resounded over the lake, each note building in unison.

Doc and Marcella were the first to appear. They were both maids of honor, dressed in similar, flowing, peach chiffon dresses. They looked beautiful.

Tori was next. She was the perfect flower girl, gliding down the isle in a white and peach, princess-style gown. It was so endearing to watch her joyfully drop rose petals along her way. Tori was always a happy child, but today, she was ecstatic! It was hard to fathom that just three months ago, this healthy, blue-eyed, blonde, little girl- was dying, without hope.

Everyone on cue, rose to their feet, and turned to see the bride emerging from a Grand staircase; built just for her.

Jane looked stunning in Axle's grandmother's wedding dress. Her smile lit up the room, as she walked elegantly down the aisle, her arm gracefully draped through her father's. She kept her eyes fixed on Axle the entire time.

A beautiful white gazebo, was now a permanent fixture at the end of a long deck, which stretched out over the water. The lake was now stocked with swans.

Her Pastor was smiling, waiting for her, as well. He told her during their premarital counseling sessions, how happy he was that she waited for God to bring the *right* man into her life.

Axle proudly stood next to his *two* best men. Max and Eli were honored to be such an important part of their wedding. All three were strong, handsome men, impeccably dressed in dark gray tuxedos.

Axle and Jane exchanged traditional wedding vows. As soon as they took their first kiss as husband and wife, the song "Bone of my Bone" played. The tears were flowing down their cheeks, as they realized that *'the wedding song'*, had a much deeper meaning for *all* of them.

The bride and groom took their first dance together; then typically the floor was opened to their wedding party, then all the guests.

The rest of the evening was wonderful. The newly married couple, drew pleasure from watching their friends and family dancing, laughing, enjoying themselves, all 216 of them.

"Jane, I can't believe how much my life has changed in just a few short months. I found the girl of my dreams, and we are surrounded by hundreds of people that are sharing this special day with us," Axle whispered to his bride of one hour.

"Look at Jack Brock? Who would have thought that he was such a good dancer? His wife is so sweet, she has a contagious smile," Jane whispered back.

"Too bad *he* hasn't caught it!" Axle joked. "And I'm so happy to see that Justin finally got a date with Ivanna. I knew from the first time I met him, that she had his heart."

Their eyes welled with tears, watching their dear friends dancing.

"Did you know that Max and Marcella actually took dancing lessons, just for our wedding?" Jane said smiling.

She's pretty good, but Max still only knows that one step," Axle laughed.

"And Dom and Rebecca are such a perfect match. I barely recognized her without the lab coat. She's so beautiful. I'm really honored that so many people wanted to attend our wedding. And, now we know how the restaurant got its name, after meeting the owner's wife. They can't stop smiling. They love their new place," Jane beamed.

"Oh, wait until you see this new feature," Axle said excitedly. He tapped a pad under the table, and the murals on the wall changed picture. Another tap and the noise around the table was filtered out. "Now, we only hear the conversation coming from this table." He tapped again, and now the music was allowed in. "I can even control the volume. It's called a 'noise halo'. Compliments of Max, he designed it just for you."

"Impressive! The new ship is going to have this, right?" she said, her eyes sparkling. "Axle, look at your grandparents dancing. Vincent is like a new man. They both look so young and vivacious!" She paused, leaned in to kiss her husband on the cheek and said "this is just what I wanted. Thank you."

"And you are just what I wanted. Someone to share my life with," Axle said kissing her hand.

33

~ BE PATIENT~

After only two months, Vincent, the Chief Emissary, called upon the crew, for the first-board meeting of the Eden Group. He was ready to issue a progress report. They were gathered once again, at Vincent's home.

"As you know, our partner, Nathan, being from Nigeria, is very knowledgeable about uncut diamonds. He put a unique and profitable business plan into practice for this new endeavor. He comprised a team, consisting of four layers, two accountants, a marketing expert and a brilliant computer specialist. Nathan took on a partner, as well. He goes by Obinwa. He's a highly-skilled, precious metals craftsman. We found it necessary to establish four corporations" he continued. "One corp purchases broken and outdated jewelry. Another corp turns this jewelry into raw material. We also formed a company called "Garden Variety Jewelry; which sells all low-end pieces." Vincent took a sip of water, and then continued, "Our principal company is called Eden Rocks. It markets extremely high-end, custom-made jewelry, by appointment only, to elite customers. Nathan and Obinwa are extremely well known for providing superior quality merchandise. Their marketing strategy is brilliant. They introduced their first six pieces to a few select circles. Each piece was numbered and limited. It created a tremendous demand. The waiting list has already exceeded everyone's expectations. These new found companies have totally revitalized Sunset Lakes, the entire community has employed just about everyone."

They all clapped!

"When will Nathan require the rest of the material?"

"Not for a long while, Eli. He only uses *that* material,

for the high-end business, Eden Rocks. He is able to filter it in slowly, to avoid complications. It also allows for a very long term business proposition. Are there any other questions?" Vincent concluded by handing everyone a chip of the minutes of the meeting.

They looked at each other, then back at Vincent. Is this '*Vinny,*' the same old man they met a few months earlier? A few breaths of that leaf could not have given him this much vitality. He is an inspiration, a man on a mission, a man with a purpose.

"Well, crew it seems we picked a winner," Captain remarked, referring to Vincent.

"More like we were *handed* a winner," Max laughed. "Vincent, I'm developing interactive games. Maybe your team can help with marketing."

"Sure anytime," he smiled.

"And, I would like to discuss setting up foundations with your legal department," Captain Eli added.

"Just let me know when, I'll set something up," Vincent remarked.

Axle was shocked that the Captain was entrusting his grandfather and friends, with *his* future plans.

"A good leader knows when to take advantage of someone else's knowledge and impartial direction," Eli whispered to Axle. "This is the beginning of your leadership training."

"Vincent, I need help launching my new science courses; which were inspired specifically for teens," Marcella said with exuberance.

"Why don't you all make a list of your questions? And I'll try to put you with the right people," Vincent said confidently.

Axle was the only one who didn't have any questions. At this point, he wasn't as assured as the others at to what his next step would be.

As soon as the meeting concluded, lunch was served. Grace had arranged for food to be catered by Sherazzada's, naturally. She was flowing in her element. She and her great granddaughter, Tori, were in the kitchen the entire time, just enjoying themselves.

"So, what new games are you developing, Max?"

"Axle, I've just finished creating 'Escape the Flood and Crash the Laser Grid'. I need help in marketing them to the youth. It's my plan to first build credibility with them, so I can open manufacturing facilities in depressed areas. I'd like to begin working with young men and women that are struggling. Maybe teach them life skills. I need Vincent and his colleagues to put this all together legally."

"Max, I'm really excited for you. Captain, explain again, what you and the Doc are doing," Axle said with enthusiasm.

"Patricia and I have been communicating with groups like Creation Science Evangelism, Answers in Genesis, Institute for Creation Research and many other organizations like these. We want to put edited copies of the highlights of our journey, into the hands of every science museum worldwide. Without letting on that we went back in time, of course. We think it will create a lot of welcomed controversy. What do you think?"

"Sounds great, you have *my* full support."

Axle was so happy to hear of all their new found exploits. He shared in their enthusiasm, yet had not felt a pull in any direction for himself. *Would being a part of the six that had witnessed creation, be his only contribution? There must be more,* he thought.

Suddenly he heard the words 'be patient'. He looked around and realized no one was talking to him; they were all busy, excitedly discussing their own endeavors.

Jane, Doc and Marcella were chatting, catching up on what they've been doing recently.

"My latest involvement has been my research. I've been developing super foods; using the original seed and the growing process we saw in the garden. It could be a major step in the fight against world hunger. My concern is that this information could be stolen and patented, preventing me from developing it further."

"Jane, I share the same worry," Doc said, nodding, her head. "I am developing herbal medicines that work with specific systems in the bodies to kill any plant-like viruses, including cancer, without harming the living tissue. I'm up against drug companies. I need to be free to work without fear of being shutdown."

Doc motioned to Axle. "We have a short list of questions for Vincent. Could you ask if he can speak with us now?"

"Sure, if I can pull him away from Max and Eli," Axle laughed. "What's the urgency, ladies?"

"We're a bit concerned that our research could be compromised, patented by others, and brought to a halt," Jane said.

"Or worse yet, being wrongly classified as a new drug. Then it would take 10 years to get approval, for a nutritional product, mind you. We need advice," Doc added.

He motioned toward his grandfather that they girls needed him.

Instead, Vincent raised his voice over the chatter, "Everyone, get your list of questions to me and I will set up appointments beginning tomorrow afternoon."

"How do you know your friends will be available?" Axle questioned him.

"They're still semi-retired. They play golf in the morning, work always waits till the afternoon," Vincent replied, as he hugged his grandson with newness of strength.

Axle was so proud of him. The crew lingered a while longer to discuss, plan, and share in each others dreams.

The Captain was now listening to Marcella explain what she wants to do with her newly comprised, interactive teaching. He called over to Axle and asked him to listen in.

"I'm writing a series of science articles, using controversial, but provable theories. My goal is to get them into public arenas, so future generations will not be limited in their thinking. Learning within a confined science theory, has halted some very important breakthroughs. Max and I want to begin with a live teaching. We have secured a room inside The Asbury, Sunday afternoons at 1:30." Directing her attention to Axle, she said, "We're counting on your support, and Jane's as well, of course. It will be a Sunday school for scientists."

"Now, that's an oxymoron! We'll be there!" he said. Axle looked over and winked at Jane. He was so proud that she had given time and attention to this couple.

Max and Marcella, now teaching Sunday school! A few short months ago, she wasn't even sure there *was* a God.

Everyone was busy going forth with multiple purposes. Yet, Axle heard 'be patient'!

The following day, Vincent stopped by to see Axle, Jane and Tori, of course. Within seconds, he pulled a new business card from his suit jacket. Vincent's wardrobe had now expanded to navy blue, black pinstripe and dark gray, three- piece suits.

The Eden Crew
Business Structuring & Counseling
Vincent Kade, Chief Emissary

"Nice, Grandpa," Axle said with a slight grin.

"What's the matter Axle?" Vincent asked, knowing his grandson very well. "I sense that something is not quite right."

"Grandpa, I realize we were all brought back for a reason. Everyone else seems to have found a great purpose, for the betterment of all. I don't have any idea what my purpose is. All I know, is that I keep reliving the same events over and over, down to the smallest detail. What am I to do with all that keeps swimming in my head?"

"Write them down, Axle," he answered, as if this was an easy question.

"Why? Everything's been recorded."

"Not everything, son. Not what you were thinking and feeling, or experiencing on the inside. The camera only sees what is happening on the outside. Write it down and you'll discover your purpose."

"That just may not happen for me," Axle answered.

"Be patient," Vincent said, as he quickly bent down to kiss Tori goodbye. As he bounded down the stairs, he yelled over his shoulder "See you at The Asbury. We were invited."

'Be Patient'! Those words echoed in Axle's head. They rang deep within him. He suddenly recalled hearing those same words back on the **XODIS!**

"Be Patient. Write it down! That's my new starting point," Axle said aloud.

34

~THE ASBURY~

Axle, Jane, and Tori arrived at The Asbury, thirty minutes early. They walked into the conference hall to find that it was already standing room only. Marcella flagged them forward. There were three seats reserved, next to the Captain and Doc. Vincent and party arrived early enough to have seats in the second row. Axle quickly helped Max set up extra seating in an overflow room.

"Welcome," Marcella smiled, "to the first series of teaching and sharing sessions. We are here to learn from each other and explore new possibilities. I do not claim to have all the answers. I will, however, pose some very interesting questions. With the help of my friend and mentor, Mrs. Jane Kade, we will try to field any questions that will arise." She motioned for Jane to stand and be acknowledged.

Axle was so proud of the woman he married.

Max and Marcella began their presentation with its title, *'Creation Makes Sense'.*

For the next two hours, they discussed the formation of granites and the micro-spheres of coloration, halos produced by the radioactive decay of primordial polonium; which is known to have only a fleeting existence.

"This demonstrates how these *halos* provide unambiguous evidence of both an instantaneous creation of granites, and the young age of the earth." Marcella spoke with strong conviction.

The focused shifted to the nonexistent, transitional links in the fossil records; and all the factors in the universe that point to a much younger earth.

"My research points to Genesis as having a realistic, historical, starting point. My studies show that Genesis is backed by operational science. I will close on that note. I challenge you to conduct your own investigation of the facts. We look forward to meeting again next week. Thank you for your participation," Marcella concluded.

She received an outpouring of support from those that attended; as they stood to their feet in applause.

In just a few short weeks, they outgrew The Asbury and moved into Convention Hall.

Three months had passed, and scientists were flying in from all over the world to attend. Thousands more joined them on interactive conferences.

~ ~ ~

"Captain, do you have time to talk?"

"Sure, Max, I always have time for you. What do you need?"

"Marcella is here with me, and we need your advice. Things are going so well at Convention Hall that we're considering renting The Dome. What do you think?"

"Outstanding. I think it's time for you to train a team."

"Okay, but why?" Marcella asked, quickly.

"You and Max planted and nurtured a seed. Now it's grown and is screaming for a life of its own." Eli answered them.

"What does *that* mean?" Max asked puzzled.

"Right now, both of you have the leadership roles. Find a few scientists you trust, to pour your knowledge and vision into. Mentor them quickly. Hold the workshop in an open forum setting; with a panel of experts representing each field of science. Now, step aside and just facilitate. This will allow the entity to spread like a virus. The groups will spring up by themselves. It will be unstoppable," Captain Eli concluded.

"Who will guide it?" Marcella questioned.

"If you engage those that are *already* schooled in the Book of Controversy, you won't have to worry about '*Who*' is guiding it," Captain declared.

Max and Marcella took the Captains wise advice.

They promptly set up a team, and within a few short weeks, were able to present their first paneled discussion.

They secured The Dome.

To their amazement, the first Sunday was filled to capacity. The crew was in attendance, along with Vincent and his supporters.

~ ~ ~

"Good afternoon, we are pleased that you have all joined us today," Max began. "We have decided to start an open discussion forum, due to the numerous amounts of inquiries that we are receiving. We have invited four experts to field questions in their area of expertise. They will be introduced, as they are called upon to answer. Let's begin with the most frequently asked, first."

"If science is exact, how could there be two opposing views?" Marcella asked.

Her gaze went to a well dressed man in his early forties. His dark blue, tailored suit went well with his cream colored shirt and deep tan. He was well built, with broad shoulders. He had a hint of a smile and an air of confidence, as if he knew more than most.

"Mr. Crosta, will you please take this question?"

"My pleasure. My name is Dr. Michael Crosta, and my specialty is Physics. Science is broken down into two categories; *Operational,* or what can be tested and proven; and *Historical,* which is entirely speculative.

"Dr. Crosta, my screen is showing a multitude of comments. Could you expand your answer in these two areas? First; couldn't *Operational Science be* used to determine *Historical Science?* Second; what does the *historical* view of science affect, if anything?" Marcella read from her screen.

"I believe *Operational Science* can be used to determine *Historical Science,*" Dr. Crosta continued, "but, only if it doesn't break the laws of physics." As he spoke, his words appeared on the large screen behind him. "Unfortunately, the current view of *science* goes against the

laws of physics, by maintaining that:
    1: *nothing* accidentally created everything.
    2: non-life produced life.
    3: things improve by themselves.
    4: nothing has a purpose.
We have found that *everything* has a purpose; right down to bees that pollinate flowers. After a comprehensive study, we are convinced that operational science confirms the first eleven chapters of Genesis, as the history of the world,"
Crosta stated, confidently.

Marcella's screen was flooded with comments. You could almost hear it gasp!

A member of the panel in his mid thirties motioned with his hand. "I would like to address the second part of that question, Miss Qui." Sporting a crew cut and mustache, an olive-complexioned man took the floor. He spoke with a slight Spanish accent and appeared to be of Latin descent. "My name is Marc Lisano; Agriculture. Those who have viewed plant life as accidental tried to improve the seed by altering DNA. Hence, the GMO catastrophe. Had these same scientists, been informed that the seed was created perfect, their experimentation would have focused on improving the growing environment, as we are starting to do now. The last famine may have been avoided."

He was interrupted by a panel member, seated at the far right of the platform, next to Michael Crosta. All eyes had been darting in her direction during the meeting. She appeared to be in her early thirties with long blonde hair, exotic eyes and a gorgeous smile. She was captivating!

"Excuse me, Marc," she said sweetly. "My name is Dr. Sierra Bonn. The accidental view of life also spills into the medical field. We treat the symptom of sickness and disease, but not the cause. Blood thinners and pain medications only treat symptoms of a much larger problem. Like putting ointment on a rash and assuming the rash came from something outside the body. When we treat the body as a perfectly created series of systems, we find what nutrients a particular system is lacking. We found that by increasing the immune system just 10%, prevents most sicknesses. The good news is, we are having great success treating patients from within, using natural extracts."

Marcella took back the floor. "Thank you, Ms Bonn. We have a lot of questions about the fossil records. Who would like to address that issue?"

"I'll take this one, Marcella. I am Dr. Constantino Pacillo, Anthropologist. For hundreds of years scientists have been examining the Earth. We have been trying to piece together a puzzle with no borders or corners, and 99% of the pieces appeared to be missing. We have been led by a preconceived misconception that the Earth is billions of years old. We've speculated that simple lower life forms evolved into complex animals and humans. Experts ignored the laws of physics, as my colleagues stated earlier. Scientists have searched the fossils records, in an effort to find the 50,000 transitional life forms it would take to go from a sea creature to a land animal. As of yet, not one has surfaced. After re-examining the Earth, in light of a world-wide flood as described in Genesis, we are now armed with a new picture of the puzzle. The multitude of pieces fit perfectly. It has now been determined, that all the fossils were formed at the time of the flood. The new evidence backs up the view of an Earth only thousands of years old."

"Thank you," Marcella said. "I have many questions concerning the construction of the eye."

Dr. Sierra Bonn, enthusiastically interrupted, "Dr. Qui, may I?"

Marcella nodded.

"Every living thing carries the signature of the Creator. They all have at least one, if not several, unique body parts or attributes that could never have evolved. Biochemist Behe defines it as 'irreducible complexity'. The most obvious being the eyes. Certain biological systems are too complex to have evolved. That organ alone is an example of extreme perfection and complication. Again, there is no credible evidence to support it evolved. Evolution is a theory that is improvable by design because it depends on an inconceivable amount of time. It fails under scrutiny because every geological dating method, including radioactive dating, is influenced by atmospheric conditions, which have been, speculated and manipulated to prove a particular view."

"Thank you. Here's another question," Marcella read. "If what the experts are saying is true, why are there still so many scientists unable to recognize creation?" Pausing a moment, she said, "I'm going to field this one. I am one of those scientists that had not recognized creation for most of my life. When asked how I could improve the Eagle; I realized I was hard pressed to think of an improvement for any living thing. So I researched DNA experiments and found that when DNA is altered there is only three possible outcomes; an unchanged life form, a defective life form, or a dead life form. I had difficulty comprehending why some things on the planet seem random, while living things perfectly aligned. After taking a look at Genesis, this is what was revealed to me; when *we* use the term *'it is good,'* we mean, it is acceptable. When the *Creator* says *'it is good'*, *He* means, *'it is perfect'*. I began to see living things as perfect. However, when I look at the Earth today, I can think of many ways to improve it. When I read about the flood and the total destruction of the Earth, I realized this is *not* the Earth that the Creator called good. Which raises some crucial questions? What was the Earth like before the flood? How high would the oxygen level have to be, to support a seventy foot dinosaur, breathing with nostrils the same size as a horse's? What would the atmospheric conditions have to be, for a man to live 969 years? The answers to these questions will be an on going assignment for us all, in the months to come."

The questions and answers continued for two and one half hours. The event was monumental! What started as a small group of 4,287 interactive participants had increased rapidly. The final viewer count by the end of the session was

192,316, across the globe. This was not spreading like a virus; it was more like a tidal wave, encompassing thousands more every minute. The interest and controversy was multiplying rapidly.

Axle, inspired by the enormity of the response, turned to his wife and exclaimed, "Jane, I know my purpose!"

Jane studied the look of determination on Axle's face. The last time she saw that expression, they were crashing the laser grid.

"I need more money!" he said exuberantly.

"More than we already have? Axle, you're scaring me."

His only response to her was, "Brace yourself, for what's about to come. It's going to be exciting. I have found my purpose!"

~ ~ ~

Axle immediately scheduled a conference with the crew. "I've called everyone together to tell you about a project I have been working on. We recorded the truth about what really happened. All of us are aware of our non-disclosure. None of us want to be sued, discredited, or written off as crazy. However, I believe I have now found a way to show the recordings, and prevent *that* from happening."

"Axle, I'm intrigued," Doc interrupted.

"For the past several months, I have been documenting all that occurred on the **XODIS**. I have prepared copies for each of you. I was inspired by Max and Marcella's last interactive panel discussion. When Marcella challenged her participants with a homework assignment to post theories on a pre-flood Earth, it opened the door for us to tell what really happened. We could submit what really happened as anonymous theories."

"Brock would know it's from us," Max said.

"I'll have a little talk with Brock, he won't present a problem," Captain Eli reassured them. "Go on, Axle."

"I have the certainty from my grandfather and his

colleagues, that Eden Rocks is a viable source of income, and will sustain us; if my new venture is not as successful as I deem it to be."

Seeing Axle's passion, brought about an eagerness for the crew to hear more about this project.

As they began to read, Axle saw raw emotions begin to surface once again. They were reliving their experiences. Axle was able to capture that in his words. Something the camera was not able to portray. He had unknowingly, been writing the draft of a screen play. They were going to embark on a new venture.

They were going to make a movie!

~ ~ ~

"Grandpa, they're in," Axle exclaimed. Vincent was the first to hear his grandson's terrific news. "I'll send you and dad the final copy."

"I'm proud of you, boy. You're patience paid off. God always has a plan! I'll make a copy for my friends. You'll need a media corporation and a marketing brand to start. There's is a lot more to it than just getting the legal in place. You will need a director that will stick to your story line. Ask God for His help on this one!"

"I already have. Thanks, I knew I could count on you for great advice."

Things could not be going any better.

Life is good!

35

~DON'T LET THIS BE TRUE~

Dom stepped into Jack's office not saying a word. He gently closed the door and slumped in the chair.

Jack immediately activated the jammer.

"You have news, and I can tell it's not good. What have you learned, Dom? "

"The Vapor intercepted a communique. They are aware that Eli and Doc have become close. They are not waiting until the Captain has completed his assignment. We are out of time. They are going to eliminate them both. An accident is being arranged. It will happen in a few days. You won't be far behind," Dom said grimly. He seemed to age as he was speaking. "They need to be warned and brought up to speed. We can't wait any longer. Is there a place they can hide till we track down the assassin?" he said with urgency.

"I have a place no one knows about," Jack said.

"Somehow I thought you might. Maybe you should plan on going with them. Take some time off," Dom suggested. "It shouldn't take longer than a week."

"Do you think *that's* necessary?" Jack asked.

Dom turned his gaze from Jack, unable to respond. He was nodding his head 'yes', ever so slightly.

"Dom, get to the point!" Jack demanded.

"The Vapor made it very clear, that Eli, Doc and you, *must* leave today."

"I'll set it up. Eli is due here shortly. I'll make sure he brings Doc," Jack said.

One hour later, Eli and Doc arrived at Hangar 14.

They were both warmly greeted by Ivanna, "Captain Hunter, Dr. Lucas, so nice to see you. Mr. Brock needs to meet with you both, immediately." She quickly ushered them into Jack's office.

"Good morning, Jack," they smiled.

"Eli, we need to talk. Both, please sit."

Typical Jack; abrupt, no smile, serious. He had a way of keeping you on edge.

"What's wrong, Jack?" Eli asked, a bit annoyed at his lack of courtesy.

"Things are not what they seem," Jack replied, getting right to the point. "Oden Zadok is part of a group that wants the time ship."

"We knew something was up. We found surveillance equipment inside the ship," Eli responded casually.

"This group is very well connected and very well funded. They are looking for complete domination. They have planned from the beginning, to transfer everyone involved with the **XODIS** project. We have reason to believe that you and Doc are first," Jack said sternly.

"We're not military," Doc mused. "We can't be transferred. We're here because we want to be on the next mission."

"I know, but there are nine people directly involved, that we believe will be eliminated."

"*Eliminated*? Strong word for just taking us off the project, isn't it, Jack?" Eli responded with a bit of a laugh.

"They want to eliminate us, *permanently!*"

"Permanently? What for?" Eli said shocked.

"It seems we know too much," Jack said. I can't answer your questions now. It's crucial that we move quickly, Eli. Because your work on the ship is near completion, they have targeted you first. They are aware of your relationship with Patricia, so she is in immediate danger, as well. And, so am I!"

"So, what are you suggesting we do?" Eli shot back.

"We have a plan, and we have to leave now."

"Are you kidding me? I'm not going anywhere!" Eli said emphatically, as he folded his arms across his chest.

"Well, exactly how much time *do we* have?" Doc asked, now sounding concerned.

"We have been targeted, and we have *no* time. We have to leave now!"

"Can't you protect us here, Jack?" she questioned.

Eli jumped to his feet, "I'm not going to let *anything* happen to you, Patricia. *I'll* protect *you*!"

"Eli, calm down. We're all in danger! The Bella Group doesn't know we are aware of this information yet, so we have a slight advantage. Rest assured, we have trusted people working diligently behind the scenes on our behalf. But for now, we need to get to a safe place."

Eli was now pacing in the office. He was clearly in distress. He could see the fear in Patricia's eyes and panic setting in. Finally, after a few moments, he relinquished.

"Okay, Jack, I'll do this for Doc. But, this *better* be a good plan!"

"I have arranged for a series of shuttle rides for us. We will take off in my shuttle first, so as not to arouse suspicion. Watch your conversation, keep it light. We know my shuttle is bugged."

"Is it safe to talk *here*?" Eli questioned.

"My office has been swept, and I have a jamming device turned on. The shuttle is equipped with a jammer, but I don't use it often. I want to keep up the facade of business as usual. The last time it was used, was when I picked you up from the **XODIS**. Hopefully, we won't be gone too long, maybe a week. Look at it like a vacation. But we have to go *now*, and I can't allow you to contact anyone."

"Jack, there has to be another way. Can't we just confront him? I never ran from a man or a fight in my life. It will take me about five minutes to straighten this Zadok out." Eli pleaded.

"Eli, please, you know me. This is the *only* way."

"Let's make the most of it. Who knows, it might just be fun!" Doc said, trying desperately to keep her emotions under control.

"Eli, we have to go now," Jack reiterated, as he stood and ushered them out the door.

~ ~ ~

Justin Sonmire was waiting patiently. He quickly escorted them into the shuttle and took his place in the cockpit. Jack seated himself behind the young pilot.

After take off, they began talking about the wonderful time they had at Axle and Jane's wedding. They reminisced about the food, the dancing. Doc asked about Jack's wife and her new job. They genuinely appeared to be at ease. This may not be so bad, after all.

Suddenly, there was a deafening noise! The shuttle stopped, and began to free-fall!

Doc reached for Eli. He tried to calm her. When she saw the fear in his eyes, she began screaming.

Without words, they both knew what was taking place.

They were all together, and it was happening now!

The shuttle dropped quickly and disappeared behind a hill. Seconds later, a huge ball of flames shot into the sky.

It was over!

~ ~ ~

Within minutes, the world was informed.

"Breaking News! There has been a tragic accident. A hover shuttle just crashed; claiming four lives. It appears among the fatalities are Eli Hunter, Doctor Patricia Lucas, Jack Brock and pilot Justin Sonmire. Four badly burned bodies were found at the scene. A private shuttle owned by the late, Jack Brock crashed and burst into flames, in a remote area. More on this story as details become available."

~ ~ ~

"Axle, did you hear the news?"

"No! Why are you crying, Marcella? What happened? I can't understand you."

"Is Jane with you?" she said between sobs.

"No, she's not. Why? What's going on? Marcella is everything alright with Max?" he pressed her.

"It's not Max. There was a shuttle accident. The Captain, Doc, Brock and Justin were killed," she said through uncontrollable crying.

"What? I don't believe it! Marcella, you must be wrong! Where did you hear this?" he yelled.

"Pull up the news, Axle." Her words were barely audible.

"This can't be true. This has to be a mistake! God, please don't let this be true!" He was crying as he begged and pleaded with God.

"Axle, they're gone!" Marcella wailed.

He stumbled into a chair. It was on every station. They kept replaying the shot of the shuttle going down behind a hill, followed by the fireball shooting up to the sky, then an aerial shot of the wreckage.

Jane came running in screaming. "Did you hear?" Is that them?" she cried. "Oh God, I can't bare to watch this. Shut it off!"

"Maybe, they made a mistake! Maybe it's not them at all," Axle hollered. He began desperately searching for another station reporting the news.

"This is Ram, reporting from above the wreckage, we have four confirmed dead. They are Captain Eli Hunter, Doctor Patricia Lucas, Mr. Jack......" before he finished, Jane screamed again, "Axle, shut if off!"

Axle muted the sound, rose and rushed to Jane.

"It's true, they're dead!" he sobbed.

"I can't believe what I'm hearing," Jane screamed, again and again. She collapsed into her husband arms, not being able to hold herself up any longer.

The newly married couple clung to each other, overcome with grief. They had fallen to the floor.

"God could have stopped it, Jane. Why did He let this happen?" Axle groaned as he held his wife. "Why were they brought back, only to die like this? God, why?"

Jane was clinging tightly to him, hardly able to speak. She placed her hand on his wet cheek, "Axle, please, now is not the time to question God, but the time to trust Him."

"Trust Him? How do I do that?" Axle moaned in sorrow. "I can't believe this is true!"

He rocked her in his arms as they sobbed.

"Doc's been *my* closest friend, Axle" she said softly, through her cries.

"My mentor is lost now, too." Axle lamented. "I can't believe my friend is gone."

"They are *all* gone." Jane wailed.

~ ~ ~

The remainder of the crew, spent the next several hours mourning the loss of their friends, in seclusion. They were distraught. They were desperately trying to come to grips with what happened, and wanted no communication with the outside world; it was difficult even speaking with each other.

The following morning, Max and Marcella, met at Axle's house to grieve together, privately. Never facing this before, they had no idea of how to proceed with funeral arrangements. Max said several times, "I'll call the Captain."

And the weeping would begin again.

They weren't making any progress.

Jane received a call from Doc's father, saying there had been a change. They are having a memorial service in five days, instead of a funeral. He was just informed that what was left of *their* remains, would not be released for quite awhile. Could she please contact his daughter's friends? She told him that Marcella would help, as well.

Their level of grief and anguish just increased.

They were inconsolable!

Axle called his family and asked his grandfather to do the same. He knew they would all want to pay their respects.

The day dragged on, but they managed to get through it somehow.

~ ~ ~

The following day, Marcella called with disturbing news.

"Jane, I just heard from Dom this morning. Do you remember Powell Tomlin, the R and D technician?"

"Yes, I do."

"Dom informed me that he was appointed Acting Missions Director, *yesterday.*"

"Really? Do you think he's qualified, Marcella?" Jane wondered.

"Jane, why is there a need for an *Acting* Missions Director, *now*? The mission is at least two years away. Wouldn't they take at least six months or so, to find someone to permanently replace Jack Brock?"

"Marcella, what are you trying to say?"

"Something's not right, Jane. It's too soon."

Before Jane could respond, Axle burst into the room.

"Talking to Marcella?"

She nodded.

"Is Max there?"

Max quickly appeared on the screen, hearing the urgency in Axle's voice. "Did you hear the latest news, Axle?"

"About Powell Tomlin? Yeah, but that's not the latest," he said enraged. "Pull up the National News."

After hearing the news, Max said distressed, "We're on our way!"

36

~FOUL PLAY~

"This is Ram reporting. We are live back at the scene, with a gruesome turn of events. What was thought to be just a tragic accident a few short days ago, has now taken a turn. Foul play is strongly suspected. Investigators now say they have *not* ruled out foul play."

"Foul play?" Axle shouted in anger. "Foul play? Who would want to kill the Captain?"

Marcella and Jane were crying openly.

The men were outraged over this horrific report.

"Do you think it might have something to do with Brock?" Max demanded. "It was *his* shuttle!"

"I always felt there was something else going on here. Losing four people from the same project, *accidentally?* The odds would be astronomical. And, Justin was a better pilot than they made him out to be," Axle cried, angrily pounding his fist on the table. Jane touched his hand, he grabbed it, and they held tightly to each other. "Foul play can only mean, its project related!" he added.

"He's right. We could all be in danger," Marcella responded, alarmed.

"Who would want to sabotage the mission?" Jane lamented.

"They're not sabotaging the project! Someone wants to take over the ship. Now, hiring a Missions Director this soon, makes sense. He must be in on it," Axle yelled.

"Let's not jump to any conclusions," Jane said softly, trying to calm everyone.

"Jane, listen, four people have already been killed, and we are probably next," Axle said, now pacing.

"What do we know? What would Powell Tomlin's

function be? Who appointed him?" Marcella said frantically.

"He chooses a new Captain for one, and probably approves all the replacements." Max blurted, kicking the chair.

"But why, Eli and Doc?" Jane cried. "And, poor Justin. Why did they have to kill him? Why kill any of them?"

"The Captain's job was almost finished. And, Doc didn't have *anything* to do with the ship itself," Marcella interjected, sobbing. "And what was Justin's crime? Being a pilot?"

Axle was still pacing, running his fingers through his hair, frustration building. Suddenly he shouted, "The laser grid!" He just recalled the access codes being sabotaged. "They tried to kill us then. When *that* failed, they decided to eliminate us one by one. They used Justin to make it look like an accident."

"But, Axle, my part is finished and the motors you and Max designed are already being developed, and nothing happened to us?" Jane said confused.

"We were next! Now that foul play is suspected, they won't make another attempt this soon. So we're safe for now. But, who could be behind it? What about Dom?" Axle questioned.

"No way, he could build the ship with private money. And Rebecca would never betray Dom. You see the way she looks at him. They don't have the power to appoint a Mission's Director," Marcella said, in their defense.

"So now we are back to the Missions Director again," Max stated. "We need to find out just *who* appointed Powell. *He's* the one behind it."

"What about those two men in military uniforms at the unveiling of the ship? They probably have access to the laser grid," Axle speculated.

"Enough! I'll just call Dom and ask him who appointed Powell. I can't hear this anymore!" Marcella was drained.

~ ~ ~

It wasn't until later that afternoon, that Marcella was able to reach Dom. Max, Axle, and Jane remained silent in the background as Marcella spoke.

"Dom, I've been trying to get you all day. I have a question about Powell's appointment."

Dom quickly cut her off. "It has been very hectic around here today. A lot of changes have been taking place, even as we speak. I can't talk now, and neither," Dom paused, "can you! There is a meeting tomorrow at two. I need you and Max to be there, bring Axle and Jane."

"But, Dom I just,"

Axle grabbed her arm, motioned her to be silent, and to end the call.

"I guess it can wait till tomorrow, we'll see you then." She clicked off.

"He knows, and he thinks his communication has been compromised," Axle said to Marcella.

"Are you sure?"

"Yes, I'm sure. Didn't you catch the pause between *neither can you?* Why would he even say that? Trust me, he knows."

"If we figured it out, so did he. He's a lot smarter than we are!" Max broke in. "What do we do now?"

"We wait till tomorrow," Jane paused, "and I'm going to trust God with our lives."

~ ~ ~

The four gathered together again the following morning. Each preparing a eulogy, as they were all asked to speak at the memorial service on Sunday.

It was raining and windy outside, but eerily quiet inside; except for intermittent weeping.

They wanted to leave early for the meeting and have a bite to eat first. The obvious place was Sherazzada's. The last time they were all there together, it was a joyous occasion. However, It proved to be too emotional for them today. They ordered, but no one could eat.

They caught a local shuttle to a central hub. Their ID cards gave them access to a private military shuttle, which took them directly to Hangar 14.

They exchanged hugs and tears with Ivanna. Her grief was evident. She promptly directed them to a closed conference room off the main hallway.

They were greeted by Rebecca, Dom, and two other men. Arianna Brock big smile and happy wave. The 4 looked at each other puzzled by Brock's wife's reaction.

"This is Max, Marcella, Axle, and Jane," Dom said, rising from his seat to make the introductions.

"Please meet Simon Rye, and this is Tink."

Simon, a man in his mid 50's, immediately stood and extended his hand. He was tall, slim, and a little balding. His jacket looked tired and was wrinkled at the lapel.

Tink remained seated, and just nodded. He was well built, rugged looks, thick black hair, and a short beard, perfectly trimmed. His eyes were deep set and the color of coal. His suit appeared to be custom made, along with his shirt.

Dom motioned for them to sit. "Let's begin. We have a lot to discuss."

"Where's Oden Zadok?" Axle demanded.

"And where is Powell Tomlin?" Max jumped in. "I need answers!"

Simon and Tink, quickly glanced at Dom.

"I told you they put the pieces together," Dom said to the men seated. "All of you, please calm down, and listen carefully. Simon is a lead investigator for the North American Union. Tink is with CHASE."

Simon took a sip of water, cleared his throat and spoke in a raspy, British accent, "You won't be seeing Oden Zadok, Powell Tomlin, Nadia Reed; as well as eleven of their associates; for quite some time. The official report will read; Oden Zadok and several colleagues were caught in a sting operation. They were indicted for misappropriations of Government funds, conspiracy, extortion, and racketeering!"

"Attempted murder and murder charges pending. More than a trillion dollars in assets were seized, and 342 bank accounts were frozen," Tink added.

"It's not clear which agency initiated the sting operation. Apparently faulty documentation in one of their minor accounts, warranted a routine investigation by the local bank examiner. That's when our agencies got involved," Simon said, glancing at Tink. "And their entire organization imploded. Members scrambled to turn states evidence, to avoid murder indictments."

"The faulty documentation that started the investigation turned out to only be a clerical error, in the banks computer," Dom added.

"What's the unofficial story?" Axle asked his voice cracking. He stared at Tink. Jane gripped his hand tightly.

Anger was building, as they waited to hear what Tink had to say. Max and Marcella, were now glaring at him, as well.

Tink's tough exterior softened slightly as he spoke, "The true story, is that you have a guardian Angel watching over you. CHASE uses an independent party on occasion, someone known as the Vapor. The Vapor obtained critical information linking Oden Zadok to the Bella Group. It was incriminating evidence. Simon discovered Bella was heavily funded and had government connections. The Vapor obtained Bella's banking records, and inserted information that would create an irregularity that would in-turn, begin a riveting investigation. The Vapor then used their surveillance equipment to plant seeds of mistrust. Then by monitoring their communications, the Vapor was alerted about the contract hit on Eli and Patricia."

The girls were visibility shaken. Max squeezed Marcella's hand, his anger fueling.

"The Vapor uncovered what account the assassins would be paid from," Tink continued. "It was carefully monitored, and within two days of the shuttle accident, payment was made. *We* initiated the foul play report. It sent panic through the Bella Group, now knowing they could be charged with four counts of murder."

"Sorry to interrupt, Dom," Ivanna spoke, trying to muffle her cries, "the rest of the group has arrived for the meeting."

"Send them right through, Ivanna." Dom answered quickly.

Tink continued, "We had leverage to offer them immunity from the murder charges, if they turned states evidence and plead guilty to lesser charges. It worked. The group is no more."

Their anger was now uncontrollable!

They were outraged!

"IT WORKED? WHO PAYS FOR THE DEATH OF OUR FRIENDS?" Axle screamed loudly.

"YOU KNEW AND DID NOTHING?" Marcella shrieked.

"YOU GAVE THEM IMMUNITY?" Max shouted, his voice now at fever-pitch.

"YOU DID NOTHING!" Axle ranted over and over.

Jane's head was on the table, her hands covering her ears. She was wailing.

Mrs. Brock, stood "Dom! You said they knew. You didn't tell them.

Just then four, very large, Military Police walked through the door. The men stopped yelling immediately.

Thrusting his hands out in front of him, Axle, said in a low, steady tone, "There's no problem here. We are okay!"

Suddenly, from behind the wall of MP's, another figure emerged, who towered over them all.

It was Eli Hunter.

The room fell silent. They were speechless.

Was this the Captain, or a body double?

You could almost see their brilliant brains trying to comprehend what their eyes were seeing.

Then, Doc and Jack Brock, appeared.

Justin followed, with Ivanna clinging to him.

Gasps, shouts of joy, now permeated the room.

The questions would wait!

Explanations could wait!

They needed to embrace each other.

Tears flowing, open weeping.

Rebecca, Dom, Simon and Tink allowed them time to reunite.

Axle, hugging Justin said, "I knew you didn't crash that way. I just knew it."

"I thought you would know that we were all still alive. You taught me all the right maneuvers the first day I met you. I used *every* one!" Justin exclaimed, wiping away the tears streaming down his face.

Ivanna, by his side, was still hugging him tightly. "I was screaming so loudly a minute ago, when they walked in. Didn't you hear me?"

"When I saw the footage and heard *foul play*, I believed *them*," Axle said to Justin, still dazed. He hugged him hard again.

Axle then ran over and pushed Captain Eli hard in the chest, "You're laughing?" Then muffling his sobs, he threw his arms around his Captain.

Everyone was crying and hugging.

Jack and his wife were still embracing, her face in the crease of his neck.

Now loud chatter began to fill the room. They wanted to know what took place, and how?

Dom asked them all to be seated.

Tink started with, "I thought you knew. Dom said you figured it out."

"How could we have figured out *that* part.?" Max questioned.

"I'm sorry. Justin assured us that Axle would know they didn't crash. I know the reports were extremely convincing, I should have made sure. It must have been agonizing for all of you," Tink apologized. "I want Justin to explain what transpired."

"Last week, while in the mess hall, with several other pilots," Justin began as he wiped his face with Ivanna's handkerchief, "I was introduced to a new pilot, who was just reassigned here. During our conversation, he said he heard of someone claiming to pull a shuttle out of a free fall. I told him a test pilot named Axle, showed me how to do that very maneuver. He said if I could prove it, he'd give me $1000. We jumped in his shuttle, and I demonstrated it. It was then, that he reintroduced himself as Tink, from CHASE."

Tink took over and began to explain what happened next. "I laid out the plan in full detail to Justin; that we had to simulate an accident. I explained there would be a shuttle with cameras positioned directly behind him and how they would be angled, for maximum effect. And that his shuttle would be bugged."

Justin spoke again. "It was an honor to be trusted, but I was apprehensive about deceiving those that came aboard that day. I knew that for just a moment; Doc, Captain Eli and Mr. Brock would endure agonizing terror. But I also knew it had to appear real, or we would fail. So, while we were free falling and everyone was screaming, I initiated the cold start procedure. I then quickly turned on the signal jammer. I pulled out of the free-fall and landed on a flatbed railroad car, that Tink had waiting on the other side of the hill. Tink immediately activated the winch that pulled us into a cave. A camouflage net dropped to cover the entrance of the cave, entirely concealing it. The decoy shuttle, already in position on the ground, exploded. Timing was impeccable! We were in the cave watching this brilliant plan unfold before our eyes."

"But what about the 'four badly burned bodies'? Jane interrupted.

"They looked real, didn't they?" Justin grinned.

Tink interrupted, "It was the Vapor who convinced me, the only way I could protect all nine people and bring the group down, was to pre-empt the hit. The assassin quickly took full credit and collected his payment. Within hours, we had him! He was arrested! And the best is; for a crime that wasn't even committed. We then threatened the Bella group with accessory to four counts of murder. They were scrambling to be the *first*, to plea bargain."

"Who is the Vapor?" Marcella questioned.

"All I can tell you, is that it's the *one* who kept you all alive," Tink smiled.

Rebecca's identity is still protected, and now only *two* people in the world know who she actually is.

After the meeting ended, Axle had the opportunity to compliment Justin again on his flying skills. "I'm so proud of you, Justin. Tell me, how did Brock handle the entire ordeal?"

"Not well, sir." Justin replied, trying to suppress a laugh.

"Was he screaming, too?" Axle pressed.

Justin looked around to make sure Brock couldn't hear and whispered, "Like a little girl."

The two laughed loudly.

37

~THE BEGINNING~

Two Years Later

XODIS II is very near completion. The crew is anxiously awaiting their next mission. The ship was built to accommodate several additional stations. A few new crew members will be added. Justin being one of them.

~ ~ ~

Max and Marcella have been mentoring qualified scientists; who are now duplicating what they began in the Asbury, Convention Hall and The Dome. There are currently three hundred meetings taking place daily, in major facilities across the globe. What began as an alternative Science class, has now become a world-changing movement.

~ ~ ~

Captain Eli, with the assistance of Doc, or Patricia, as he likes to call her; are establishing True-Science Museums in schools, colleges, and in major cities.

~ ~ ~

Vincent, in his old age, seems to be in the *prime of his life*. He is not only the Chief Emissary, but now the CEO of Eden Rocks Media Productions.

~ ~ ~

Axle persevered with what he believed to be his purpose. Jane has been his constant source of support and encouragement. Tori is showing tremendous interest in their quest, and is helping Jane create super foods in the Botany Lab.

~ ~ ~

The movie premier was last evening. All six crew members, family, and hundreds of friends were in attendance, including Lt. Joe Cat and Franklin St. Marten.

Vincent had limo's pick up all of Eden Rock's employees at the Sunset Lakes. They were all fashionably dressed. They looked like Vincent's entourage!

The audience laughed, cried and cheered.

It was all over the media.

It was a tremendous success!

The critics were raving; "Don't miss The Genesis Chip! A must see for everyone. The special effects are breathtaking. camera crews and movie makers alike, are determined to find out the mystery behind the special effects."

However, You and I know, it was actual video shot...

"IN THE BEGINNING"

Based on a true story
By

Butch Buordesco

About the author

Thank you for reading "The Genesis Incident" Feel free to leave a review. For more information on Creation vist. **CreationMakesSense.com.**

The Berardesco team just finished a short story prequel entitled **"A.K.A. The Vapor".** Follow the amusing journey of Madison Marino,as she transforms herself into Rebecca Weege, one of the many colorful characters featured in **"The Genesis Incident".**

Butch Berardesco, graduating from Asbury Park High at the bottom of his class, is the most unlikely writer of our time. Voted the most likely to die before the age of 30, and educated on the streets of the Jersey shore with priorities that valued partying above all else, he quickly fell into a world of bikers, drinking and drugs.
Shortly after his first child was born, he had an after death experience that should have changed his life; it didn't. He remained trapped in a world of drugs and riotous living. Five years later, he overdosed again.

With God's mercy, he was given a second chance - a second time, and began a new life.

"Face to the Floor", is Butch's true account of his raw and incredible journey from real-death to real-life. It is currently being read and studied by inmates to help them overcome addiction and the sin that so easily besets us.

Acknowledgments

Kennan Burch, Founder/ President of Dream **Builders** and **Brand Catalyst Partners.** Kennan has inspired so many men to pursue things much bigger than themselves.

Nicole Mascioli, a/k/a Nico Mas, our Jr. proofreader and editor. What an amazing young lady you are. You have been a source of encouragement to me. I do believe you have a great career ahead of you.

Nathan Obinwa, My first reader. You read the first draft, which was *incredibly rough.* "I finally get it"- is what motivated me to continue. Thank you for those words, young man.

Kim Joseph, Missionary/Youth Leader. Your constant words of support, and enthusiasm of just how far The Genesis Chip can travel, opened up a bigger vision.

Michelle Melver, Stephanie Smith, You two were answers to prayer for me. Thank you for stepping in at just the right time with your proofreading skills.

Christian Bulkholtz, You stirred me to pursue this dream. You told me to put it in print and here it is. What a great friend you are! Thank you.

Mary Summerville, Thank you for your inspiring words many years ago. It has come to pass!

A very special thanks to **Dr. Kent** and **Eric Hovind** of **CSE drdino.com** and **Ken Ham,** of **AnswersInGenesis.org** for their endless supply of resources.

To my children, **Rebecca** and **Justin Berardesco** and **Michael DeCrosta,** and my grandchildren, **Tori, Hunter, Arianna Berardesco, Vinny Anglisano, Isabella DeCrosta** and **Jordan Sullivan. I love you all!**